JENNY BUNTING

Editing: Lopt & Cropt Editing

Proofreading: Horus Copyedit and Proofreading

Cover: Kari March Designs

BOOKS BY JENNY BUNTING

Here in Lillyvale

Here (Zoey and Jonathan)

Hustle (Taylor and Malcolm)

Home (Addison and Kirk)

Hubby (Makenna and Dan)

Stuck in Love

Please Be Seated (Erin and Landon)

In Case of Emergency (Cassie and Smith)

For Your Safety (Raegan and Henry)

Finch Family

Fool's Gold (Annie and Cameron)

Gold Rush (Whitney and Reid)

For Candice
When I saw your intense desire to be a mother, I knew I wasn't
meant to be one.

And for that, I am endlessly grateful.

A NOTE FROM JENNY

Thank you so much for reading *Gold Rush*! I hope you enjoy it.

This book deals with themes of parental abandonment and generational trauma from the societal pressure to be a parent. It also includes situations and conversations, including a brief mention of medical gaslighting, that may be triggering to childfree-by-choice folks.

If you are sensitive, please take care of yourself.

REID

"I can't believe Jackson is missing this!" Mom shouts.

My brother Cameron croons, badly, into the microphone, slowly rocking his hips to the vocals of "I Want It That Way" by the Backstreet Boys. If I'm cringing, it will make my other brother Jackson shrivel into a mummified corpse.

"I thought he was coming," she shouts again.

That's my cue. Mom wants me to check on him.

"I'll see what he's doing."

Cameron's off-key singing follows me outside into the night air. For the first time tonight, I can breathe. Being around lots of people was never my thing, but our annual staff appreciation party, always scheduled for the weekend after Labor Day, is mandatory. "We have to show our employees that we care about them," my dad says. It was Cameron's idea to get the karaoke machine, and it's been a hit so far.

There's no way they're getting me up on that stage, though. Cameron is the equivalent to a candied ham when it comes to performing, so he's the family representative when it comes to embarrassment.

Since Cameron planned an epic and successful nineties-themed adult prom in May for our family's business, Woody Finch Brewery, my parents have put him in charge of all events. It was his idea for a karaoke night to celebrate surviving a Goldheart summer for our employees. It was crazy busy this summer, our taproom full of tourists and locals drinking our beer, hanging out with their friends, and having a good time. We had our most profitable tourist season yet, and everyone is tired but happy. Our little brewery, on the edge of extinction two years ago, is finally in the black and making a profit. The whole family is involved in the running of the business, but Jackson sits out on all social events. He left the prom early, and he's a no-show again tonight.

Jackson is the oldest out of the four of us, stoic and quiet. He prefers to be left alone with his numbers, and I'm not surprised he skipped our party at all. Too many happy people having fun. I am a little jealous that he can say no so easily, when the thought of saying no makes my chest pound.

My loafers crunch the fallen leaves as I open my phone and scroll to my brother's phone number. I scratch my beard as I wait for the dial tone.

My brother grunts when he picks up the phone.

"Hey. Mom said you were coming."

"No," Jackson says. I wait for more and even check my phone that Jackson hasn't hung up on me.

Mom will be mad if I don't try to convince him a little bit. There's nothing more awkward to me than my mother angry.

"Please come. Cameron is currently gyrating to the crowd. He might get in trouble—your favorite," I say.

"I'm good," Jackson says. "I bought some Macallan's if you want to ditch."

Oh, that's tempting. The only other kind of alcohol I drink, besides beer, is really good Scotch. Invitations from my oldest brother are few and far between.

He knows I won't leave, though. Whatever my family wants, I do, no matter what I want.

"Thanks for the offer, but I should stay here. Keep up appearances," I say. "At least I can tell Mom I tried."

"You did," he says, and the line goes dead.

I slip my phone into my pocket and head back inside. The taproom is stuffy and overbearing. It's too cold to open our overhead door, but too full of people to be comfortable. Walking past the picked-over pizza, I grab a fresh Solo cup, and walk behind the bar. A sweet female voice drifts from the speakers.

Cameron's girlfriend, and my good friend, Annie has taken over the microphone.

The stage lights reflect off of her golden-red hair. She is luminous. Annie holds the microphone lovingly with both hands, her gaze locked with Cameron as the opening chords of Mariah Carey's "Always Be My Baby" starts.

I had a tiny crush on her back in the day, but it all worked out.

I can admit it—Cam and Annie may be total opposites, but they're perfect for each other.

Annie sings along, laughing in between lyrics. At one point she puts her hand up and kind of hits a high note, which causes our slightly tipsy crowd to go berserk. Cameron is the loudest of them all.

She stares at my brother, singing only to him.

It might be cringy, but I would love to have a relationship where someone sings to me. I might appear like I'm dying of embarrassment if it ever happened, but it would make me feel really good.

After her song, Annie steps off the stage, handing the microphone to Dan, our investor. He picks the song, and the opening chords of "Cry Me a River" by Justin Timberlake blast through the speakers.

"I'm bringing sexy back," Dan yells into the microphone.

"Wrong song, Dan," Cameron shouts through cupped hands.

Dan begins singing the lyrics, not even reading off the prompter. His wife, Makenna, is in the front, and I see her shaking head from here.

Dan is a ball of energy, who charges through life. He landed a beautiful wife and has a successful business he built himself. I've always admired his courage. There's so many things I've wanted to do—travel, finish my novel, create something for myself.

Somehow, along the way, I got stuck. And I don't know how to get unstuck.

"Are you going to get up there?" a female voice asks inches from my ear.

Annie stands next to me, flushed from the beer and singing, the mirror ball creating fractures of light on her face, like she's an angel. Annie has always been beyond beautiful to me, even when we were kids.

"Why would I take the stage from this guy?" I ask, pointing to our investor, beer in one hand, and microphone in the other.

We watch Dan channel Justin Timberlake, popping his knee out and dragging the toes of his shoes across the stage. Annie laughs. "He's too much."

"Really," I say, chuckling. "You looked like you're having fun."

"Yeah, I realized that embarrassing myself is okay if I'm having a good time. You should try it."

I shake my head. "No, I'm good."

"Is Jackson coming?" Annie asks.

"No," I answer. "He has some new Scotch, so he's not leaving his place tonight."

"That's too bad. I remember..." Annie trails off. We both remember what Jackson was like.

Before.

Annie turns to me, her face dead serious. "So, I don't want you to freak out..."

Oh no. The last time she said that, I went on a terrible date with a lady who took her rats everywhere. My soul left my body when she opened her jacket to reveal a rat coming out of her bra.

"Whitney is coming to Goldheart." Annie grimaces, and my smile falls.

Whitney Ferguson. *That* woman. The only person my people-pleasing does not apply to.

"Why?" I squawk out.

Annie grimaces harder. "She just sold her house because she got divorced, and she's trying to figure out next steps. She says that Goldheart worked wonders on her productivity, and she has a book to finish that's been giving her a hard time so..."

"It's fine," I say, although my nostrils expand and twitch at the mention of her.

"You're flaring," she says, pointing to me.

"No, I'm not," I say, covering my nose. "I'll be civil if she's civil."

"What happened between you two, anyway?"

I hoist my beer up. "I need at least two more of these before I can talk about that."

"Well, fine. She arrives tomorrow. And she'll want to work at Gold Roast, so I told Tara to play referee if you two have a run-in."

"I guess I'm drinking iced coffee from home now."

"At least *try* to be friendly," she says. "You're my friend, and she's my friend."

"I can't make any promises if *she* starts something."

Annie rolls her eyes, but rubs my back anyway. Her touch tugs at my insides. "Please try."

Cameron climbs the stage again.

"I need to tell Cameron to give other people a shot. Excuse me."

She scampers off to peel my brother away from the microphone.

Whitney is moving to my town, *and* infiltrating my coffee shop. She's not even here yet, and my blood already boils.

When I first met her years ago in my Short Story Writing class at Byron University in San Diego, I was mesmerized. Long dark hair, glacier-blue eyes, pouty pink lips, a killer body.

Then, I read her writing.

It danced on the page. Made me jealous as hell, even if it wasn't my normal genre.

Romance.

I found her work clichéd, having seen the same things happen in romantic comedies and love stories girls I spent time with made me watch. I said so in my feedback, because that's the only thing I could find wrong with it.

I also said it out loud as we went around a circle and voiced our feedback.

I was mid-sentence, explaining my thoughts, when she

interrupted me. She didn't even let me compliment her on her use of language and how lyrical I thought it was.

"Those are tropes. It happens in genre fiction," she spat, like I didn't know what those were.

Back then, I was way more defensive than I am now, so I fired back, "Tropes are overdone. You should try to do something fresh. Subvert the genre."

"You don't understand," she said with a dismissive hand flip, and any interest I had in the intriguing woman behind the beautiful prose evaporated. For the first time in my life, I didn't mind that someone hated me, because I hated her right back.

While I was critical of her story, she eviscerated mine the next week. She harped on for ten minutes, pointing out where I was unoriginal and called it a "Salinger-Faulkner-Steinbeck circle jerk". That made me drink heavily with my buddies at a frat party that weekend.

Mostly because she was fucking right.

I spent so much time paying homage to writers I admired, I didn't take the time to be original. She may have used tropes, but I lifted my inspiration from writers who did it better than me.

I had unknowingly awakened the beast of a pissed-off woman. She was a few inches shorter than me, but I've never been more scared of a person. Ever.

When Annie mentioned her author friend Whitney, I didn't connect her friend with *that* Whitney I knew in college. When she came to my family's brewery for the nineties prom, I almost shit myself.

Her author friend, the one who made over a million a year according to Annie, was the same girl who gave me death stares and dressed me down harder than a troll on the Internet.

Now she's moving to my town, and I'll have to be around the only person who hates me. I've lived my life in a way that I never ruffle feathers, I never rock the boat. I cannot stand people being mad at me, so Whitney moving to town makes my throat close up.

Annie comes back. "Crisis adverted." Instead of my brother, our newest employee, Shiloh, takes the stage, a tiny blonde with big hair and a big heart. The opening chords of "Jolene" strum, and Shiloh smiles to the crowd, unleashing a killer singing voice.

Annie smacks me on the chest.

"You should ask her out for coffee or something. Clear the air."

"Who, Shiloh?" I ask. "She's not my type."

"No, Whitney."

I laugh from deep in my gut. "You're hilarious."

"Seriously," Annie says. "College was so long ago."

"And it went so well then."

"Come on. You have so much in common. The writing. And she runs too."

I picked up running after the brewery started doing booths at different races in our area. I've thought about training for a race one day, but I need to be in much better shape to do it. I go to a twice-weekly running group with runners of varying ages. I'm barely faster than Miriam Oliver, a woman in her mid-seventies, who runs a ten-minute mile. It helped me shed some pounds, though.

"I barely run," I say.

"I'm just saying you could relate to each other. You just went through a traumatic breakup."

"I wouldn't call my breakup *traumatic*."

Callie, my ex, was part of my life for three years, fading in and out of our relationship like water through a cheap paper towel. For the last seven months of our relationship, we lived together, but for the last three months of it, we barely spoke, only communicating about her twelve-year-old son, Isaac.

I picked him up from school and watched him while Callie worked as a manager of a local restaurant. Isaac frequently did his homework at the brewery, surrounded by rowdy regulars. Because I loved Callie and her son, I filled the role Isaac's dad vacated. I thought I had finally found the family I wanted.

One day Callie told me she didn't feel the way she needed to feel. To get married. To build a life together.

I still go to Isaac's baseball games, and he hangs out at the brewery sometimes when Callie needs to work late. It's not the same, though. Isaac and I used to watch the History channel together and go to the Ernest Wyatt Mine, just to be alone with our thoughts. While the role of "dad" never sat right with me, I promised Isaac and Callie I would still be there for him.

Now my nights are free, and my life is lonely. The only thing keeping me company is Dwayne "The Rock" Johnson's entire filmography. *The Scorpion King* is oddly soothing.

The way I'm going, I'll be a bachelor for the rest of my life. But then, everyone said that about my knucklehead brother, and now look at him. If he could find someone, I surely can.

It's tough though, in a small town, when everyone couples up after high school and has kids before they're twenty-three. I wasn't interested in that when I was younger, but now, it might be too late.

In the meantime, I have the family I was born into, including a mother with a crazy look in her eye coming toward me. Our mother loves us. It just comes out as meddling and nagging most of the time.

"Reid, did you call Jackson?"

"Yep. Not coming."

"Oh well. We're doing a family song," my mother says, taking my arm. My feet feel like cement as she pulls me toward the stage, where my sister Emily, her daughter Olive, and my dad stand. Cameron is chugging a beer on the wing of the stage.

The beginning of "We are Family" by Sister Sledge begins, and I roll my eyes. Emily smacks me on the arm and hands me a microphone. My niece Olive bounces on her feet, her pigtails bobbing.

I quietly sing into the microphone, making sure my voice is overpowered by my family. Between Olive's shouting and Cameron's off-key vibrato, I fade into the background like I always have. It's why I enjoy the brewing so much. It's quiet, it's solitary, and I don't have to talk to people.

After the song ends, my dad takes the microphone.

"I want to thank everyone here for the hard work they put in to make this Woody Finch's best summer yet. We did 134 percent better than what we projected, which is amazing, and it's because of you all here."

My dad gets choked up frequently, and today is no exception. He wraps his arm around my mother and pulls her in.

"Let's have some fun! The karaoke machine is open! Please sing something so we don't get any more of my son making love to the crowd," Dad says.

I clap politely as the crowd cheers. Our part-time staff, under Cameron's direction, makes Woody Finch a fun place to get beer and socialize. I make the beer, but our team makes the brewery.

The lights make it difficult to distinguish faces from up here, but I can see Annie by the bar where I left her. Annie has assimilated beautifully into our brewery as an employee and our family as our sister, which I knew she would.

She's clapping and looking lovingly at Cameron. My mom has said it's only a matter of time before Annie and Cameron get married and have a family of their own.

I look at my dad, surrounded by his family who quit their jobs to make this brewery dream of his come true. I hated teaching history, but it was the only natural path for my history degree. Turns out you must love kids to teach, not just your subject. I don't mind children, one-on-one, but no one warns you how scary middle-schoolers can be in packs.

My siblings didn't need coaxing; we just did it. For him.

No matter how wacky and extra my family can be, I love the shit out of them. I'll do anything for them, even if it's at my own expense, sometimes.

I look at my dad, who took a chance a few years ago, a risk, and it's finally paying off.

I'm envious of my dad. He has everything I could want.

A family who loves him.

A purpose that makes it easy to get out of bed in the morning.

Happiness.

All I have is an empty house.

2

WHITNEY

"It was a beautiful home," my friend Jodie says, appearing from the kitchen.

"Yeah, it was," I say, glancing around. This house, empty and cavernous, is no longer home. It feels like a stranger's place.

When Brad and I bought this house, we picked out everything—the real hardwood floor, the travertine tile in the kitchen, the dark cabinets with quartz countertops. We filled it with expensive, taupe furniture and painted the walls a soft grey. My readers oohed and awed at the crispness and cleanliness when I posted our space on social media.

I wished we were as happy as I made it seem on Instagram.

Walking into my empty office tugs at my chest. It was every writer's dream room. I ordered built-in bookshelves that reached floor to ceiling with a rolling ladder so I could be like Belle from *Beauty and the Beast*. The shelves are now empty. My desk used to face a window that overlooked our slate-colored pool. Now it sits in storage.

This office was supposed to turn on a faucet of words, but I spent the first few weeks after it was fully set up just staring at my computer. The words didn't flow through my fingers like I thought they would. When deadlines loomed, I would just go to my tried-and-true Starbucks.

After a month, I gave up trying to make my office work. I just took Instagram pictures in there and used it for TikToks.

I touch my naked ring finger, rubbing a white spot on my skin. It used to hold a giant diamond wedding set that Brad upgraded on our fifth anniversary.

With my money.

It was also right after he told me he wanted a baby. The moment I knew my marriage was over. He thought a giant diamond would save it.

Tears dust my cheeks as I hear Jodie walk in.

"It might not seem like it, but this is the best thing that could've happened to you," Jodie says. "I would've never met Lucy if I hadn't divorced Weston."

Jodie and I met when our husbands were in residency together through University of Nevada, Reno. We realized we had similar interests—wine, the Real Housewives, running. We didn't know three years later that we would have divorces in common and that our ex-husbands would both leave the state and we would stay.

"I hope I can be happy now," I say.

"You will be. I promise."

Jodie pulls me in for a hug, her floral perfume surrounding me. Between Jodie and my good friend Annie, I know I can get through this. One step in front of another. Even when I don't feel like getting out of bed most mornings.

"The words are finally coming again," I say. "That's good."

"Absolutely," Jodie says. "Hopefully Goldheart will be good for you. Although I'll miss you terribly."

"I'll miss you too. But it's only two hours away. You better visit me."

"You know I will," Jodie says. "Lucy and I are already discussing a little weekend away."

"Good," I say.

"You'll have your friend Annie. She seems sweet."

"She is."

My friend Annie lives in a magical town in California called Goldheart. When I announced I was getting a divorce, she invited me for some time away, and I wrote six thousand words in a cozy coffee shop there in two hours. Prior to my visit, I was barely managing five hundred a day, my mind a whirl of thoughts and emotions distracting me too much. I already had to push a release back once; any longer, and I'd lose my preorder privileges. I *had* to be on time with that book, and Goldheart saved me.

Plus, my readers would find me and break my ankles with a mallet if I didn't deliver a manuscript to them. Most of them were understanding with the first push after I announced my divorce. One reader, who is literally named Karen, left a message that I heard the loudest: *I don't care. Give me the next book.*

As I've gotten more popular, I've gotten more demanding messages, pressuring me to release more, to write faster. It comes in cute comments here and there: *I hope your vacation goes well so you're fresh to get us a new book,* or *I'm (impatiently) waiting for the next book! I don't want to read anything else.* Sometimes, they're nasty, like *Stop doing those stupid dances and write your next book.*

Readers wonder why I can't produce a book every other month like I used to, why I haven't announced my next series yet.

It's impossible to write about love when you think it's bullshit.

"Did you forward your mail already?"

"Not yet." It's on my list, impossibly long with items that put one more nail in the coffin of my marriage.

"I'll go check it so you can have a moment." Jodie takes my mail key from me and walks out.

Crossing my arms, I look around. This was the first place I bought with my book money, and now I'm splitting the equity with my doctor husband. How quickly the power dynamic shifted. Everyone expected Brad to be the bread-winner, but I was the one who brought home the sour-dough, the rye, and the wheat bread. It's sickening how much I had to pay to be free.

Whatever I paid, I vow to make it back. Twice.

"There was a lot," Jodie says, handing me a stack of flyers and junk mail.

I flip through the flyers and see a plain envelope, scrawled with black lettering. The return address catches my breath.

Angie Singleton, Castle Pines, Colorado.

What? Why now?

"Anything good? Looked like a lot of junk," Jodie says.

"I'll need to look at this later," I say, tucking the envelope in my Celine micro luggage handbag. I used to covet this piece, thinking I would feel successful if I had it.

Now, I look at it and feel nothing. It's just leather and stitching, and it does nothing but represent a life I wish existed.

One in which I was still married and happy.

Jodie peers over my shoulder. "Did you get a weird fan letter? Your readers are *persistent.*"

"It's nothing. Probably a sneaky HVAC company making it look personal. Or something about my car warranty."

My friend brushes it off, but my heart screams.

My mother found me. As if this year couldn't get worse, she reappears like a fungal infection you thought you conquered. She must've sensed I was having a rough patch and decided to time it perfectly.

"I know you love selfies, and I can already guess what the caption will be, so let's take a photo," Jodie says. "I put on mascara, just in case."

I heave a breath before finding my camera, one I use for Instagram and use its wi-fi to transfer to my phone to post. Buzzing around my now-empty family room, looking for the best natural light, takes a few minutes as Jodie fluffs her hair and applies a new coat of a sheer lipstick.

When I find the spot, I angle the camera toward us, giving my best fake smile, tilting my head to its best angle. I take several shots, tilting my head slightly with each click. I will look happy in these photos, but I am not.

When I flick through all the options, I find the one I like the most and transfer it to my phone.

Jodie watches me in a wonder as my thumbs flick through the editing—brightening here, eliminating a shadow here. I've perfected my Instagram aesthetic, and I'm not about to ruin it because I got divorced.

My career is the one thing I have left.

"I'm in awe of you," she says, watching me. "No wonder my Instagram looks like crap."

You spend too much time on there, Brad, my soon-to-be-ex-husband, used to say when I answered messages while we watched TV. *I mean, you're here with me, but you're not* really *here.*

"Done," I say, showing her the post. Usually, I like to spend more time on the captions or schedule posts. Today, I write: *Onto the next chapter* with my signature emojis trailing it.

"I don't need that eyelid surgery after all with what you did to my face, goddamn," Jodie says.

"It's all editing," I say. "I can show you sometime."

"No thanks. That looked like too much work."

Jodie hugs me again. It's like she knows I need one. My speeding heart calms when I feel her arms around me. She's been the older sister I never had.

My phone buzzes in my hand, and my head tingles with who it could be. Brad calls once in a while to check up on me, but it always unravels. *We can get a surrogate if you're scared to be pregnant. Or we can adopt. Just please, don't leave me.*

It took a long time to realize forcing motherhood on me was his way of trying to control me.

The phone call is actually from Annie.

Annie was one of my first readers when I was a nobody. I was questioning what I was even doing, self-publishing a captive-captor romance, when she emailed me and told me she loved it.

I printed her email and tacked it to my wall and at our apartment. When I had my first six-figure year and we moved, that email came with me and I got a frame.

When I could finally retire my hell of a job as a claims examiner for a major personal auto insurance company, I invited her to Reno and met her for the first time in person.

It was like our souls recognized each other.

Now Annie is letting me live with her, even though her place is a studio with one bed and a foldout couch.

When I told her I had no idea how long I was staying, she said, "I would love it if you stayed forever."

Forever. I just might.

I'm not sure how long I'll stay, or if I'll crash at Annie's the whole time or find a place of my own. I just need Goldheart right now. It might be different than I remember, but I need to chase peace right now.

I desperately need it.

I click Accept and hold it to my ear.

"Hi, Whitney!" she says. "I'm just checking on when you think you might get into town. I have to work late, but I sneak away to let you in."

"Um, I haven't left yet," I say. "Just looking through the house one last time."

"Oh, okay. Just wanted to let you know that Tara is closing her shop at noon today."

My heart sinks. When I go to Goldheart, I usually swing by Tara's coffee shop, Gold Roast, first to bust out some words while I wait for Annie.

I do believe most writers are superstitious, and my muse can be a fickle bitch. But when she pulls up a seat at Gold Roast, she usually bestows me with all the beautiful words, clean words, passages that remain untouched after loads of revision. That six thousand words I wrote my first day there were written with minimal edits—a word change here, a comma there—and now that unassuming coffee shop holds more magic than all of Hogwarts for me.

I'm sad I can't start my time in Goldheart at the coffee shop.

Oh well, I'm going to be there for a while anyway.

"You can always go to the library! It's open until five.

Mrs. Epstein, the town librarian, is so nice. I can tell her you're coming. She could put a reserved sign on the best table she has."

"Sure, that sounds great."

Annie adds, "I don't think Reid will be at the library today. I know he's in the middle of a couple books so he won't have any to return. I'll see you later!"

Reid Finch. That fucking asshole.

When I first saw him at my Short Story Writing class in college, I thought he was cute. He had shaggy brown hair that fell in his green eyes, his lips parted like the world gave him inspiration.

I couldn't help but smile at him.

Then he opened his mouth.

In our first week of workshopping, I wrote a romance story, a short, five-thousand-word snapshot about a military hero who left a woman and came back for her after his tours in Iraq were complete.

He called it clichéd.

After I spent a full afternoon crying on my tiny dorm bed, I pulled that story out, the copy he wrote all over, and I sat down and started revising.

When I got his story the next week, I read his with deep interest.

And it was just what I thought.

Pompous. Arrogant. Delusional about his own talents.

The whimpering song of a mediocre white man.

After one too many wine coolers and the sounds of my roommates engaging in one-night stands, I may have called it "a Salinger-Faulkner-Steinbeck circle jerk" in aggressive, red pen.

Something I completely forgot about until I read my feedback out loud.

Then he ripped apart my subsequent two stories.

And I ripped his next ones apart as well.

So much so that the professor kept us after class one day toward the end of the semester.

"Is there something I don't know about? Some lovers' quarrel?" Professor Eldridge said, taking her glasses off of her face and cleaning the lenses with her silk scarf.

Reid's arms folded like a petulant child. "No."

I crossed my arms as a defense. "Absolutely not. He's the worst."

"This is a community of writers," Professor Eldridge said, her hands floating through the air like she was conducting a symphony. "You are the same. While I appreciate honest feedback, it doesn't help to go for each other's throats. Try being kinder. If you do publish, reviewers will be mean enough as it is."

Reid drew the first line in the sand by saying "Pass" when we presented a revised version of one of our stories with the original. When the professor asked why, he didn't speak, refusing to give his opinion. I remember the feeling well. The blood drained from my face. I worked so hard to swallow my pride and make changes, even adding things that he would like, motifs I noticed in his work.

I wanted him to acknowledge how I fixed it.

He didn't give me anything, and I didn't even get my story back with his feedback.

His refusal to critique my work still haunts me.

I never thought I would see Reid again, and then by chance he lives in Goldheart and is friends with Annie.

Telling him I was a famous romance author felt like vindication for that girl in college. Over the years, I'd enter his name into Amazon once in a while and find nothing.

When you type my pen name into Amazon, I'm everywhere. I've received countless messages that my books have lifted someone up when they were feeling down, gotten women through divorces and parent caregiving and deaths of spouses and children, that my book had changed their life.

Reid never did that with his writing. He never even came close.

All I have to do is avoid him in Goldheart. Hopefully he'll steer clear of Gold Roast once he knows I'm in town. He's not interested in finding me or confronting me or even apologizing. He's just a whiny little boy who never had anything go wrong for him.

I worked my ass off for this life, and it crashed around me. But I will pull myself back together. I always do. Nothing can touch me, not even Reid Finch.

I take one last look around at my empty house. I turn to Jodie and pull her in for a hug.

"You let me know if you're having a hard time, and I will be there," she whispers into my ear. "No questions asked."

"I'll be fine," I say, a tear slipping down my cheek.

I hope to God I'm right.

3

REID

"Hi, Mrs. Epstein!" I say, holding up a hand, my other hand cradling my overdue library books. "I'm afraid I'm late on these."

I set the library books down with a thwack.

"Wow, those are some honkers," Mrs. Epstein says, putting her glasses to her nose. They usually dangle from a beaded chain tucked into her cardigan. "I understand why you were late."

Having a late library book is not the end of world, Reid. Breathe.

"I didn't have as much time as I thought this week, and this one has a hold list a mile long. This one took so long, but it was worth it."

I tap the top book, a book about Old West gunslingers. It was dense and took me three renewals to get through before I finished, and I was still late. I finally feel like I'm close to dusting off my manuscript again, now that I understand the psyche of my main character even better.

One more non-fiction book is coming in the mail, and

after pulling research from it, I will be ready to get back on that horse.

I think.

I've been writing a book about a fictional vigilante gunslinger in the Wild West for years, but I keep getting stuck. Lots and lots of research is what I need.

Mrs. Epstein takes the books from me to check them back in.

Reading and researching are two of my favorite past times, and I love huge volumes, deep involved stories I can really sink myself into, far removed from my quiet life in the town I grew up in. The Wild West is endlessly fascinating to me, and I never get tired of learning about it.

Mrs. Epstein punches the numbers on the library's ancient computer, peering over her glasses. "That will be three dollars and fifty cents, son."

"Okay," I say, pulling out exact change and handing it to her. "Has it been busy today?" Busy for the Goldheart library is three people in the library at a time.

"Just one person," Mrs. Epstein says with a discreet point. "Typing away like she's mad at her computer."

I turn around to see dark hair, covered by large headphones over her ears, peeking over the top of an Apple MacBook. Mrs. Epstein is right—she's banging the keys like she's Jerry Maguire typing his manifesto.

The face shifts, and my blood runs cold.

Whitney Ferguson.

I didn't know she was going to be here. First, my coffee shop is off-limits, the best place in town to get iced coffee, and now she's here, in my other sanctuary.

My hands sweat and my throat closes.

"Dear, you look like you saw a spirit," Mrs. Epstein says.

I turn back and give a tight smile. "No, we used to know each other."

"What happened?" Mrs. Epstein asks. "Did you used to date?"

I shake my head. "Writer problems in college."

Our hatred for each other in college became a game, a fun push-pull where both parties participated and both parties took shots. I wasn't guilt-free, nor was she.

Until our final story, a revision of one we wrote earlier in the semester.

Whitney's story went from good to luminescent.

Her story sang on the page. I could even pinpoint specific changes that I had suggested.

I couldn't stop our game, though. When it came time for my feedback, I just said "Pass," and I could see her shoulders hunch and her spirit crumple. I didn't give her the story back, either. I still have it, tucked away in my school papers.

I'm not sure why.

Then we saw each other in May at Woody Finch's nineties prom and got in a spat. It was college all over again —me bringing up my inspiration trifecta of Steinbeck, Salinger, and Faulkner, and Whitney mentioning my trite and clichéd comments on her work.

I never fight with anyone, but she inspires me.

Now, my throat swells as I look at her. She just types away, never looking up.

"She's very pretty. You should go chat. It's been so long, and I'm sure a nice boy like you can make it better," Mrs. Epstein comments, opening a historical romance and burying her nose in it. "Go be your sweet self. I'll just be here, reading my book."

Bullshit. She'll be listening the second I say hi. Mrs. Epstein has gossipy friends, which encourages me to speak low. Nothing that sounds remotely like flirting. Just profuse apologizing.

"Thanks, Mrs. Epstein," I say. I straighten my shirt and walk over, my heart pounding.

Whitney had only gotten more beautiful in the years since college. Last time I saw her, she was in costume at the nineties prom, dressed as Annie Bates from *Misery*, but I much prefer her without the jumper and the mallet. Less chance of my ankles being smashed.

Her long dark hair looks like it would slip through my fingers, it's so silky. Her dazzling eyes, the color of aquamarines, are focused on her screen. Her shirt clings to her curves, and I try not to look.

It's time to apologize. Bury the hatchet. I really want to get my iced coffee without fear.

I stand next to her, waiting for her to sense my presence. She doesn't; she's wrapped up in her story and her music.

"Hi," I say.

Still nothing.

I touch her shoulder, and she jumps clear out of her chair, throwing her headphones.

"Jesus," she yells, grabbing her chest. "I almost peed my pants."

"Sorry I startled you."

Her porcelain skin flushes the colors of roses. Her eyes narrow as she looks at me.

I'm really glad she doesn't have the mallet.

"I thought I would come over and say hello. Officially welcome you to Goldheart," I say, adding a smile. Whitney's lips part in confusion. Her stare makes my throat fold into itself, and I cough. "Annie told me you were coming. She didn't say you would be at the library, though."

"Gold Roast was closed for the afternoon," she says,

crossing her arms. "I very much like this library too. Mrs. Epstein is nice. She asked me some deeply personal questions, but overall, nice."

"That's small-town life for you. Everyone thinks they're entitled to your business," I say with a chuckle.

She glares at me. This might be harder than I thought.

"Why are you talking to me?" Whitney asks, crossing her arms tighter.

I grumble into my hand. "You're Annie's friend, and Annie is my friend, so I thought I would welcome you to the neighborhood."

"You thought you would play nice."

"I guess," I say. God, this woman was intimidating. And words aren't working right now. "Why'd you pick here?"

"The library?"

"Goldheart," I say.

Whitney lets out a heavy sigh. "This is literally the only place I can write. I'm not leaving town until I finish this book I'm publishing at the end of the year."

I look over and Mrs. Epstein dips behind her mass market paperback. She was obviously listening in so she can report back to Miriam Oliver, Goldheart's biggest and nosiest busybody, and discuss it over lunch with the rest of the Bad Biddies.

The Bad Biddies is a term my siblings and I made up for a group of ladies who trade gossip like baseball cards. Mrs. Epstein will definitely mention us to the group later.

"I heard you published some romance. That's really cool," I say. "I wouldn't have guessed you would do it."

Her eyes narrow. Damn, I said the wrong thing.

"You didn't think I could do it?" she asks.

I pull at my collar, which suddenly feels tight. "It's just a lot of people in that class were never going to publish anything. Myself included."

"Have you ever finished a book, Reid?"

Since college, I've tried several times to start novels, usually from a kernel of an idea I get really excited about. I get about ten thousand words in and freeze, going back to edit the same words, tweaking them, making them the level of greatness I pictured in my head.

Then, if I didn't know a fact or I was unsure of the historical accuracy, I would read five books on the subject just to write a sentence.

This has been my cycle for three years.

My stomach churns at her abrasiveness, but I still stand there, and shake my head. "Writer's block."

"Well, I *have* finished books. Twenty-five, to be exact. When you say 'Lila Madden,' my pen name, people take notice. For me, writer's block is not an option," she says, smugness crossing those plush lips. "When I find a place that works for me, I have to capitalize on it. I'm sorry if that makes you uncomfortable."

"I'm not uncomfortable," I say. "It's just that..."

"It's just what? You can't handle me being here?"

"No, I...."

"No, you what? Can't stand seeing a woman more successful than you? Is that it?"

Heat crawls up my neck to my ears. People have razzed me, antagonized me, my entire life. *Reid is so easy to tease. Look how he turns red.*

Reid won't say anything.

All the while, my blood boils. Anger is ever present, but I never express it because I care what people think too much.

I close my eyes, feeling the pull of old patterns. Back down, give in. No conflict. No fighting. No matter how much someone pisses me off, a family member, a friend...keep your mouth shut. Peace is the most important thing.

I tried to be polite; I tried to apologize. Whitney still acts superior and smug, and I've had enough.

"Please stop interrupting me."

"Excuse me?" Whitney asked.

"I said, stop interrupting me," I say, louder this time. Loud enough that Mrs. Epstein drops her book. Whitney and I both look at her, and she shakes her hand.

"I'm not listening. Go ahead and keep fighting," she says, opening the paperback again.

I turn back toward Whitney. I don't care who hears about this later. It's time to take Whitney down a notch. Just because she's a successful romance author doesn't mean she can treat me like shit. No matter how uncomfortable this makes me, it's time I tell her how it's going to be.

I lean over the table, place my palms on the faux wood, and lean toward her. Our faces are inches apart.

"This is my town," I say, my voice low. "You can't come in here and treat me like this. If we're going to live in the same place for a little while, I demand some common courtesy from you."

Her face lengthens, and her bright blue eyes widen. I watch her throat swallow. I hope an apology tumbles out, but it doesn't.

I shouldn't have expected it.

She leans back. "Admit it. You look down on romance, but it's a billion-dollar-a-year industry. It keeps publishing afloat."

"Romance is not my thing. It just seems far-fetched. Not everything ends in a happily ever after. Falling in love is the easy part. It's staying in love that is hard."

"No shit," she says. Her shoulders relax now that I'm standing straight. "You may be more jaded than me."

Her stare could eviscerate any man. But I'm done being any man.

"What happened, Reid? Did some woman dump you and break your heart because you're *literally the worst*? Or are you terrible in bed?"

Not matter if this is a real fear of mine, she can't know.

Channel The Rock. Dwayne wouldn't put up with this shit. I pull my shoulders back.

"You'll never know," I say, leaning over the table. I notice a slight hitch in her breath. The air sizzles between us, and it confuses me. Why did I whisper? Why did I try something I saw Cameron do once at a bar?

I have zero romantic interest in Whitney whatsoever.

"What a relief," she says.

That's my cue. Any more fighting, and my mother will be hearing from Miriam. I'm already tempting the Goldheart rumor mill.

I knock on the table. "Have the day you deserve, Whitney." I walk away, Mrs. Epstein's gaze lasering in on me as I leave. I don't have any reading material for the week, so I hope that book I ordered comes soon. I'll reread something on my shelves in the interim rather than spend one more moment in the same building as Whitney.

My temples pound as I walk out in the muggy air. My heart thunders against my chest, and a wash of relief floods my system as I breathe in.

When I get in my car, I look around for witnesses, before I hit my steering wheel in frustration so hard, I yelp, shaking my palm to alleviate the pain.

Whitney Ferguson may be beautiful, but she's ugly on the inside. When I look back up, Mrs. Epstein is tilting her glasses toward me, holding a bag of trash in her hand as she heads to the dumpster.

She looks at me like she just witnessed the beginning of a love story.

Far from it. If I never see Whitney again, it's too soon.

That woman is the opposite of what I want. I don't care if she doesn't like me, because I know I can't stand her.

Before I start my car, I find my brother's number in my phone.

Jackson grunts when he picks up the call after two rings.

"Do you still have that Scotch? I can bring over stuff to make dinner. Maybe pasta?"

"Any food I don't have to cook sounds good to me."

"I'll stop by the market after brewing."

"Sounds good."

We arrange a time and I head back to work, nerves shooting through my fingers as I replay our spat, over and over again.

4

WHITNEY

"This market is so cute. And tiny," I say to Annie as she holds the door open so I can take a cart inside.

"Get used to it. It's all that's close for ten miles."

I breathe in and out. Perfect.

Tonight, we're making dinner together at Annie's. Annie is off and her boyfriend Cameron is working late, so I have her all to myself. We're planning a delicious dinner with wine, after-dinner popcorn and chocolate, and watching *13 Going on 30*, a modern classic.

I'm in a great mood. I wrote seven thousand words at the Goldheart Public Library, got my library card, and checked out the new Louise Penny. I've *almost* forgotten about the letter from my mother. My first day in Goldheart was perfection, except for my run-in with Reid Finch.

I clench my fists every time I think of him.

He looks different, better out of his costume he wore to the prom. He even grew a beard, and I hate to admit it, but it looks fantastic on him. All I can remember is him hovering over me, whispering to me so the librarian couldn't hear, insinuating he would never sleep with me.

My mind cheers, but my pussy is confused.

Damn those dark romance novels.

I've been writing too many alpha males lately. Rude, mean men who are also sexy have warped my vision of healthy lust and healthy relationships.

All I know is toxic.

Let's just say I need a glass of wine the size of my head.

Annie unfolds her list and places it in the purse basket, right next to my handbag.

"Okay, tomatoes," she says, pointing to the produce.

We turn the corner by an endcap of cheese puffs to see Reid, touching every dang tomato in a pile. Watching him squeeze a plump tomato does something to the apex of my legs.

His big hand on my breast, massaging my nipple with his thumb...

"Whitney," Annie says.

I blink furiously. "What?"

"Reid is over there," Annie says.

"I know. I already saw him today."

"And?" Annie asks, her eyes lighting up like a Vegas billboard.

"It didn't go well. We argued. He was being a dick."

Annie's face twists in confusion. "Huh, that's weird. He's usually very sweet."

"Reid? We're talking about the same Reid, right?"

She nods as she walks over to him, her purse swaying on her shoulder.

"Hey, Reid," Annie says. When he looks up, he grins, his teeth annoyingly straight.

That smile must be reserved for people he likes.

He closes his mouth when he sees me.

"You again," I say, unable to hide the disdain in my voice.

"Me," Reid says, holding up a tomato in each hand. He cradles them gently, and I bite my lip.

God, Whitney, you are a romance author cliché. What now, you write "the hero lifts her breasts like tomatoes at the supermarket"?

"Why are you... touching everything? You're getting your germs all over the produce."

"There's already pesticides," Reid says, putting a tomato back on its pile. He looks down and grumbles. It's almost... hot. "What are you ladies up to?"

"We're having our first official celebration of Whitney being in Goldheart. We're making homemade sauce with pasta, your favorite. Garlic bread too. Do you want to come?"

"No," we say in unison. I turn to Annie and whisper, "Why would you invite him?"

"He's lonely," Annie whispers back through gritted teeth.

He deserves to be lonely with *that* personality.

"I have plans tonight anyway," Reid says. He puts the handle of his basket on his forearm. His delicious forearm.

That makes me pause. Is it another girl? It makes my skin tingle to think of him with another woman. Potentially lifting her tomatoes.

I wonder what she looks like. I wonder if she has as great tomatoes as I have.

I doubt it. My boobs are pretty fantastic.

Annie asks, "Is it her?"

Who is *her*?

Reid shakes his head. "Jackson. He has good Scotch."

My skin flushes harder. Goddammit, why am I sweating over a terrible man in a supermarket?

"That's nice you guys are hanging out," Annie says. "Come on, Whitney."

She pulls me away from the produce, leading the cart to one of three aisles to hide. She looks around before getting in my face. I can count the freckles on her nose.

"What...was...that?" Annie asks, gritting her teeth.

Instinctively, I cross my arms. "Nothing."

"That...was something," Annie says, pointing. "I thought you were going to be polite."

"We argued in the library."

"Was Mrs. Epstein there?"

I nod.

"Oh no. This could be bad."

"Why?"

"The Bad Biddies Club."

"The Bad Biddies Club?" I ask. "What is that?"

Annie leans in closer. "There's a group of women over sixty who get together and knit and talk crap. They bring wine and gossip. Miriam Oliver spearheads it, and she roped in Mrs. Epstein. It's a whole thing. I almost crapped myself when I saw them all together at Betty's Café, talking on the patio. Those women know everything that goes on in this town. I'm surprised Reid's mom hasn't called me yet about you two."

"Oh God," I say, covering my mouth. I always thought small-town gossip networks were a myth. People really do know everyone here. I've been here for less than a day, and I've already seen Reid twice.

Annie nods slowly. "Miriam Oliver is the worst. She saw Cameron and me when we were fake dating and told Kit, Cameron and Reid's mom. It all worked out for us, obviously, but the less that woman is in your business, the better."

"Please," I say, flipping my hand. "I've dealt with bitches. I can handle this Miriam lady."

Annie shakes her head vigorously. "You don't understand. You do *not* mess with Miriam. It just turns out badly. She holds a grudge, and now she has her minions. It's like a geriatric Plastics."

"Like *Mean Girls*?" I ask. "I haven't seen that in a while. We should watch that tonight too."

"Definitely," Annie says. "Let's head over to the meat section."

As we go to the small section of meat, all locally sourced and fresh, we see Reid at the eggs. Inspecting them like he must have to inspect the vagina to find the clitoris.

That man definitely doesn't know where the clitoris is. Or he has to go on a treasure hunt because he doesn't retain general female anatomy from sex ed.

"Ladies," he says.

"Ugh," I say. Annie, ever the peacekeeper, smiles and laughs.

"Small-town life," Reid says, throwing up his hands. He seems to have forgotten the eggs are in his hands and flings a full carton in our direction. It drops to the ground like a grenade. Annie's quick reflexes get her out of the way, but I'm not so lucky. Egg slime goes flying, nailing me.

He covers his mouth with his hands. "I am so sorry. I didn't mean..."

"It's fine," I say through gritted teeth.

"I'll go get a towel or something," Reid says, scampering off.

In dread, I look down. He got my beige shorts and my new white top, both obtained through a wine-induced shopping spree the night I signed my divorce papers. Chicken goop is all over my leather sandals.

"First day in Goldheart," I say.

Annie muffles a laugh behind her hand.

"What's so funny?" I ask.

"This would only happen between the two of you."

"There's nothing 'between' the two of us," I say. I stand frozen as Reid jogs back, a white towel in his hands. The cashier follows him with a rolling bucket and a mop.

"Whitney, this is Bea. Her family has owned this market for fifty years."

"You new in town?" Bea asks, looking me up and down. I open my mouth to speak, but Annie beats me.

"She's staying with me," she says. There's a protective tone in her voice.

"Where are you from?" Bea asks. Wow, the questions sound like an interrogation.

"I live in Reno, but I'm originally from Oregon."

"Thank you, Bea," Reid says loudly. "I'll clean up for you."

"You don't need to."

"You know what my mother always says. You break it, you clean it up, and pay for it."

"Are you sure?"

"Of course," Reid says. Bea smiles and pats Reid on the cheek before shuffling down the aisle.

Well, at least he's polite to his elders.

Reid hands me a towel, and I snatch it from his hands. I try to remove the sludge from my legs, but the egg just spreads.

"She's one of them," Annie whispers.

"What?" I ask, my eyes wide.

"The Bad Biddies," Reid says. "Mrs. Epstein is one of them too. You and I will be a hot topic at their next Wine and Dine."

"They have nothing to talk about," Whitney says.

"Doesn't stop them. They create whatever narrative they want. Like you do," Reid says.

Now he's patronizing me. *Stay calm, Whitney. You can do it.* I breathe in and out through my nose.

"Are you okay?" Annie asks.

"I'm just trying not to give him a tongue-lashing. Hurt his feelings."

"You can't hurt my feelings. I grew up with two older brothers," Reid says.

"You want to try me?" I ask, taking a step toward him. My head feels like a boiling tea kettle, the water bubbling so close, about to burst out.

Why am I taking a step toward him like I'm going to kick his ass? I'm not strong; I'm hunched over a computer for eight hours a day. Reid doesn't look like he spends hours at the gym, but I saw a hint of a bicep at the library, and he has some nice forearms.

I blame all the thirst traps my readers post in my reader group. I wrote nice forearms on a Russian mob boss once, and *they will not let it go.*

"Will you two stop? Please?" Annie asks. "You are being ridiculous."

"Okay," I say, pushing my hair away from my face. I close my eyes to take a deep inhale and exhale. "I'm cool now."

"Good," Reid says, his mouth slightly parted with a gaze that could burn a hole in my face. He looks angrier than I feel right now.

"You are my friend." Annie turns to Reid. "And you are my friend too. You both need to get over your beef and chill. In front of this beef."

We turn to find ourselves in front of the steak section.

"I doubt it, Annie. Whitney is the only time I've questioned your taste."

"Oh, now it's on," I say, reaching to take out one of my earrings.

"Keep your earrings on," Annie says. As she pulls me away, I stick out my tongue at Reid like an eight-year-old. He not only sticks out his tongue, but he raises me moose ears. Then, I pound my fists together like I'm a character on *Friends,* and he does the same thing.

"Get away from him," she says. Once we're safely in another aisle, she turns to me. "What is *wrong* with you?"

"What?" I ask. My breath slows, but my heart races.

Hatred is kind of fun. As an author, I have to be positive and nice to fans all the time, so being nasty feels liberating.

"You and Reid. You turned into third-graders who secretly crush on each other."

"I *do not* have a crush on him," I say. "I never want to be around him again. He got egg on my new sandals."

"That will come out. I have just the thing in my cleaning cabinet," she says. "It's a shame, really. I wanted you to be my partner at the Woody Finch Olympics."

"The Woody Finch Olympics?"

She nods. "It's the first one. Cameron planned it all on his own. He'll be working it, so I need a partner. Reid will be there, though."

"When is it?"

"Sunday," she says. "It's the last weekend before football starts, and then I'll really never see my boyfriend again."

"Sounds like fun," I say. Worry etches her face, and I feel terrible. Annie is a good friend, and I let my temper get the best of me. Once it's turned on, I can't stop it. I lay a hand on her shoulder. "I promise I'll be on my best behavior. As long as you talk to Reid and tell him to stay away from me."

"I promise I will talk to Reid." Annie throws her arms around me, resting her chin on my shoulder. "No matter how funny your fighting is, you can't fight at the brewery."

"I promise. As long as Reid promises."

Annie pulls away, reaching around me to grab a box of brownie mix off of the shelf and holds it up.

"Yes," I say with a point. "Definitely yes."

"Let's go back to the tomatoes," Annie says. "Reid has probably moved on right now."

"We'll just have to find the ones he didn't fondle."

Annie smirks at me as we wheel the cart back toward produce.

"Dude, get out of dreamland and serve the people!" my brother Cameron says, slapping my back as I shake out of my mind daze.

The brewery has a line fifteen people deep, all fifteen minutes before our Woody Finch Olympics start. Ever since Cameron planned the adult prom, he's been a student of Pinterest and event-planning Instagram pages. It went from simple trivia nights to out-there ideas, some more popular than not. There was a mac-n-cheese/beer pairing night that gave me acid reflux for two days, a ventriloquist with a dummy that creeped me out that *nobody* came to, and my personal favorite, a dog fashion show that gave my dad pure joy.

That one made a lot of money. At one point, my dad was showering the dog models with dollar bills, all money that was donated to the local animal shelter. It was Cameron's idea to have donators shower the dogs with cash, like they were in the champagne room at the Low High, a strip club just outside of town.

Now, the Woody Finch Olympics.

This event is a way to get some of the locals in our doors now that the tourists have dwindled down due to the end of tourist season. Cameron's master plan is to do a dry run and then bring it back next year at the height of our busy season.

He made Olympic rings out of the tops of kegs, almost burning his hand when he welded it together with his buddy, Thumper. Thumper needed to blow off some steam after being locked in a room at the town bank for three hours when the bank was held up by a person in a chicken costume.

It's a long story better suited for another time.

The setup looks great, all the stations are clearly organized, and I'm seeing faces in our taproom I've never seen.

Thank God I talked Dad into putting an alcoholic seltzer on the menu for the White Claw-loving folks. Goldheart loves their boozy seltzers.

"Distracted with a girl?" Cameron asks, putting two beers in front of Pete, who usually hangs out at The Swift more than our taproom. Winston, his usual drinking buddy, must be around somewhere too.

"No," I say. The less I say about it, the better.

Truthfully, I'm distracted that Whitney will be here today, and I don't know how I feel about it. Mentally, I'm cupping my balls in case she tries to take a sharp boot to them verbally.

Pete takes his beer and gets out of line, revealing Miriam Oliver.

"Not it," Cameron says, calling the person behind her in line.

My entire family has a problem with Miriam, except for me. Sure, she gets into everybody's business and prods people for gossip, but I've never been a target of hers, since I'm the most boring guy in Goldheart. I remember one night at book club she chatted with me about Callie, telling me I deserved better.

Now, all of the Bad Biddies give Callie the stink eye around town.

"Oh, hello, Reid. How are you?" Miriam asks.

"I'm great, Miriam. What can I get you?"

Miriam stares at the menu like she just noticed it even though she's probably been standing in line for fifteen minutes. She squints as she tries to read it.

"Which one is your favorite?"

"Gold Dust IPA," I say, recommending our most popular beer. This woman probably wouldn't like it. The hops are overpowering, and if you're not used to that flavor, hops are all you taste.

Miriam winces. "Is Dan the Man good?"

I grumble, but mask it with a smile. We put Dan the Man on our menu because our investor Dan likes mild beers. His palette ranges from Coors Light to Bud Light. Dan the Man has zero flavor to me, but then I like my hops to punch me in the face.

"It's very light. Refreshing."

"We'll just get Dan the Man. Two of them, please." She pauses and asks, "So, are you seeing anyone special nowadays, Reid?"

I go to turn toward the taps, when I see dark hair enter the brewery. Dark hair that belongs to the most beautiful woman I've ever seen. The beautiful woman I don't get along with at all.

Whitney is wearing short shorts that barely cover her round behind, and her tank top clings to her curves in a way that makes my mouth water and my brain short-circuit.

"Isn't that your girlfriend's friend, Cameron?" Miriam asks my brother, busy pouring a cider. "What's her name?"

Blood drains from my cheeks. Cameron says, "Yep. Whitney. She's cool."

Cool as in stone-cold toward me.

I don't care that she hates me. I really don't.

"Reid, do you need me or the ladies to put in a good word?" Miriam says, leaning onto the counter. I see several people behind her, tapping their feet and growing more and more impatient.

I turn to the taps. "She hates me."

"How could anyone hate you? You're the best man in Goldheart."

Cameron's head snaps toward Miriam. "What about me, Miriam?"

"You're working on it. Frankly, you dating Annie Stewart and treating her like a queen makes me like you more. However, you haven't done half the nice things Reid has."

Blood floods my cheeks again. I bet they're neon pink.

It's nice to be recognized. I try to be a good man, a generous man, and while I don't expect accolades, I'm glad someone notices.

My parents don't seem to be aware what my siblings and I contribute to this family. They've barely acknowledged how Cameron has single-handedly turned this brewery around with his fun community events, or how Emily juggles her work at the brewery with her jewelry business and with raising Olive. How Jackson returned for our dad, even if the town holds bittersweet memories.

They've always expected a lot of us, even into adulthood.

"Here you go," I say, turning around with beers for Miriam. "Do you want to open a tab?"

"Just close it out," she says, handing over a card. I run the card and present her with a receipt to sign. Miriam tips seven bucks.

"Go buy that girl a drink," Miriam says with a wink. "I can't wait for the Olympics. I hope my dear Leland doesn't embarrass me."

We wait for her to walk away, studying her like a science experiment.

"Is Miriam terminally ill and worried about meeting her maker?" Cameron asks. "She even *tipped*." She never tips. Ever.

"That was weird, right?" I ask.

"Absolutely. She knows something." Cameron takes the next customer's order while I watch Miriam drop off her beers to her husband, Leland, who is sitting uncomfortably close to Annie and Whitney. She's definitely going to say something.

You give the Bad Biddies *one* little clue, and they run with it.

Cameron finishes the cider, and starts tapping our IPA, tipping the beer to let the foam off so he can fill it with more liquid. Usually, he's faster than this. I take another order, give a recommendation, and turn toward our kegs. I pull two fresh glasses from under the bar and begin tapping another Dan the Man. For such a weak beer, it sure is popular tonight.

"Dude, are you into Whitney?" Cameron whispers.

"Absolutely not. We got in a fight at the market," I say.

"I heard from Annie. Did you throw eggs at her, bro? I didn't know you had it in you."

I know I'm tomato-red now. "It was an accident. You know how I hate confrontation. Makes me nervous."

It wasn't the confrontation; it was everything about Whitney. The way she ran her tongue over her lips to wet them, the way her stare challenged me. I want to wring her neck, but I also want to touch her skin to see if it's as soft as I think it is.

Emily appears from the back. She handles the social media and is the only parent out of the four of us, mother to our eight-year-old niece, Olive. Olive almost never gets screen privileges, but when it comes to events like this, Emily sticks Olive in the back with an iPad and lets her watch as much as she wants.

"Wow," Emily says, looking at the line.

"Can you step in? I'm going to bring some drinks over to Annie and Whitney," I say, wiping my hands on my jeans.

Miriam is leaning in, chatting with them, like she's Brutus plotting against Caesar. There is a good chance she's talking about me. Whitney and Annie lean in, captivated by the old gossipmonger.

I need to get over there as soon as possible.

"Why is he worried about Miriam talking to Whitney?" Emily asks. Cameron gives her a look. "Ooh."

"There's nothing going on, I promise. She hates me. I don't hate her, but I'm done dating women who hate me."

"Uh-huh," my siblings say in unison.

"Leave me alone! Do you know what they want?" I ask Cameron.

Cameron pulls his phone out. "Annie texted me. A cider and Night Music."

Without a word, I pour the cider and our stout, Night Music. Annie likes our cider, and any woman picking the Night Music instantly intrigues me. It takes a special kind of woman to enjoy the rich coffee and licorice notes of our stout. While a stout has little to no hops, it's my second favorite style to a solid West Coast IPA.

It's an excellent choice.

And my stout is superb, if I don't say so myself.

I walk the drinks over to them as Miriam is chatting with Annie and Whitney.

"Here you go," I say, putting the drinks down in front of Annie and Whitney. I watch Miriam. She doesn't look *that* guilty, but I wouldn't be surprised if she was in the CIA.

Miriam Oliver is everywhere.

"Thank you so much, Reid," Annie says. Her gaze zeroes in on Whitney. "Isn't Reid so nice, Whitney?"

"The nicest," Whitney says through gritted teeth. Annie has fully prepped her like a plaintiff for a deposition. Excellent.

"Are you going to participate in the Olympics, Reid?" Miriam asks, looking up at me with folded hands.

"Yep," I say. "Jackson promised he would come out of hiding to be my partner." Dad wants some participation from us kids in the event and nominated me and Jackson, since we were the only ones not involved with the planning or promo of the event.

The area between Whitney's eyebrows creases when Miriam explains to her, "Jackson's the oldest Finch. Doesn't like to be out in public much."

"Oh," Whitney says. She turns toward me, smoldering smoke in her eyes. "Well, I hope that I beat you."

"If I don't beat you first."

"Care to wager?" Whitney asks.

"Oh, definitely."

At this point, I don't care about Miriam and Leland or even Annie watching. All I want is to fight with this woman, get under her skin, make her so angry that her cheeks turn pink and she looks at me with that infuriating glare again.

It's just so fun.

"If we win," Whitney says slowly, "you have to read one of my books."

"And if I win, you have to name one of your male leads after me. A really hot one."

"It's on," Whitney says, holding out her hand to shake.

"It's definitely on." When I take her hand in mine, heat crawls up my arm. Our gaze locks on each other, and there's a moment—a miniscule, tiny moment—where I want to crush my lips to hers. See if this heat transfers into passion.

I'm so tired of being nice.

She drops her gaze and hand at the same and coughs, taking a sip of her dark beer. She licks the foam from her lips, and I look away.

Nothing would give me more pleasure than Whitney having to name a character after me. Talking about his cock. His swagger.

Truly, nothing would make me happier.

The line dwindled in the time I talked to Annie and Whitney and is now a manageable five parties in line. Emily scurries from the bar to the taps to our computer like she's on two-times speed. She gives me a thumbs-up, and I point to the office and mouth, "Jackson."

Focus is what I need now. First, though, I need a partner.

I pass a couple customers in the hallway, since it leads to the bathroom as well as our offices. When I get to the family office, I knock before I open.

The office is completely dark except for the glow of the computer screen. I see the outline of my brother staring at it, his fingers clicking the keys. He doesn't turn; he doesn't say anything.

Over the last few months, since he came home from Seattle, no one else seems to be worrying about him, not like I've been.

"Jackson," I say, "we're about to start the Olympics."

"I'll be out in a sec. I'm almost done with this budget."

I pause. "You'll come out for sure?"

Annoyance dances on his face as he turns around. "I'll be out once I'm done with these numbers. It will be a few minutes."

"I'll see you out there," I say, closing the door.

My other siblings' eyes bore into me as I walk around the bar.

"Is Jackson coming?" Emily asks, pouring one of our IPAs into a sniffer glass.

"He said he was, but you know him."

"I will drag him out myself if he doesn't," Emily says.

"Good," I say. "Do you think we baby him too much?"

"Absolutely," Emily agrees. "It sucks what happened. Absolutely. But it's been ten years."

"I agree." I take the next customer's order, a flight of four beers. I go to the next customer as the flight-purchaser fills out their card with their sample choices. After ten minutes, we finally clear the line, and Cameron looks at Emily and me.

"You ready for this?"

We nod.

I breathe in and out as I look across the room at Whitney, laughing so hard it makes her eyes sparkle.

That's what she looks like happy. When she's not being mean, she's enchanting.

I don't hear Jackson until he's next to me. His hair is tied back in a tiny stub of a ponytail, and his dark circles under his eyes aren't as pronounced as usual. I wonder if that means he's been getting sleep lately. His glasses slide down his nose.

"Are you ready to play some games?" he asks, monotone, and his hands shoved in his pockets.

"Yeah," I say, smacking him on his chest that feels

deceivingly muscular. "Are you ready for some corn hole? I think that's the first event."

"Sure," he says, his jaw flexing. Nowadays, Jackson participating in anything but financial systems and reports is like childbirth: arduous and a miracle.

We walk outside to three separate lanes of corn hole, each surrounded by red, white, and blue garlands.

Cameron rushes outside with a bull horn, announcing that the first event is going to take place.

"We're going to do heats and brackets ...."

Our names aren't called in the first round so we watch the first batch of teams play, and I rush inside to get us some beer to help with our aim. I know I'm always better a little bit tipsy when I bowl, and it must be the same for corn hole.

When I come back with the beers, Jackson grumbles a thank-you, and we cheers.

Looking to the side, I see Whitney watching me. When I turn away and look back, her eyes haven't moved from my direction.

"God," I say to myself as I pound more beer. How I can be so annoyed and aroused at the same time?

"What?" Jackson asks.

"What?" I repeat.

"You're acting strange." Jackson's face is long and expressionless. He looks at Whitney, who is biting her lip, maybe to be sexy, maybe to plot my murder. I can't tell.

"Who is that?" he asks.

"Who?" I say innocently.

I know damn well who he is talking about.

"The woman with Annie."

"The infuriating, dark-haired woman? Oh, that's Whitney."

"Oh," he says again, pursuing out his bottom lip before taking a swig of his beer. "She's cute."

"She is. And she uses it for evil."

"What are we talking about?" Emily asks as she comes up behind us, throwing her arms around our shoulders even though she's half a foot shorter than us.

"Reid might hate-fuck Annie's friend later," Jackson says, taking a sip.

Emily leans over in shock and almost takes us down. "Hey," Jackson yells.

"Sorry, I just...that was surprising. From you, I mean, Jackson," Emily says.

"Next up, we have Team Clit and Caboodle and Team Finch Bros to start us off at this corn hole," Cameron reads off.

Whitney and I lock eyes with each other and mouth "Fuck" in each other's direction.

"*Definitely* hate-fucking," Jackson says, sipping his beer. I glare at him.

Cameron repeats the rules—team members stand at the end of each corn hole, diagonal from their partner. Each partner takes turns launching a beanbag to get on the board or in the hole. Through the hole is three points. A beanbag that lands on the board and stays on is one point. For brevity's sake, we will not do the cancellation scoring and each team gets two beanbags per partner. Partners need to be on opposite boards for fairness. The team with the most points after two rounds wins.

Jackson speed-walks to Annie's side while Whitney walks toward me gingerly, like I might be rabid.

"You're going down, Finch," Whitney says.

"It's on," I say, rubbing my palms together. "I'm going to knock all your beanbags off of the board."

"That doesn't win the game, asshole."

"I don't care. My new mission in life is to piss you off," I say, narrowing my eyes.

"You can croak now."

"Oh, bite me."

"Chew on barbed wire," Whitney retorts, and I shut up.

That was pretty good.

Jackson is pushing up his sleeves and rubs his hands together. I point to my eyeballs with my pointer and middle fingers and point to him, and he reciprocates.

"Ladies first," I say, motioning to Whitney.

"I don't participate in patriarchal ideals," Whitney says, with crossed arms under her amazing breasts. Is she pushing them up on purpose to get in my head? "You go first."

"Fine," I say, gritted through my teeth. I launch the first beanbag, and it goes clean through the hole.

I pantomime taking a foul line shot. "Nothing but net!" Then, both of my arms go up in victory as Whitney rolls her eyes. I retreat back, arms outstretched. "That's how it's done."

"Whatever," Whitney says. Her body goes still as she contemplates the physics, priming to launch at the opposite corn hole. She swings back her arm, and the beanbag goes up in a perfect arch, hitting the wood with a thud. Jackson and Annie watch it slide up the platform, stopping inches from the circle.

"So close!" I yell at her as she rolls her eyes again, her lips pressed together in fury.

"We'll get that back," Annie says, clapping like she's a kiddie soccer coach. Whitney fumes.

Perfect.

"Jackson, you're next," I call. "Sink it like the Titanic."

Jackson launches the beanbag with no stance, and it lands on the platform in front of us. That does get us one point, if it stays.

"Another one," I yell in Whitney's face, bending my legs so I can get face level. I expect her to disregard me, but she pushes up against me, tilting her head.

Her breasts press into my chest, and she looks up at me with defiance. I clench my jaw because this is too close for comfort. My dick is very confused.

"Are they going to fight or make out?" I hear Tom, one of our part-timers, ask. I wish I could stop antagonizing her.

But I can't.

"You think you can be all cocky." She looks up at me like she's done time in prison. With her temper, I wouldn't be surprised if there had been an overnight visit at least.

"You suck so far." I jerk my head for emphasis. I think some spittle may have accidentally left my mouth.

"At least I've published books."

Then her body is gone, and she refocuses on her partner, cheering Annie on.

What the fuck just happened? Does she want me? Or is she fucking with me? Or both? I shift in my jeans, my cock pushing against my zipper.

Whitney is objectively hot. It's totally normal for my dumbest organ to misunderstand.

"Come on, baby!" Cam yells in the bullhorn, morphing into a boyfriend instead of a MC.

I scowl at Cameron, and he throws up his hands and then points at Annie. "Annie lets me have sex with her. I have to cheer her on."

"Honey!" Annie says, the beanbag cradled in her hands like a fresh-laid egg.

"What? Everyone knows you have sex with me, baby. I

mean, look at this," Cameron says, sweeping his hand from head to toe. Annie matches her partner's rolling eyes and concentrates. Whitney and I watch her intently, me trying to will the beanbag away from the platform and Whitney praying for a clean dunk.

Annie pulls back her arm and lets go, the beanbag's curve almost flat. The bag lands on the platform, avoiding Jackson's, then bounces clean through the hole.

"Yes, YES!" Whitney screams. She throws hands now. "Suck on that, Finch. Suck on that shit."

"There are kids in the audience," I say. "Keep your voice down."

"I can say whatever I want." Her voice is low, meant only for me. Her eyelids lower, her blue eyes peeking through slits. Those pouty pink lips are parted slightly, and I can hear her breath.

She's back to hate-flirting with me.

I can't take this.

"It's my turn," I say, holding up a beanbag between the two of us. I lean in closer, and I watch her eyelashes flutter. Maybe she wants me to kiss her too. "I plan to destroy you."

"I would like to see you try."

Turning away, I stare at my target, visualizing the beanbag sliding through the hole again like last time. I'm Kobe Bryant. I'm Michael Jordan at the foul line. Looking at her, I kiss the disgusting beanbag, making eye contact with Whitney.

"Stop flirting and go!" Cameron says.

I chuck the beanbag so it goes high. It lands several inches away from the hole and then slides onto the ground.

I drop to my knees and shake my fists at the sky.

Whitney dances around me like a witch at a bonfire.

"Don't get too cocky, woman," I say. "You haven't won yet."

"Oh, I will win. I eat excellence for breakfast," she says.

"What, eggs?" I ask, touching the sore spot. How I accidentally egged her legs.

"Fuck you. I liked those sandals," she says.

"I'll buy you some new ones."

She freezes, unable to react. It disarms her, even more than the insults and the jabs. It dawns on me. Kindness messes her up more than insults.

A smile crosses my lips, a smile Tim Curry would be proud of.

"You can do it, you strong, independent woman," I say.

"Shut up, Finch," she says.

"You are so skilled in everything you try."

"What are you doing? Are you being sarcastic?"

"No. I want to bow down to you, you capable empress," I say.

Whitney is flustered. My compliment-bombing is working. She shakes her head, her cheeks flushed, the red traveling down her throat. She pulls back her arm and tosses the beanbag, which falls short but and lands on top of my fallen beanbag.

"That was oddly satisfying," Whitney says.

I grit my teeth. Jackson is our only hope.

"Jackson, you gotta save us. You gotta clinch this!" I say, standing up. Getting Jackson to participate at his full potential is something none of us expect so when Jackson actually squares up so his beanbag sails through the air and clears the hole, I run over and attack him, wrapping my legs around his waist like we did when we were kids.

He actually holds me around my torso and jostles me with an arm outstretched. It feels like nothing has changed.

Whitney runs over to Annie and gives her a pep talk, so low I can't hear. It doesn't matter because even if she sinks a beanbag through the hole, we win.

Still, Annie nods once and pulls back her arm. Her beanbag lands on the box, then slides off.

"We win! We win!" I say, yelling. Whitney and Annie congregate, hugging each other. I walk over and extend my hand.

"Good game," I say. Annie takes me in a hug after Whitney hesitates. Whitney's arms are crossed, her breasts pressed up, and I try not to look.

"The Olympics aren't over yet," Whitney says. "Annie and I will get our victory back."

"I love your confidence," I say.

Whitney lets out a tiny scream and stamps her foot. "Stop patronizing me."

"Can't I compliment you?" My smile reaches to my eyeballs, because this is angering her more than any insult I could hurl. Plus, it doesn't feel gross. My people-pleasing loves to give compliments.

"Those are not compliments," Whitney says. "Say what you really feel. I know you want to say something snide."

I wink at her. "If I say something snide, will you press your body against me again?"

Whitney's cheeks slack, and I walk away, wrapping my arm around Jackson.

"I don't want to be a chess piece in this weird flirting ritual," Jackson says.

"Come on, it's fun," I say.

"Whatever," Jackson says. "How much longer?"

"Two more events, and then you can go back to your spreadsheets."

Jackson nods once. "I need another beer. You want one?"

"Of course."

I look back at Whitney, and our gaze catches. It lasts a beat longer than I expect, and I don't know if it means we want each other or we still hate each other. The latter is confirmed when Whitney sticks her tongue out and I stick mine out back.

"You two are insufferable," Jackson says, returning with a beer for him and me. "I might need two beers."

6

WHITNEY

My irritation is at an eleven.

I'm also ridiculously turned-on.

Reid was inches from my lips, and there was a brief moment I thought we were going to kiss. My lips parted like my legs did in college and I would've lost my mind and let him, if we were alone and our hatred wasn't so well-documented.

Then, he started complimenting me on my personality, my strength, and I could not contain my anger. People see the dark hair and the blue eyes and the boobs and think I'm less than. Reid complimenting me exactly the way I've wanted to be complimented my entire life grates my nerves.

His comments destroyed me in college, and while I've gotten several, stinging ones since then, none of them hurt quite like Reid's.

Growing up, I had always loved to write, but that class was the first time I showed it to anyone. Reid's feedback was the first time I had heard criticism, and it branded me. It shook my confidence.

I hate the sight of him, but I can't stop looking.

Jackson and Reid lose in the first round to a couple guys wearing backward caps and work boots, who play with a beer in their free hand. They're suspiciously good at beer pong. Reid sees my gloating as I bobble my head, and he bobbles his back, sticking out his tongue at me again.

Maybe the compliments are over. Damn him.

Annie and I are defeated in the second round of beer pong, after being paired with a couple of women just happy to be there, but I don't even care, because that puts us even with the Finches, and it all comes down the final, tie-breaker event.

Because we played an extra round of beer pong, my head is woozy and light from all the beer.

It also makes Reid more attractive to me, despite his horrible personality.

The final showdown comes down to Jenga, a super-sized version I've only seen in backyard parties my ex and I attended sometimes. Brad was the VIP when we played Jenga, all steady hands and strategy.

I'm like Miley Cyrus—a wrecking ball of chaos.

A cocktail of excitement and disgust swirl inside of me when I realize the final showdown is me and Annie against Reid and Jackson. Standing next to Reid makes my heart beat fast like a hummingbird's wings.

Why does he have to smell so good?

"So we meet again," Reid says. His voice is low and gravelly.

Don't flirt. Don't you dare flirt with him. "Are you ready to lose, Finch?"

"I never lose at Jenga," Reid says. "This is my family's brewery. Guess whose idea it was to have Jenga as part of the Olympics?"

I glare at him, unsure if he's bluffing or not. Reid is prob-ably good with his hands.

No. I shake my head. *You cannot think about Reid's hands.*

"Do you want me to go first again?" Reid asks.

"No, I'll go," I say. I tap a middle block at the base, and after I pull it out cleanly, I place the block on top. Reid's eyebrow flicks up.

"The base, already?" he asks.

"I came to win," I say. "Slow and steady."

Reid steps forward and picks a block halfway up the tower, pulling out an end block. He's playing dirty, picking out a side block so soon. Annie takes a safe block, another middle one, and then Jackson picks another middle one. I inspect the level that Reid picked out the end block and chose the block on the opposite side, so half of the tower balances on one block.

I'm never so bold so soon at Jenga, but Reid brings it out of me.

It's the first time it wobbles. Along with my confidence.

Reid stares me down. "You're playing dirty. I like it. Makes it a challenge."

"Shut up and play," I say. I cross my arms again, pushing my breasts up, hoping it distracts him. I want to get in his head, I want him to be intimidated with me. I want him to obsess about me.

Why, I don't know.

Reid picks another side piece, uncomfortably close to the unstable level. When he pulls it out with little drama, he drops it on top, cavalier in his skills.

His arms open again, like he's a gladiator who just defeated his opponent.

He really needs to stop that if he doesn't want a facial bruise.

"This game makes me so anxious," Annie breathes out. "You and Reid are not helping."

"Come on, this is fun," I say. I point out a couple blocks that are good options. Annie goes for a safe one, selecting another middle one and putting it on top.

The game continues with Reid and me taking chances and Jackson and Annie picking safe bets. The tower wobbles a couple times, usually after Reid picks a dangerous block that shouldn't work and then does.

Why is he so annoying?

Reid and I give each other taunting looks after we pick our difficult blocks. The tower looks like a spinal column with barely any complete levels. The audience watching with beers in hand can feel the suspense.

Now, it's my turn again. I walk around the tower, looking for a viable option, but there really are none that I could choose without losing epically.

Studying it like I used to do with Britney Spears's dances, I look at every angle.

"Come on, Lila. You're going to lose."

I stand up with a quirked eyebrow. How dare he call me by my pen name. How dare he.

Annie leans in. "Simmer down, Whitney. He's just trying to get in your head."

"You're right," I say, refocusing on the oversized blocks instead of Reid's beard.

It would look great under my vulva.

Focus, you whore.

Finally, I locate one that is promising. I crack my knuckles, and Annie massages my shoulders as I zero in on my target.

Please work. Please don't make me lose.

The crowd holds their breath with me as I tap a block and the tower only moves slightly.

When I pull it out, it shifts enough to make my heart stop. I grab my chest when it settles. Barely. I place the block on top of the tower and step back.

"Suck. On. That," I yell, now opening my arms at Reid. Reid's bottom lip purses out, like he's impressed.

It's technically Jackson's turn, but Reid pushes Jackson out of the way. "Let me," Reid says. Jackson backs away with his hands up, while Reid leans over to analyze the best move. It's technically against the rules, but I want to see Reid tip this over, lose in front of me. I want to see the fear in his eyes.

Annie slings an arm around my shoulders as we watch Reid walk around the table a few times to find the best block, but there really isn't one.

I can't help but smirk when he looks up, at a loss.

Then, I see it. A block that is so convenient, so perfect, that it could be picked out with little stick, little problem. I feel so foolish I didn't get that one. Of course, Reid will see it.

He spots it and looks up, seeing my pleading eyes. We won't survive another round. Annie is next, and she will crack under the pressure.

There's a moment of recognition. He knows that I saw that block. Instead, he picks a block near the bottom. I can practically hear the Jenga creators yelling from their corporate offices "Don't do it!"

The whole crowd stops breathing as he pulls it out. The tower topples with a chorus of groans and exhales.

The wood blocks scatter everywhere, one falling right by my foot.

He could've picked the easy one. Instead, he picked the block bound to fail.

"Why the hell did you pick that one?" Jackson asks, as Reid backs up.

Reid looks at me after looking at his brother, and I can read it all over his face.

He let us win.

We can move forward with the competition, because Reid picked a block and forfeited himself. It feels romantic, even if it's Jenga.

No, it's *not* romantic. I'm fully capable of beating his ass at this game.

After the match, I grab his arm. I try to ignore the sparks that I feel. It has to be our banter, our anger toward each other of why I feel like this.

"I saw what you did there," I say. "Why did you do it?"

"Do what?" he asks innocently. "You and Annie won, fair and square."

"Good game," I say, extending my hand. Reid looks at it and grabs his beer instead and walks away.

Asshole.

I just beat Reid. Why am I sad?

Because it wasn't fair. I didn't beat Reid because I was better than him. I beat him because he was a gentleman.

Not sure how I feel about it.

Reid is laughing with his brother, smiling, drinking his beer. I know he feels my eyes on him because his eyes flicker toward me.

Please look at me. Show me this isn't all in my head.

He deliberately fixes his gaze forward, acknowledging that we have shifted to something new, something uncharted.

All because of wood blocks and beer.

"You and the Finch boys were so fun to watch!" I turn to find Miriam, the lady we chatted with earlier. She seems nice, but Annie did warn me she meddles, so I should keep any secrets close to my chest.

"Thank you. They were good competitors."

"That Reid is such a sweet boy."

I nod because I can't agree with her.

Miriam rests her wrinkly hand on my forearm. "Dear, I would love you to come to our book club as our special guest. Please bring a book of yours you would like us to read."

I bite my lip. Not many of them are safe for a group of older women to read. One of them always thinks I sacrifice babies in the woods because I have explicit sex in my books, and most of the time it's taboo.

"Sure, I would love that," I say. "How many members?"

"We have ten. We'll pay for your books."

"No, it's okay. My treat. I think I have some stock. And Goldheart has been so welcoming to me," I say. "It would be an honor for you to read them."

"Great. Goldheart Public Library. This Wednesday. Seven o'clock."

"Perfect. I can't wait."

"Goodbye, dear," Miriam says, smiling warmly.

Maybe she's not as bad as everyone makes her out to be.

7

WHITNEY

The small parking lot is filled with cars, and the library glows as I sit in my car, gathering my courage to go in. I arrived fifteen minutes early so I could freak out in my car.

I breathe in and out, shaking my hands.

Large groups of people I do not know makes my palms sweat.

Multiple copies of my book, *Love, Lies, and Contracts*, sit on my passenger seat. Besides the obvious taboo of a woman in her early twenties dating her dad's best friend, it is the tamest of my books, even though he eats out the heroine on his desk during a Christmas party in his own home. While the heroine's actual dad is in the hero's living room, schmoozing with eggnog.

There's also an eggnog scene.

I've been to a few book club meetings, and most of the time, they spend ten minutes discussing the book and the remaining fifty minutes drinking and talking about non-book-related things. I always loosen up after a while, but the anticipation spikes my anxiety. I come off as outgoing and friendly on social media, but I'm secretly a reclusive bridge troll in person.

The best one I ever went to was in Lillyvale, about an hour from Goldheart. They discussed my mafia romance, *Brutal Lover,* and the conversation was lovely and welcoming. My reader, Addison, kept that whole meeting on task like a wedding planner played by Jennifer Lopez, and her friends were the type of people I would want to be friends with.

Annie warned me that most of the attendees of this one were the Bad Biddies, so I'm allowing myself grace for being so nervous.

"Get it together, woman," I say to myself as I look in the rearview mirror. I pull the elastic out of my hair and gather it, smoothing down the fly hairs and bumps. I open my social media to check my notifications, and clear out five DMs.

I'm stalling, and I know it. It starts in five minutes, and I'm hearting messages on Instagram instead of putting my big girl pants on and getting in there.

Still, my stomach clenches like I ate dairy.

"You can do it," I say to myself in my rearview mirror before exiting my car. Dread nags at me, but I shake it off.

This will just be a bunch of harmless women.

The library is different in the nighttime, the windows framing darkness, but still warm and inviting. A tray of goodies sits next to three bottles of wine. From what I know about book clubs, that's not nearly enough.

My bag of books is heavy, so I drop it on one of the tables and go to the refreshments table to grab a small chocolate croissant. It's dry, sucking all the moisture from my mouth, and I cough on the crumbs.

I'm in the middle of a hacking episode when a bottle of water appears in front of me.

"Here," a female voice says.

I look up at a woman I don't recognize. She has dark hair and vibrant green eyes, framed by lines that indicate she's smiled more than she's frowned.

"Thank you," I say.

"You're Whitney, right?"

"Yes," I rasp, twisting off the cap and taking a sip. I hold out my hand. "Whitney Ferguson."

"Kit Finch."

I cough again. Oh no. Reid's mother.

I smile and nod, once my throat settles. "Nice to meet you. I've heard so much about you."

"I know you're staying with Annie. I just love her. She's been so good for Cameron, and she's been Reid's friend for ages."

I smile because I don't know what to say. I love Annie with my whole heart, and I could never understand why she was such good friends with Reid. He's snotty and pompous, the exact opposite of my dear friend.

"Reid is my sweet boy. He's around here somewhere."

My soul leaves my body. I just assumed this book club, especially one with the Bad Biddies, was women-only. Yes, Reid lost our bet, and he technically has to read my book as part of our deal, but I wasn't planning to hold him to it. Just taunting him with the possibility that he would have to read a romance novel was enough psychological warfare for me.

His forfeit disguised as a Jenga fumble crowds my brain at night and has made writing a struggle since the event.

Usually, an onlooker at my coffee shop of choice can't tell if I'm writing a sex scene or a murder scene, but since Reid entered my life, I've been skipping the sex scenes. I tried to work on them once, but all I imagined was Reid in place of my hero, hovering over me, breathing heavily, and I slapped my laptop shut.

"He's here? At book club?"

Kit nods, smiling. "He comes to humor me, but he's recommended some amazing books, and he always brings discussion questions. He lets us talk about menopause and pretends to look somewhat interested."

Aw. That's kind of...cute.

We turn and a group of four elderly women stare at us, holding disposable wine glasses filled with red wine.

Kit touches me, and it feels motherly and warm. I can see why Annie speaks so highly of her. Kit points to the wine. "I'll get you a drink. You'll need it."

"Why?" I ask as Kit leaves me alone and the women approach me like hungry crows.

"Whitney, darling, what are you doing here?" Mrs. Epstein asks. "Are you joining our book club? It will be so fun to have a real author amongst us!"

Miriam appears next to Mrs. Epstein, linking arms like a mean girl high school posse.

These must be the Bad Biddies. Well, they seem harmless.

"Estelle, I invited her. We had a nice little chat at the brewery the other day. She's a hoot."

"Nice to see you again," I say to Miriam, who takes me in a half-assed hug. I'll take any physical affection at this point.

"I have my books," I say, pointing to my large bag. Oh no, I filled the wrong tote. I have two identical ones, both beige, with two totally different sayings. One says "Unapologetic Romance Reader." I grabbed the one that says "Smut Slut," a gift from one of my readers when she opened her Etsy store.

"What does your tote say?" Mrs. Epstein says, squinting behind her glasses.

"It doesn't matter," I say, turning the tote bag quickly, and pulling two books out to hand to Mrs. Epstein and Miriam to distract them. They look at my books like I handed them a magical tablet. "As promised, I brought enough books for your group. It's one of my most popular."

"Perfect," Mrs. Epstein says, looking down at it. "What kind of books do you write?"

My discreet covers aren't obviously romance, so I don't fault her for asking.

"Um, they're steamy romance." I add, "Like really steamy."

And by steamy, I mean there's anal sex in eighty percent of them. If there isn't, I ran out of time. Thank God, the one I'm giving them has no anal. It does have daddy kink, though.

Why can't I write romantic comedy? This crowd would love a romantic comedy.

"Oh, I love steamy," Miriam says, clapping her hands. "Do you read Nora Roberts?"

"I mean, who doesn't?" I ask.

"I blush when I read hers," Miriam asks. "Are they like that?"

"Um, kinda." My voice cracks on the K. If she thinks our queen Nora is steamy, she'll have to be re-baptized in the church after reading *this* one.

Mrs. Epstein grabs my hands. "It's so special having an author here. Goldheart's only author is Pete, who wrote a bird-watching manual twenty years ago."

"Your books are way more exciting," Miriam says.

I try not to burst out in laughter. Just wait until she gets to the wine bottle scene. I was going through a phase with this book where I thought sex play with liquids was hot.

"I can't wait for us to read it. We'll need a break from the depressing books Kit Finch recommends."

"It's because of that sweet, sweet boy. Wonderful man, depressing taste in books."

"Reid?" I ask.

"He's here, honey," Miriam whispers.

"Yeah, you didn't mention it when you invited me." My voice matches her quiet tone.

"I know," she says, her evil genius grin giving her away. "I saw the heat between the two of you at the Woody Finch event. I thought I might, you know, orchestrate something."

I swallow since the moisture in my mouth evaporated. "Miriam, I..."

Miriam points to the stacks. "He's over at biographies. He's always looking for something to read. Smart one, that one. He's tutoring my grandson in American history. Poor Gavin's eyes glaze over when Reid gets going, but his grades are improving. It helps Reid taught at the middle school before he quit to work at the brewery."

"Oh," I say. Reid tutoring a kid in history is also kind of cute. He was a teacher? I've always thought that was a hotter profession than being a firefighter.

"Reid just picks the wrong women," Miriam says. "Remember that Callie woman, Estelle?"

"Not good enough for him," Mrs. Epstein says, leaning in.

"Not good enough at all," Miriam says. "She always took advantage of him, and he's still being a father figure to her son. He was such a good man to her."

Interesting. Knowing Reid likes to be around children is a relief. It calms me to know that Reid can't be an option if he turns out to be a good person. If he likes kids, he probably wants them.

I decided to never have children when I was sixteen. My friends constantly talked about what they would name their children, but I was only interested in naming characters in my stories. Having an absent mother was just part of it. I never felt a maternal urge. Babies are fine, but I never want to hold them, and I only ever want to interact with children for fifteen minutes, tops. As my friends dropped like pregnant flies, I grew more and more sure of my decision.

The fact that Reid willingly hangs out with children and acts a father figure to one is attractive, yes, but it makes me pause. I've been down that road before, trusting Brad when he said he didn't want to be a father, and I have no desire to go back that way.

The next man I get involved with will be so childfree, he's gotten a vasectomy before meeting me. I can't start anything with any man who wants them or on the fence. My heart can't take it.

"You should go say hi. Come on, dear," Miriam says, pulling me by the arm.

I dig in my heels gently but the Bad Biddies are surprisingly strong. I jump three feet when I see Reid, looking like a guy who would end up on the Hot Guy Reading Instagram.

He's wearing a blue button-up shirt that hugs his biceps and jeans that stretch across powerful thighs. This man's presence heats my body like a microwave, causing my horniness to explode like a potato. His beard is full and thick, and I want to rub my hands down it.

There's nothing more dangerous than a horny romance author.

"Hi," I say.

He looks bewildered. "What are you doing here?"

"I came to drop off my books. For book club. But I'm not sure how they will take it. It'll at least give them something to talk about," I ramble. "Dad's best friend, age gap. A scene in a library. There's enough copies for you to have one. For our bet."

I peer through the space between the shelf and the books to see Miriam and Mrs. Epstein standing by the circulation desk, chatting. Bea from the market joined them, pantomiming something, maybe our argument by the tomatoes and the eggs.

"Whitney," Reid says.

"Yeah?" I say, snapped out of my Bad Biddies distraction.

"Get ready for the side-eye," Reid says. "I doubt they're used to exhibitionism and daddy kink in their books. Bea went through an Amish romance kick for a while."

My mouth drops. "How do you know that?"

"Bea tried to recommend different Amish romances for six months."

"No, my book."

"Oh." He looks down. I notice how long his eyelashes are. When he looks up, his gaze almost knocks me over. "I already bought a copy, and I'm halfway through it. *Love, Lies and Contracts*, right?"

I nod, my throat drying to an off-brand cracker. I run through all the sex scenes I only vaguely remember, since I wrote the book two years ago. I want to run away now.

Reid has peeked into my head, read my book. Without being prodded.

This library feels like it's a thousand degrees now.

"What do you think?"

Reid looks down, shoving his hands in his pockets. His

jaw muscles twitch, and he grumbles, "It's very well-written. It is *very* sexy."

My heart blips with excitement. Reid is complimenting me. He didn't say that romance isn't his thing. I didn't have to shove my book down his throat like the hero in this book shoves his cock in the heroine's mouth *once,* in a totally consensual way.

I wonder if my writing turned him on. Sweat trickles down my back.

"Thank you," I say.

"You're welcome."

He pulls another book out, flipping through it. I know he's not reading it. Whatever moment we had is gone, like a butterfly fluttering away faster than I can grab it, and I want to recapture it.

I was so quick with my wit at the brewery, and now I'm a weirdo that blurts out, "Did you lose at Jenga on purpose?"

"What? Why do you think that?" His voice is husky, but rich like an expensive bourbon. I want to hear him say "Good girl." Just one time.

No, you hoe. Knock it off. This is the enemy, remember? At least I think *he is.*

"There was a block that you could've pulled safely, and you knew it. You said you play Jenga all the time."

"I made a mistake," he says, putting the book back on the shelf. He can't even look at me now.

This man is infuriating.

"Really?" I ask.

His green eyes bore into me, burrowing a hole into my chest, and his lips rub together. I stare into his eyes. His gaze strips away our past and our conflict, leaving only heat behind.

He breaks our connection as his focus drifts to the

yellow and gold carpet. "I promise, you won, fair and square. Hopefully, this means we don't need to fight anymore."

"Five minutes!" Mrs. Epstein says from the main study area. Reid does not move. We stand there, stuck in our dance. If my anger has been stripped away, if I don't have hatred toward him anymore, what's left?

Just lust, gnawing at my insides.

"Well, I hope you enjoy my book," I say, turning away. "I have to go now. This was awkward."

"No, you should stay. We're discussing *A Little Life*."

I suddenly feel better about my book being offered.

I read *A Little Life* years ago and cried and cried, since the author Hanya Yanagihara put the main character, Jude, through copious amounts of graphic abuse of all kinds and trauma. It's the bleakest novel I've ever read, and while a father's best friend romance might be scandalous, at least it's happy.

Turning, I say, "Was that your choice?"

He nods with a smile. "I think everyone DNF'd at the first trauma scene. So there will be lots of gossiping. You should stay. Get a sense of how the Bad Biddies operate." His eyes crinkle at the sides. "Please?"

Staying is a bad idea.

But I want to stay. Explore if the feeling in my gut is correct. Reid might not be a trash human. He might be exactly my type.

With one problem: he might want kids.

"I'm going to skip this one," I say.

"Reid, are you coming?" Mrs. Epstein asks, appearing in front of me.

"Coming," he says. He walks past me, his shirt brushing against my sweater. I shiver and turn, watching him glide around the bookshelf. "See you around, Whitney."

He looks back. There's the familiar spasm of my kitty recognizing something she likes before my brain lets me do it, and I let out a tiny gasp. I can*not* stay. My head needs to be on straight if I spend any more time with Reid Finch.

I float above myself as I walk up to Mrs. Epstein.

"I'm going to get going," I say.

"I understand. I would love if you could join us for next month. I'll make sure we pick your book soon. Thank you for dropping them off."

"You're welcome," I say.

I'm walking to the exit when Mrs. Epstein says, "Reid is a good man, you know. What he's done for his family, how he's been a father to his ex's son. The way he humors us old ladies." She walks toward me and continues, "Take it from an old woman who has seen many assholes in her day. He's a good one. Whatever happened between the two of you might've been a misunderstanding."

I almost laugh, hearing an elderly woman curse. I want her to say it again.

Mrs. Epstein takes my hand. As a woman who didn't have a mother figure growing up, I'm not used to any kind of maternal affection. Holding her soft hand feels like a warm hug. "You're a smart woman. I know you can forgive him. He deserves your forgiveness."

"Thank you, Mrs. Epstein," I say. I hug her, probably way too hard for a woman in her late seventies.

Growing up, I ached for my Grandma Ginger's approval. Even after my mother left, my dad tried to give me a female figure in my life and would take me to see my mom's mom. That old woman spat verbal poison at me, making me cry constantly as a child. I finally asked to stop visiting her when I was eleven. Six months ago, my dad called me to tell me she died alone in a nursing home.

I'm the last in a long line of women who should've never been mothers, and the only one who figured it out before it was too late.

When I finally let her go, Mrs. Epstein cups my cheek like I'm hers.

"You're so sweet, dear. I knew you needed that."

I know if I speak, tears will spill. So, I just nod.

We say goodbye, and I wipe my eyes as I walk past the group. Reid is sitting next to his mother, who smiles and waves at me. I don't know if I'm hallucinating, but I can feel Reid's eyes on me as I leave.

8

REID

"Finch siblings, out on the town!" Cam says, holding up his hand up for a high five. Jackson looks up from his phone and smacks it. Cam offers that same hand to me and then Emily, and we unenthusiastically hit it.

We all have a rare Saturday night off, thanks to Cam. He mentioned it to our mother, and she agreed to giving all four of us the time off with two stipulations: we all hang out together, and we don't talk about work. We practically kidnapped Jackson, but we made it.

Ever since the brewery has become more popular, my siblings and I have become more coworkers than family. Rarely seeing each other outside of the taproom, only talking about work at Sunday dinners. Cam and Emily hang out since they live on the same property, and I hang out with Jackson, mostly to drink Scotch and watch the turkeys who wander onto our parents' property, but we rarely all get together as a sibling group. We see each other so much at the taproom, we don't feel the need.

Our mother insisted on it at our last meeting, claiming we were working too hard. She also offered babysitting to

Emily and shortly afterward, she texted us in all caps in the our group chat: "MOM IS BABYSITTING. WE'RE GOING OUT AND GETTING SCHMAMMERED."

We just happened to get the night off when The Swift, Goldheart's most popular and only decent bar, has karaoke. Jackson and I groaned when we walked in to a regular, Pete, singing an off-key version of "Living on a Prayer," and we knew we would be pushed on stage at some point. Especially me. I avoided it at the employee appreciation party, so I know it's inevitable tonight.

It's why I start drinking alcohol immediately.

"Shots!" Emily shouts. Carl, the owner, sets down a tray with four shot glasses, all filled with clear liquor.

My stomach turns. Vodka and I don't get along. Vodka turns me into a snarky sasquatch. I grunt mean jokes. I hurt feelings. I'm the worst version of myself. Logical me hates Vodka me.

"What is that, Em?" I ask, pointing to the liquor.

"Don't worry about it," she says, taking a shot from the tray. We all grab one and hold it up. "To the Finches getting out and drinking something other than beer."

"I'll cheers to that," Cam says, kicking the liquor back.

Jackson studies the liquid, but shrugs a shoulder and tips his head back with the shot. I take the shot, and it burns down my throat. Yep, it's vodka.

I waggle my tongue, the taste bringing back repressed memories of ill-advised nights in college that usually led to me puking into the ocean in San Diego after partying. I don't say anything though, because I'm scared of my sister, one hundred percent.

"Who's getting up there?" Emily asks. "I can't decide if I want to do Britney or Christina."

"Britney," we all say in unison. The stray cats will come

out of hiding if my sister even attempts a high Christina Aguilera note.

"What are you going to sing, big boy?" Cam asks, smacking Jackson on the shoulder.

"Don't taunt him. It's a miracle we got him out at all," Emily says.

Jackson pushes his glasses up his nose. "This is my own personal hell."

"Well, you're here with us," Cam says, pulling him in.

Jackson scowls.

I find a binder of karaoke songs on one of the tables and hand it to Emily, who smiles in thanks and starts flipping the laminated pages.

"Hot damn, look at the love of my life!" Cam yells over the noise of the bar. I look to the entrance, and my heart drops.

Annie and Whitney stand at the entrance, their eyes scanning the crowd. Annie lights up when she sees my brother waving like he's lost at sea. Whitney's expression matches mine, the "Oh shit" expression plastered on her face.

Whitney looks beautiful, with her long dark hair down around her chest, a chest I try to avoid looking at about ninety-five percent of the time. She wears a low-cut dress that hits her mid-thigh, so I can see her toned legs. Now I have to avoid looking at those too.

My blood heats from the quick glimpse. My dislike for her has morphed into a confusing mess, something I can't analyze without driving myself mad. She's been mean, vindictive, spiteful, but I saw her soften at the library, and now I'm willing to forgive everything. I read her work, and I'm so in awe of her and her talent that I want to forget our entire history.

I'm willing to say I'm sorry.

I didn't, though, and I acted so weird at the library that I've been cringing ever since, going over and over our interaction there and kicking myself for behaving the way that I did. No wonder I have issues with women.

"Hey, baby," Annie says, her grin from ear to ear as she kisses my brother, snuggling into his arms.

"Hi, Whitney," I say, friendly as I can.

"Hi, Reid," she mutters, looking at the ground. "I promise I'm not stalking you. I didn't know you would be here. *Someone* forgot to mention all of the Finches would be here, not just her favorite one."

Annie smiles slyly and turns her head back to goose my brother.

"I feel like you're stalking me, though," I say, leaning in. The vodka is working its sorcery on me. Oh, Lord help me.

"I am *not*," Whitney says, her voice escalating.

"Why did you run out of book club?"

She crosses her arms. Whitney wants a barrier between us. "I changed my mind. There was just a lot of...observation."

I laugh. The Bad Biddies told me a couple months ago they wanted to find me a good girl to marry and have babies with. Nothing happened, so I figured they had forgotten about it.

I laugh, thinking about the Bad Biddies setting me up with Whitney. "I think you're their target."

"Target?"

"They're trying to set me up with you," I say. Usually, I have great restraint, but... vodka. I continue. "They're trying to find me the mother of my children."

Whitney flicks an eyebrow. "Well, they should know I'm a terrible choice."

"I agree," I say, resting my chin on my hand. Yep, she still hates me. "It's too bad, though."

"Why's that?"

"Because you're beautiful."

The words float away from me before I realize what I said. I slap my hand over my mouth.

She definitely knows she's attractive, but I can't let her know I think she is. Sure, she has dark, silky hair, those blue eyes, pouty lips, and a figure with curves in all the right places. However, she'll use my attraction to her for evil, throwing it back in my face in an inevitable fight.

"Looks like we need more vodka," Jackson says. "Reid saying stupid shit is the only reason I came. I'll help the process along."

"Anything but vodka," I call out.

"You're on the vodka train, better ride it out," Jackson says, walking toward the bar.

"You can't handle vodka?" Whitney asks.

"Not since college. I threw up at Mission Beach, and I vowed no more vodka for the rest of my life."

"Until tonight?"

"Until tonight," I say. I'm probably red as a tomato by now.

"If I have to listen to this, I'll join you."

She points to another bar-goer, Justine, who is singing "Love Shack" like she's one of those deliberately bad singers on a talent show.

"Not into karaoke?"

Whitney shakes her head. "I can't sing worth a damn."

"Wow, there's something Whitney's not good at?"

"Har har har," she says, punching me in the arm. She smiles, though so we're getting somewhere.

"If it makes you feel better, I suck at it too," I say, placing my hand on my chest.

"Like you suck at Jenga?"

"Har har har," I say, mimicking her.

I press my lips together. I did throw Jenga. Halfway through the game, I realized the competition was fun, but I wanted it to end. I don't want to fight with her anymore. For some reason, I want to get to know her. What makes her tick.

After I flew through *Love, Lies, and Contracts,* I became fascinated with her. I'm barely on Instagram, but I started following her, and scrolled through her photos, seeing how much love she gets from her readers. She's come so far, she's so talented, and I am in awe of her success.

That's why I acted so weird at the library.

Jackson sets down a shot glass in front of me. "Here you go, little brother. Another delicious shot for you."

I hold up the shot. Is this a good idea? Yes, I decide. I can't be the soft pushover I usually am. I can't let Whitney know I'm close to surrendering.

Vodka will save me from myself.

I take the shot, and the burn is less, which is a terrible sign. Once it stops tasting like vodka, your hours are numbered.

"Reid took another vodka shot? Gird your loins, friends," Emily says.

"Why?" Whitney whispers to her.

Emily points to me. "Reid says sassy things when he's drunk."

"I prefer the term snarky."

"They're sassy," Emily says, leaning forward.

I hold up my hands. Whitney leans forward into the group. "The Bad Biddies think Reid and I should date. Isn't that hilarious?"

Cam and Annie's faces stretch as they look between us. "That's hilarious," Annie says tonelessly.

"Please don't provoke him," Jackson says to Whitney. "Reid is too pretty for jail."

He's right. Either I would be easy to pick off in prison, or I would run the place. There is no in-between.

"I can't see myself with her," I say, outstretching my arm to a shaky point.

"Me either," Whitney says, crossing her arms. "Nothing's going on."

"Absolutely nothing," I repeat. "I mean, I just became okay around her."

"Me too," Whitney says quickly. "Indifference. That's what we have."

Annie looks at me and then Whitney. "That's good, I guess?"

I add, "Completely indifferent. Nonchalant, even."

"Unbothered." Whitney searches my face for my reaction.

"I mean, I would be open to being friends," I throw out there. Whitney's eyes grow large as do my siblings'. I cross my arms because all of their gazes make me uncomfortable. "I mean, I would be if Whitney was. If not, no big deal."

"This is the most awkward start to a 'friendship' I've ever seen," Jackson says, taking a sip of a Diet Coke.

"You know what would make this even more awkward?" Cam asks, sitting back with his arms crossed.

Our arms fall at our sides. My eyelids close, because I know what is coming.

"Singing a duet."

Emily's mouth outstretches. "Singing a duet."

Jackson's head snaps toward us. "Singing a duet."

I swipe my hands in the air. "Absolutely not."

"I'm a terrible singer," Whitney says. "You don't want to

hear me sing."

"Doesn't matter. Singing talent rarely matters in karaoke. It's about the stage presence. All the best karaoke performances I've seen, the person was a terrible singer," Cam says.

"It's true," Emily agrees.

"If I'm required to be in this hellscape for two more hours, let me do the honors of finding the song," Jackson says. Emily hands him the binder. This is the most animated I've seen Jackson in a while. It's like he had a brain transplant. I even saw a smile.

Jackson flips a few pages before he stabs his finger at the page. "This is the one."

"Is it a song you know?" I ask.

"It's a song you know *very* well," Jackson says, taking the binder to the master of ceremonies. He points to a page, and the man nods. Jackson ushers us up, and I look at Whitney, who looks at me.

"I won't do it," I say.

"What about our friendship bonding?" Whitney asks. She's dead serious.

Although I really didn't want to do karaoke, Whitney's request is enough to get me up there.

"You better bring it," I say. "Or this friendship is over before it began."

"I won't let this friendship down," Whitney says. We clasp hands like we're Power Rangers. It feels like a volt through my arms. We rip our hands apart and plaster them to our sides. Did she feel that electricity too?

"This is already awkward. I love it," Jackson says, rubbing his hands together.

We walk up to the stage. We're handed mics and

Whitney takes the exact opposite of the stage to me. The tiny screen in front fills with the song.

"You asshole," I say to my traitor brother. Jackson lifts his hands with a shit-eating grin on his face.

The opening chords of "A Whole New World" from *Aladdin* plays.

I was obsessed with *Aladdin* as a kid. I used to pretend the oriental rug in my parents' living room was a magic carpet, moving the coffee table out of the way. I went as the Genie for Halloween once, and my skin was blue for a week. I know this song by heart, and Jackson knows it.

My first few lines are shaky as I hold the microphone, barely above a whisper. I'm sweating under the lights, everyone in this room is feeling sorry for me, and a woman I want is seeing how much I suck at karaoke.

After I sing about showing her wonder, I hear Cam yell, "Show them some pizzazz!"

Fuck it. I need to sell it. Dogs may start barking at any moment, but my voice grows louder. I try to hit the high notes.

Whitney holds out her hand to me, and I take it.

I sweep my arm like I'm showing her a fantasy land and smile along, pretending like there's stars on the ceiling of The Swift. I echo the movements from the cartoon. I don't even need to look at the lyrics.

When she takes over the singing, finally, she snuggles up to me like she's Jasmine falling in love with Prince Ali. Her voice is just as bad as mine, but she doesn't care. Damn, she feels good in my arms, even if she's trying to win crowd approval.

I go into the crowd and grab my jacket, spreading it on the stage. I turn to the audience and say in the microphone, "Pretend this is a magic carpet."

The crowd cheers.

I sit down on my spread-out jacket. I open my arms like I'm Jack Dawson, pretending the air in this bar moves. She looks at me, unclear if she should play along. It's not clear who looks sillier, a man in his thirties pretending a jacket is a magic carpet, or a woman of the same age refusing to play along.

The crowd giggles, while my siblings lose their shit at our table. I can pick out Cam's cackle anywhere. When it comes to the part we have to sing back and forth and together, I grab her hand since she is still standing.

I tug gently and she gets the hint, sitting down between my legs. She's stiff as I am, but I circle my free arm around her waist. We continue to sell it, getting more and more into it as the song concludes. She settles into me, and I pull her closer. She smells like grapefruit. When her back rests against my chest, a smile bursts with my high notes.

I nestle my chin on her shoulder, an intimate move that she receives willingly. For a split second, it feels like she's my girlfriend, watching a movie on the couch, content in my embrace.

I like this. I really like this.

When the song winds down, she faces me, putting her hand on my cheek.

I want her.

When the chords end, the entire bar stands to a standing ovation.

We stand, and I drape my jacket over my arm. We bow and return to our table.

"Wow," Cam says. "That was... confusing."

"Outstanding," Jackson says with a slow clap.

"Bravo," Emily and Annie cheer in unison, clapping.

"Thank you," I say. I hold up my hand to Whitney.

"Good job."

She smacks my hand, and we're back to being buddy-buddy. There was nothing real in the karaoke, and her energy now conveys that.

Still, I lean in. "Can I get you a drink?"

She nods and follows me to the bar. Carl is busy making a couple of margaritas, so I turn to Whitney. We're inches from each other, and I want to touch her again, but it doesn't feel appropriate.

"How did that feel?"

"Uncomfortable, but then fun. In line with every karaoke experience I've ever had."

"Seriously," I say. It's on the tip of my tongue. It's either the fun of the karaoke or the vodka, but I say, "Now that we're friends, I want to let you in on a secret. I did throw Jenga."

Her eyes widen in surprise. "Why did you lie?"

"Didn't want you to know I did a nice thing for you."

I brace for something snarky, but she says, "Thank you. I wasn't going to make you read my book, though."

"I always hold up my end of the bargain. It's who I am. And I finished it already, anyway."

"I appreciate it," Whitney says, sipping her drink.

"Do you forgive me for throwing Jenga?" I ask. "Does this drink settle it?"

"I don't know," she says. "I'll think about it."

"I thought we were friends now," I say.

"We are, but I'm not sure our friendship will last," she says.

"Oh, really," I say. "Why?"

"Because I think you're beautiful."

She leaves me with my mouth gaping at the bar. I don't know how to act around her the rest of the night.

A woman has never called me beautiful. Coming from Whitney, it unravels me.

9

REID

I'm on our step ladder, mid-pour, when Cameron wanders into our brew room.

He never comes in here unless he and Annie are looking for a private spot. I once caught them mid-strip in between the tanks. If I ever see Cameron's ass again, it will be too soon.

It reminds me of how long it's been since I had sex and of the woman I currently want to have to sex with.

Whitney.

I can't stop thinking about her body pressed to mine, sitting between my legs. How I want to be between *her* legs.

Lost in thought, I'm startled by a grumble behind me.

I turn to see Cameron, standing with his hands in his pockets. "Hi, Cam. What's up?"

"Isaac's here," Cam says.

I stop pouring the grain. "Really?"

Isaac still hangs out at the brewery once a week at one of our corner tables when his mother works late. Today is not Callie's usual late day, though.

"Isaac wants to talk to you."

"Let me start the boil, and I'll be right out."

I exhale as I walk down the hallway. Isaac is a cool kid, but he's desperate for a father figure. Stepping into that role when I met Callie was more than I bargained for. I knew she had a kid when we had an epic first date that lasted all day, starting with coffee, into lunch, into a drink into dinner.

However, when we started dating, I was treated like his parent immediately, helping him with his homework, picking him up from school. Watching him while Callie ran errands. I never knew how to fit in that role respectfully and it never felt right. He even called me "Dad" a couple times and it unsettled me.

It's much better now that we're just friends.

I honestly like the kid. He likes history, so we always discuss what he's learning in school. He's also into classic cars, like I am, and we look for our dream cars sometimes when the brewery is slow. Isaac wants a '67 Mustang, I want a '69 Bronco.

It's nice to have someone to talk to about it, even if he's twelve.

I care about him, and he can always hang out when his mom is working late. However, Isaac showing up to talk worries me. Callie's new boyfriend, Todd, is a guy I know in passing, and he seems nice enough. If he's hurting Isaac, I'll kill him.

Isaac stands in the middle of the brewery, shifting on his feet, unable to stand still. He only does that when he's nervous.

"Hi," I say, approaching him, taking him in a side hug.

"Hi, Reid," he says.

"I heard you want to talk. Come here," I say. We walk to his usual table. Isaac doesn't take off his backpack but clasps his hands together. He says nothing, just stares at the table.

After a few painful, quiet moments, I ask "What can I do for you?"

"Um," Isaac says, his knees bouncing under the table.

"Is something wrong at home?" I ask.

"No, not really."

Good. I don't have to commit murder today. Again, too pretty for prison.

"Reid, I wanted to talk to you about something."

"Okay," I say, crossing my arms.

"It's, just, can you and my mom get back together?"

I grumble, coughing into my hand. The only time Callie texts me is to ask if Isaac can hang out at the brewery. There's absolutely no way us getting back together would happen.

Usually, I would sugarcoat this because I hate hurting feelings.

However, it's time to be kind, by being honest. She's moved on. I've moved on.

"Isaac, your mom and I won't get back together."

"Why not?" Isaac asks.

Your mom never saw me as a romantic partner is the truth, but it's so much more than that. Something I can't explain.

Looking back, I was so unhappy. I never felt anything other than friendship from Callie. Whitney has shown me what was missing. The complete system shock I felt touching Whitney. How my whole body buzzed when she took my hand at karaoke. How the thought of seeing her makes me so damn excited.

Whitney makes me feel alive. Callie didn't.

"Isaac, your mom is a great person. You're so lucky to have her. She cares about you and she's such a good mom. We didn't work, bud. Your mom and I won't be getting back together."

Isaac sniffles and wipes his eyes.

Damn it, I made a kid cry. I offer a hug and Isaac walks into it.

"I like you so much more than Todd," Isaac says between sobs. "He doesn't talk to me about the Wild West or cars. All he cares about is my mom."

What an asshole. I firmly believe that if you date a single mom, her and her kids are a joint package—you can't pick and choose.

However, it's no longer my business. As long as the new boyfriend isn't hurting Isaac, I have to let it be. It's Callie's life and ultimately, she's his parent, not me.

"Your mom deserves to be happy, bud, and she wasn't happy with me," I say. That used to hurt, but oddly enough, it doesn't anymore. "We can still be friends, as long as your mother is okay with it. I just can't be with your mom anymore."

"Promise?" he asks.

"Of course," I say. He cries softly against my flannel as I rub his arms. I ruffle his short, brown hair and he pulls away, sheepishly looking at the ground.

"Can I come do my homework on Thursday? Like usual?"

"Of course."

"And you'll still come to my baseball games?"

"I wouldn't miss them."

"Cool. Thanks Reid."

"Anytime, buddy."

We say our goodbyes and I walk back to the brew room and stand with my hands on my hips. My body seizes when I feel hands on my back. When I look behind me, I breathe out a sigh of relief.

"Did you say hi to Whitney?" Cam asks.

"What?" I didn't see her in the brewery at all.

"She was here. Just now. Came in, then turned around and left. Had all her stuff too."

Whitney only writes at Gold Roast and the library. Why would she come to write here?

"That's weird," I say.

"Really?" Cam asks. "It makes perfect sense to me."

Blood drains from my face. "How?"

"Dude, it was obvious at karaoke. You two like each other. I thought I'd have to get the fire extinguisher," Cam says.

"No," I say. Yes, she did call me beautiful at karaoke, but we were both tipsy.

"Yes," Cam says. "She wants you, man."

"No way."

"Stop being so dense. There was some hardcore flirting at the Olympics."

"It was more arguing than flirting then, I think."

"It was flirting, you idiot," Cam says.

I climb the ladder to the top of the tank and shake my head. "There's no way."

I pause and wipe any expression from my face. Cam, being Cam, would take any reaction from me and run with it, and my mother and sister will eventually conspire, and then I might as well buy the engagement ring now.

"Whitney cooked dinner for Annie and me the other night, and we talked about you."

I can't ask what it was about. That's a dead giveaway.

Cam says, "She just showed up to work and lost her nerve. She's trying to talk to you man."

"Do you think so?"

"Yes," Cam says with a stupid grin. "Don't deny it. You think she's smoking hot, and you want to fuck her."

"I do not," I object, my voice entirely too high-pitched to be convincing. "Okay, maybe a little bit."

"I knew it," Cam says, shaking his fists like a kid who ate too much sugar. "Whitney is planning a surprise birthday party for Annie at Culver Lanes. Whitney asked for a guest list, girls only, but I want to go. My booty shorts are at the dry cleaners as we speak. I figured it was only fair that we crash their party because they crashed a Finch outing."

"You can't get naked in public anymore, Cameron." The last thing Cam needs is to get kicked out of another Goldheart business. He's already banned from the pool hall.

"I won't. Probably," he says. "Anyway, I want you to crash it with me."

"Uh, no," I say. While I do think our time together on stage was a good sign, the idea of approaching her for real makes my stomach twist. I don't even know how to begin to make a move with a woman like her. My skills are not that good.

"Come on, Reid. Whitney is recently divorced, so she might be looking for novelty dick. Some of the best sex before Annie I have ever had was with someone I hated. Much better than being turned down constantly by Callie, am I right?"

"Shut the fuck up," I say.

"Look, all I'm saying is it might behoove you to be at the party. Where tequila is involved. Tequila is our friend, not our foe."

I squint at my brother. "Since when do you use the word 'behoove'?"

"I'm dating a smart woman. She uses big words." Cam pauses. "Come on. It'll be fun."

I groan. Culver Lanes is a bowling alley/margarita bar that people frequent to get trashed and have fun with their friends. It's only five lanes, and it's dead most days, but at night, it thrives off of the bar food and the eight different flavors of margaritas, mostly from mixing machines.

I've had the worst hangovers of my life from that bowling alley. Even worse than the vodka nights in college.

But I'm lying when I say I don't want to see Whitney again. I wonder why she ran off while I was talking to Isaac.

I weigh my options. Showing up at my friend's birthday party with my friend's boyfriend who also happens to be my brother is completely reasonable.

"When is it?"

"Saturday," Cameron says. "I'm the present."

"Please don't strip. And don't hold two blue balls next to your junk like you did last time."

"It's an amazing gag," Cam says. "Are you going to hit on her?"

"I don't know." It still feels sleazy to be so forward with a woman, especially with Whitney. I like women to tell me they're into me before I go for it. It's why I never said anything to Annie when I had a small crush on her. It all worked out since Annie is perfect for my brother, but who knows how many women I could've dated if I just made a move.

"You are wound too goddamn tight, bro. Plus, you've been having vanilla sex for too long. I want my little brother to get fucked properly, and I can't think of a better person for that than a dark romance author. You are in for a treat."

I got a taste of it from the book and a half I've read, and I'm honestly a little scared. I've never tried dirty talk, but it's apparently a thing with Whitney. I'm not sure I can call any woman "a good girl" and not bust out laughing.

"You look like you're going to puke. You just need some of my confidence," Cam says, slapping me on the shoulder.

"Without my height and charm, I'd probably be a solid six on a good day. You're not as good-looking as me, but confidence can be taught. You need to realize you can hit it. You can hit it real hard."

"That sounds abusive."

Cam rolls his eyes and then says, "You might have to spank her. There was a lot of that in the book I read of hers."

My eyes bug. My brother, reading? He barely reads the instructions to a complicated kitchen appliance, and he's read a whole book?

"Don't look so shocked. I read it...for research," Cam says. His cheeks flush. "Anyway, the guy, Nico, super alpha. Like a badass motherfucker. Women want that. You need to be that. Take charge."

"Which one is that?"

"*Brutal Knight.* Bodyguard romance. I fucking love bodyguard romances."

"You've read multiple?"

"No, but I've seen *The Bodyguard*. I know how you are about Kevin Costner."

I love Kevin Costner. I've seen all of his movies multiple times. *Yellowstone*, his TV show, is my religion.

"Be like Nico. Be the alpha."

I pause for a moment. My whole life, I've reacted instead of acted, waiting on the first moves from people, never a take-charge person. It's why I hated teaching, was miserable for years, and only quit when my dad asked me to join the business. It's why Callie had to break up with me, even though our relationship had been over for months.

It's why I'm drawn to Whitney. I love a woman who takes no shit and deals it back when it's given to her. That kind of strength is sexy. Maybe I'll need to pretend I'm an alpha to become like that.

"Do you really think Whitney could be into me?"

Cam nods with a smile on his face. "Absolutely. I've been studying women for years, and that woman could be into it if you took the initiative. Hanging back and waiting for life to happen won't help your situation. It's time to do things differently."

Whitney's so exciting, so breathtakingly beautiful, so sexy, that I can't let her get away. I can't let her leave Gold-heart without seeing if this could be something. If the chemistry I feel simmering underneath the surface could become a huge explosion.

"I'm in," I say. "Let's crash the party at Culver Lanes."

Cam slaps me a little too hard on the chest and dances around. "What flavor am I going to get? I love the regular margarita they do, so I could get the Cadillac, maybe fancy? But I also love the strawberry."

Cam might be in a committed relationship, but he's still goofy and immature. He got Annie because he went after what he wanted.

I have to do the same thing.

10

WHITNEY

My knees bounce in excitement in Annie's car. I'm having a great day.

I had the best writing session I've had since before the separation.

Ten thousand words.

I rarely hit that number since I tend to lose steam around six thousand words, and even when I've hit it in the past, the words were never that good.

The words today weren't just good. They were *excellent*. As the love story flowed from my fingers, I know there will be no huge rewrites, just a polish that would take maybe half a day, tops.

To add onto my already fantastic day, I'm taking Annie to her surprise birthday party at Culver Lanes, Goldheart's small bowling alley attached to a bar where they make eight different types of margaritas, according to Cameron.

I love margaritas, and I love bowling. I also love Annie and want to celebrate her.

We're meeting some other women there, friends of Annie's, and I'm excited about that too. In Reno, I had a hard time finding women I could relate to. Without the excuse of a playdate or mutual attendance at a soccer game, I don't see my friends who have become moms all that often, sometimes six months between visits. I'm so happy for my friends, crying with some of them who struggled with miscarriages or infertility. I've thrown baby showers. But my friendships with women always morph once children come in the picture, because they have to.

While I'm happy to be childfree, I can't deny it's lonely when you don't have a big part of your life in common.

It's more than my friends scaling back because of motherhood.

It's lonely to have a mother who considers writing one letter enough effort after years of silence.

It's lonely to have a father who tried his best, but only checks in every couple weeks. It's lonely to have no extended family to visit or chat with once in a while.

So, I cocoon into myself to fight the loneliness, masking the pain with my own fiction. At least I did, until even writing didn't take away the heartache.

The writing definitely didn't make me forget about my confusing feelings about Reid.

Something was brewing, manifesting within us and I couldn't concentrate directly after karaoke at the Swift. One day, I decided to go to Woody Finch with no strategy and no script. I had no idea what my objective was or what I want.

All I know is I needed answers about Reid.

Since being childfree is such a dealbreaker, I need to be clear, create my boundaries, and determine if something will happen with us. I have a tendency to latch onto people with a death grip, and I can't do that with the wrong person again.

Then, I saw Reid embracing a child, comforting him

through emotion, and I got my answer. Annie mentioned that Reid dated a single mom and that could've been his ex's child. However, it made everything clear for me.

He's so comfortable with kids, that he must want them.

It can never work with us. I don't want to hurt him, and I don't want to get hurt.

Once I realized that, the words flowed again.

We pull into the gravel parking lot of Culver Lanes. The only illumination of the building comes from the lit sign, with letter placards spelling out "Happy Birthday, Annie!"

Annie's lips purse as she points to the sign.

I can't help but smirk. "I let them know it's your birthday."

"That's so sweet," she says, taking me in for a hug. "I'm so excited to go bowling."

The bar is dark when we walk in. Signs advertising different beers are the only light source in the room.

"It's not usually this dark," Annie says as we walk further into the bar. The lights flick on, and a small group of women huddle together, each holding a different colored margarita.

"Happy birthday!" they all yell, and Annie's face immediately turns red.

"What is going on here?"

"Well," Tara, the owner of my favorite coffee shop Gold Roast, says, "it's a surprise party."

She drapes a sash over Annie that says "It's My Birthday, Bitch" and hands her a large margarita in a pink plastic cup. Annie inspects the rhinestoned cup, which matches the sash in color. Annie is swallowed up by her friends, and I smile widely.

I hug Tara, who comments on how focused I was today at her coffee shop. I meet the other women—Izzie, the editor of the town newspaper, a tall woman with golden hair down her back, and Shiloh, a smaller blonde woman, who looks like she's not old enough to drink.

She's drinking a soda, so that might be the case.

"Shiloh is one of the newest employees at Woody Finch," Annie says. "She's the best."

"No, Annie is the best. Whitney, it's so nice to meet you. I've heard so much about you," Shiloh says, taking me in a surprisingly tight hug. "I'm so honored to meet such a prolific author. When Cameron invited me, he told me about you, and I immediately ordered a paperback of one of your books. Can you sign it for me when I get it?"

"Of course," I say. Shiloh's energy feels like direct sunshine, so uplifting and positive.

I turn to Annie and whisper, "Is she old enough to drink?"

"Yes, but she doesn't drink. She's twenty-six."

"Maybe laying off the booze and being bubbly helps you stay youthful."

"Absolutely," Annie says. "I really like her. She's a good fit for our team."

"Sorry I'm late," Emily Finch says, walking into the bar. "Single mom here."

Annie squeals and tackles her. The only Finch sister, Emily, is so sweet and nice. It's evident she grew up with protective brothers, but not the type that turned her into one of the guys. I've been interested in getting to know her more, but being a single mom has to be unbelievably tricky. It's why I've been hesitant to invite her out for lunch or coffee, although I've really enjoyed the conversations I've had with her. She's everything her daughter has, and I don't want to rob her of her of that precious time.

"Good to see you again," Emily says, taking me in for a

hug. "Well, I think a birthday calls for tequila shots. Dad drove me here so I plan to get schmammered."

"Annie, I'm driving you home even though you insisted to drive. I'm not taking no for an answer," I tell her.

"Okay," Annie says hesitantly. "Can you drive Emily home as well?"

"No problem," I say.

"That would be awesome," Emily says. "That means I can get shit-faced, which is a step up from schmammered."

"Where does drunk fit in?"

"Drunk is lowest," Emily says. "Then, it's schmammered, then shit-faced."

We order a round of tequila shots from the bartender, and once all of them are passed around, Annie looks at me, and I know she's going to say something that will make me cry.

"I'm so blessed to know such an amazing group of women. Whitney, you are so special to me. Thank you for planning this," Annie says. She takes me into a side hug, and a tear slips down my cheek. This kind of thing is what I was missing.

For four years, I worked my ass off to get my writing career off the ground. Sleeping for three hours a night for months straight, working on the weekends, saying no to parties and social events to get my words in and my marketing done.

One day I looked up, and no one was left. My husband saying he wanted kids was his last-ditch effort to show the situation we were in was not working. *We* were not working.

Now, I'm in a town that feels like a comfy blanket, surrounded by women who might become my friends.

It's time to live a little in the real world, not only in my stories.

We clink our glasses and knock the shots back. The tequila scorches my throat, burning on the way down. I wiggle my tongue to help with the burn. I'm immediately handed a margarita that rivals cocktails I've had at fancy bars. I'm cutting myself off so I can drive us home, which is a good thing since the drink makes my head and chest warm and my limbs loosen.

Annie talks to the bar owner, and we walk to the rear of the building with the five lanes.

There's a family eating hot dogs with a pitcher of soda between them, and another lane open.

"We're on two," Annie says, pointing to the lane, second from the left.

I see a large "Reserved" sign on the number one lane. Is it necessary to reserve a lane in a small-town bowling alley?

I'm pulling on my shoes when I hear, "Sorry we're late!"

I turn around to see Cameron walking out from the bar area, holding a huge frozen margarita, followed by Reid.

"I said no boys allowed, Cam!" I yell, hands on my hips.

"You crashed the Finch extravaganza; this is only fair." Cameron kisses Annie's neck, grabbing her butt in the process. "Happy birthday, baby."

Reid is in another blue, checkered, button-down shirt, with the sleeves rolled up.

Is he trying to torture me?

"Hi, Whitney," Reid says. Butterfly wings flap in my stomach at the sight of him. I feel like I'm in high school again, seeing my crush in the halls, wishing he would talk to me, pay attention to me.

This can't happen. Don't you dare let anything happen.

"Hi," I say, putting my hands on my hips. "What are you guys doing here?"

"We were in the mood for margaritas and bowling."

"In the *reserved* lane next to us?"

"Correct," Cam says. Reid follows Cameron to his lane, picking a ball from the shelves behind the lane seats.

I pull Annie to the side. "Why is Reid here?"

She shrugs.

Reid's gaze captures mine. I can't stop staring at him and he can't stop staring at me. I tried to sneak out when I saw him with the kid, and I don't think he saw me.

Now he's here. And he knew *I* would be here.

"What are Cameron and Reid doing here?" Tara asks, emerging from the bathroom. Annie told me that Cameron and Tara were involved before Cameron started dating Annie. They're cool now, but Tara isn't exactly thrilled to see him.

"We're here to bowl. And Reid has something to say to Whitney," Cameron says.

Reid smacks Cameron hard on the chest.

Act chill. Act nonchalant.

"Whitney, can I steal you for a second?" Reid asks, touching my arm for a second. It feels like a brand on my skin. He definitely saw me.

I cannot act chill. This is not me chill.

"Sure," I say. I take a sip of my margarita for courage, and we walk through the bar and out in the night air. It's still warm outside even though it's mid-September and pumpkin spice is already taking over. Reid points to a corner of the parking lot, dimly lit by a lone bulb.

If I didn't know this man, I would've thought I was getting kidnapped or murdered. Without question. But this is what happened when you write dark romance and don't talk to other people and fall asleep to true crime podcasts.

I turn toward him, crossing my arms in front of me.

"How are you?" Reid asks.

"I'm good," I say. "How are you?"

"I'm great," he says. "Look, I heard you stopped by the brewery."

Why lie. "Yes, I did."

"Why?" Reid asks.

"I, um," I fumble, looking down at my feet. I take a deep breath and say, "It's been really confusing the couple weeks between us."

"I can agree," he says.

"Like we hated each other and then we didn't. I don't know."

"I can agree with that. Why didn't you stay to talk to me?"

I wave it off. "You were busy with the kid and I didn't want to interrupt."

Reid nods. "That was Isaac. I dated his mom and we're still friends. Is it weird I'm friends with a twelve-year-old?"

"No, I think it's sweet." I catch myself as I look through my eyelashes. *Stop flirting with him, you don't need to flirt with him.*

"So, we officially don't hate each other anymore?" Reid asks.

"Correct."

"Good. Let's start over," Reid asks, stretching out his hand. "I want to truly start over. Hi, I'm Reid. Reid Finch."

"Whitney Ferguson," I say, putting my hand in his. His palm is smooth and warm, and we don't pull away from each other. The same tingles I felt when I touched his hand at karaoke are still there.

"It's a pleasure to meet you," he says, continuing to shake my hand.

"So nice to meet you too," I say, swallowing hard. "Why are we still shaking hands?"

"I have no idea."

"You stop," I say, not pulling my hand away.

"No, you."

Our hands continue their bobbing up and down. He looks down at our hands and back up at me. My breath stops, my lips part. He's wetting his own lips, and my core clenches at that. Our hands are still touching, and I close my eyes to get my wits about me.

"I like you," he says.

I break into a smile. "Really?"

He nods, his eyes pleading.

"Even after I was terrible toward you?"

He nods again, in beat with our hand shaking.

"Are you going to show me a whole new world or what?" I ask. I have no idea what I meant by that.

It all happens in a split second.

Suddenly, his hands are on my face, the tips of his fingers tangled in my hair. His lips crash into mine before I can process what's happening.

He kisses like a goddamn romance hero.

Hot breath, hot moans. Our tongues fumble in a frenzy, and my hands are in his hair, my body pressed against his. Overwhelmed is an understatement for how I feel. He kisses me like he's punishing me, hard and relentless. Any moment his brother or any of the women could come out and see us making out like two horny teenagers.

I can feel his erection against my belly as we attack each other's mouths, a messy, slippery dance of tongues and breath, melding together. When he pulls his lips away, pushing my hair away from my face, he's breathing like he just ran away from zombies. The fast kind.

"Was that okay?" he asks.

I'm not sure what he's talking about, whether it's our

connection or the passion or the off-the-charts chemistry. All of it was unbelievable to me. He's flummoxed and can't look at me. It's kind of cute. "It's just...I'm not sure if you wanted to kiss me or..."

"That was a whole new world," I say and immediately cringe. His cheeks bloom with pink. I shift because my underwear is so wet and uncomfortable, my pussy responding to the best kiss of my life. I feel like I might die if he doesn't fuck me against this brick wall immediately.

"Did you like it?" I ask. Our arms are still wrapped around each other, and one of Reid's fingers in wedged in my waistband, inches from my ass.

"Very much," he says. He lets me go, the impression of his arms and hands on me still present on my body.

"Don't you want to kiss me again?" I ask. *God, Whitney. You've been out of the game for a few years, and now you're desperate.*

"Yes, but I won't," he says, and my heart sinks. Then he lights me on fire. "Next move is on you."

I lean against the brick wall like I'm a musician on an album cover.

"I want you to ask for it. *Beg* for it." He grins. "Good night, Whitney." He walks off, with a swagger I've never seen on him.

"What if I don't make a move?" I call after him.

"I really hope you do," Reid calls back as he goes back inside Culver Lanes. He doesn't even look back.

I'm reeling.

I let my fingertips trace where he kissed me, where he kissed me for a good minute and I smile. His cock—which felt impressive, by the way—pressed against me, and now I'm imagining what it would be like inside of me. Reid over me, rocking in and out. If I ever had sex with him, I won't be leaving his body for at least four days. I don't care how sore my pussy gets, I will take that dick beating over and over again.

Until then, he wants to play a game.

I *love* games.

Maybe he's interested in something casual. He did just get out of a long relationship. The kid issue doesn't matter if it's not serious in the first place.

Still, I can't give in right away.

Instead, I'm going to finish those three sex scenes I've been neglecting and some time with my hand in the bathtub. Maybe light a candle too, to romance myself. Really analyze if I can get back to my college roots and sleep with a man once, instead of latching on like a leech, and never letting go, no matter what red flags I notice.

When I walk back into Culver Lanes, the number one lane is empty.

"Where did Cam and Reid go?"

"They left," Annie says. "Reid was acting stranger than usual. What did you talk about?"

We didn't talk as much as we kissed. "I guess you can say we had a collision."

"You look weird," Annie says, her head tilting in study. I shrug my shoulders. I kissed her friend. Her ridiculously handsome and straightforward friend.

"You're up, Whitney!" Shiloh shouts.

"Okay," I say, looking down the lane at the bowling pins.

I take a twelve-pound ball and hold it up like I used to see professionals when my dad watched bowling competitions on TV. I approach and swing back and let it go. It doesn't have the same satisfying crash as it collides with the lane, but the pins fall down. All of them.

"Divorced bitches get it done!" Izzie screams like she's at

a Magic Mike show. Annie told me Izzie married her high school sweetheart, for it to end after three years of marriage.

I turn around, holding up my arms in victory. In the darkness of the doorway from the bar to the bowling lanes, I see a flash of Reid, watching me. Our gaze catches, like it always does, and then he's gone.

I didn't imagine it. He is as wrecked about us as I am.

Two can play at this game. I can make a man pursue me. If it's not serious, I can pull a move I have long since retired.

Make a man jealous by showing up with another man.

"Hey, ladies," I say. "Does anyone know of a single gentleman who likes beer?"

"Reid does," Shiloh says.

"Not Reid," I say, my dry throat making it difficult to swallow. "Let's just say, for appearance purposes."

Annie snaps her fingers. "Thumper."

Izzie, who was mid-laugh with a chip to her mouth, stops. Her face drops.

"Thumper is a great idea," Tara says. She points behind her to Izzie, who is sitting there. "Izzie was stuck in a bank vault with him a couple weeks ago."

"There was a robbery," she adds, breaking off the chip.

"Oh my God, are you okay?" I ask.

Izzie nods. "I mean, the woman was in a chicken costume, and it was as pleasant as bank robberies can be, I guess."

"But she was stuck with Thumper in a bank vault for three hours," Annie adds. She laughs and says, "What I wouldn't give to be a fly on the wall for that."

"It was nothing," Izzie says. Her face is white as the walls of a model home.

"Okay, I would love Thumper's number," I say.

Annie takes my phone to input it. "You'll have to call him because he doesn't text."

Who doesn't text?

"Is this to make Reid jealous?" Tara asks in a whisper.

I can't help but smirk before lifting a shoulder in a shrug.

Izzie takes a ball and walks to the lane without saying anything. She's been a great bowler all night, but this swing goes right in the gutter. When she walks back to the chairs, I pull her to the side.

"You don't mind if I go out with Thumper, do you?"

Izzie smiles and nods, but I don't entirely believe her. "Thumper is a great guy. I'm sure you'll have a fun time with him."

"Good," I say. "It was really nice to meet you, Izzie."

"You too," she says. "We should go to that sushi place sometime."

"Sounds good," I say. We look at our respective calendars and decide on a date next week. The whole time we schedule it, Izzie looks at me with sadness in her eyes.

I'm not sure what happened in that bank vault with Thumper, but I intend to find out while also making Reid wildly jealous.

So many wonderful things are happening. This town is magic.

11

WHITNEY

"Fucking with Reid is my favorite past time," Eugene, also known as Thumper, says, offering his arm to me.

Thumper is Cameron's best friend, who agreed to join me for a beer at Woody Finch Brewery. He's a country boy, wearing cowboy boots and a stained baseball cap over scruffy dark blond hair. When I called him to ask him to help me torture Reid, I didn't even have to finish my invitation before he responded with "Hell yes."

He's already called me pretty three times, and it didn't feel creepy. This will work out just fine.

"So, what is the plan?" he asks. "I take my fake-dating duties very seriously. Look what happened with my motherfucker of a friend."

My cheeks hurt from smiling.

"We're just going to have a beer," I say. "I'll buy."

"Nonsense. I'm buying."

"No," I say. "I invited you."

"Woman, let me buy you a beer," Thumper says, rubbing

his hands together. "Are you sure Reid can handle you? You might be too much woman for him."

"He can handle me," I say. At least, for one night.

Thumper laughs as he opens the door to Woody Finch for me. I walk in.

I stop right inside the door like I'm Jennifer Love Hewitt in a nineties romcom.

My outfit might be ridiculous, but it's going to get the job done. Leather leggings, strappy Louboutins, a simple T-shirt tied right above my waistband, and my favorite red lipstick. I did not come to play.

Mission accomplished. Reid is frozen behind the bar like a statue.

"What do you want?" Thumper asks, looking at the board.

"Night Music." I'm obsessed with that stout, ever since I drank it at the Olympics.

"Nice choice," Thumper says. "I'll be right back."

I grab a high top next to a group of locals, deep into a competitive game of Connect Four. My gaze flicks over Reid, standing behind the bar next to Shiloh, who is doing more work than Reid is. Reid just stares.

After I do a full scan of the room, I look back to the bar. Thumper is there. Shiloh is there.

Reid is not.

I look around me, and then I stiffen. Feeling heat behind me, I don't move but my pussy immediately clenches.

"What are you doing?" Reid asks.

"I'm getting a beer. With Eugene."

"With *Eugene*?" Reid repeats and scoffs, shifting on the stool.

"Aren't you supposed to be working?" I ask, resting my

chin on my hand. I make sure to tap my nails against my cheek.

"Yes, but I can't. You're here."

"Am I bugging you?" I ask innocently. I widen my eyes and jut out my bottom lip.

"You come in here looking like that. You know what you're doing."

"I don't even know what you mean," I say. Reid's Adam's apple bobs. My presence has the desired effect. I lean in, making sure his eyes are transfixed on my mouth, and lower my voice. "I know you want me."

"If you're here with Thumper, I'm already questioning what happened at the bowling alley," he says. He looks up and swallows again. He wants me and he's fighting it.

"Thumper told me I looked pretty already tonight. You can too."

"Nah," Reid says, suddenly playing it cool again. He's turning into a different man, and it's a thrill to watch.

I lean forward, so he can get full view of my cleavage. The bra I call my "evil tits bra" pushes my breasts high, and I'm testing its powers by leaning over—a nipple might pop out at any moment. When I was married, this bra was guaranteed to get me laid.

It's not working as well as I hoped on Reid. He won't even let me catch his gaze.

"This doesn't do anything for you?" I ask.

"I'm not looking."

I lean over more. "I wish you would."

"Whitney, you're going to be the death of me," he says, slapping the table like I wish he would smack my ass. "Still your move, *Lila*."

I point to my cleavage. "What else do I have to do?"

"You just have to beg for it." There's that deep, raspy

voice, dripping with raw power. I bite my lip, and he leans into me. "What do you say?"

"I'll never ask for it."

"I can wait. I'm a patient man." Reid walks away, and I fan myself.

Thumper passes Reid as he walks back with the beers in his hands. He turns his head to look at Reid. He sets my glass down in front of me as I look past him, checking out Reid's ass as he walks back to the bar.

I want to smack it too. And bite it.

"I'm gone five minutes, and you two already flirted. I know we're just friends, but you need to put those things away," Eugene says, pointing to my cleavage. I slouch and stuff myself back into my shirt. He lifts his beer to his lips. "Damn."

I take a sip of my own beer, the malt heavy on my tongue. Knowing Reid brewed this, used his talent and hands to mix this, makes the beer all that more delicious.

It's time to hit my second objective for the night. "So, I heard about the robbery."

Thumper laughs. "What a shitshow that was. Holy nutsack."

"You were stuck with Izzie? She seems really nice. Was that the first time you met each other?"

Thumper nods. "She is." He sips his beer and blushes.

"Any romance potential?" I ask. He glares at me, and I hold up my hands. "I'm a romance author. I love love stories and people getting together. It sounds like the bank vault was your meet-cute."

"What the hell is a meet-cute?" Thumper asks.

"It's usually the scene at the beginning of a romance novel when the couple meets for the first time."

"Well, we met when a woman I used to sleep with came in dressed in a chicken costume holding her son's BB gun."

"Still," I say, "you should go for it with Izzie. She seems saner than this ex of yours."

Thumper looks off and chuckles. "Well, Izzie did just ask me out on a date."

I hold up my beer. "That's great. Cheers to that."

"What should I do for our date?" he asks.

"Make it private. Romantic."

He takes his hat off to readjust over his head. "I have just the idea."

"Perfect." I change the subject. "Do you ever worry you'll be single the rest of your life?"

"Do you worry about that?" Thumper asks.

It's something that's brought up constantly when I say I don't want children. *Who will take care of you when you're old?* Having children doesn't guarantee you a caretaker when you're older. The only prayer I have is the money I make from writing will get me some decent around-the-clock care and good people to oversee my estate.

My dad is an only child. I have no siblings, no cousins I know of.

"Do you think there's one person out there for us?"

"I don't know about that." Thumper turns his beer with his fingertips. "I won't settle for anything less than what my daddy has with my momma. He still smacks her ass when he passes her, and they've been married for forty years."

My heart squeezes at that. I thought I had that with Brad, but he couldn't handle me being more successful than he was. I remember the look of devastation on his face the first month I made twenty thousand. His career would eventually catch up, but he was supposed to be the breadwinner as the doctor, not me, the person who started publishing romance novels for fun.

"I want that too. Same as you, though. I'm not sure if it will happen," I say. "I didn't have the greatest childhood."

"I did," he says. "I didn't mean it to rub it in your face. I just don't want to bring any kids into this world without knowing my kids will be as happy as my sister and I were."

"I get that," I say. "I'm never having children."

"Really?" Thumper asks.

I nod.

"It's not for everyone." He sips his beer and looks off. My shoulders relax. Whenever I admit that to someone new, I always brace myself for some comment trying to talk me into having kids. When someone accepts my decision, without questioning it, it makes me like them more. Thumper turns back to me and asks, "Does Reid know that?"

I shake my head.

Thumper knows something I don't. I don't think men who are acquaintances sit around and talk about wanting to be a dad like women do. However, there's something about Reid I've been glossing over. He was a teacher, he tutors. He's still involved with his ex's son's life. He likes kids. That usually means a person wants them.

There is no way my thing with Reid can be casual. I take a sip of beer, hoping it numbs the twinge in my chest.

Thumper looks at his beer. "Reid is a good guy. I kid when I say I like to get under his skin. He's just so funny when he's mad."

"I agree," I say, clinking my glass with his.

"You're completely out of his league, though."

"Maybe," I say.

I've never talked with a guy like this before, as a friend.

Every male friend I've had secretly wants to fuck me and has pulled a move on me. It's refreshing to be with a guy like Thumper. He compliments me but respects boundaries. Maybe he's already gone for Izzie and doesn't even know it yet.

If I can't have a love story with Reid, I might as well encourage one for Thumper and Izzie.

Out of the corner of my eye, I see her watching us while Tara tells a story.

"Do you like Izzie? Like, like her?"

Thumper nods vigorously. "She just asked me on a date, so our little stunt worked for both of us."

"Maybe," I say.

I look to the bar now. Reid is nowhere to be found, and Emily is now working alongside Shiloh. Emily's mom comes out and wraps her arm around her daughter, laughing and smiling. It makes me ache inside to see the relationship between Kit and Emily. How close they are, working together. Helping to raise a bright little girl who I met once when I ate dinner over at Emily's with Annie and Cameron.

The letter from my mom still sits at the bottom of my luggage, under a pile of T-shirts and toiletries. I can't even hope that I'd ever have a sliver of what Emily has even if I did reach out to her.

"Are the Finches as happy as they seem?"

Thumper nods. "They're a family like any other family, don't get me wrong. Still, nothing's better than being invited over for dinner. That family loves each other."

I bang my glass against his again. "Thank you for coming with me."

"You're welcome, darlin'," Thumper says, winking at me.

I laugh and take a sip of my beer.

I stand up and grab my jacket, taking a last sip of my beer.

"You should go hang out with Izzie. She's been staring at you this whole time."

Redness covers his cheeks. "Really?"

"Yeah," I say. "Have a great night, Thumper."

"You too," he says. He takes me in a polite side hug, and I leave him to walk to the exit. Thumper pounds the rest of his beer and shoves his hands in his pockets, walking over to Izzie and Tara. A smile crosses my lips.

I love this town.

12

REID

"I'm going to write for a little bit," I say, pointing to my laptop in my hand. Emily, my sister, stands at the bar, her eyebrow arched in surprise.

"Have fun," my mom says, not looking up from a binder that holds our part-time staff's schedule.

"Where are you going to write?" Emily asks.

"Gold Roast." I hold my laptop up. "I'm going to finally finish my book."

"Hmm," Emily says, knowing damn well why I'm going to that coffee shop. My sister has a big mouth, but she knows better than to say anything in front of my mom.

It's common knowledge that "a romance author" has a designated table in the corner at Gold Roast, consumes cups and cups of coffee, and hits her keyboard like she's mad at it. There's also rumors she orders salads to be delivered to said spot and tips the delivery kids twenty dollars, so they rotate who gets to deliver to her, to make it fair.

Emily is smart, and she could see the guilt on my face when Whitney and I came in separately after our kiss at Culver Lanes.

That kiss that I've been obsessing about since it happened. Why did I walk away? What if she never begs? Guys like me don't say stuff like that to women like her.

We cave at the first moment of missing her, hence, why I'm "running" into her with my laptop.

Then, she came in to the brewery with Thumper, apparently on a date, wearing what she wore. She's taunting me.

It's time to taunt her right back.

"What, Emily?" Mom asks, still not looking up.

"Oh nothing. It's just interesting, is all. Why now, Reid? I don't think you've dusted off that manuscript for a year."

"I'm feeling inspired," I say, clutching my laptop close to my body.

"Huh," Emily says. "Just make sure you're inspired in private. If you know what I'm saying."

I shake my head, glaring at Emily. Mom finally wised up, lifting her head to look at both of us. "You're up to something. Good try at doing it while I'm trying to concentrate. Very sneaky."

"*I'm* not up to something," Emily says, pressing her hand to her chest. "Reid, on the other hand…"

"I got to go," I say, a little too loud.

"You could always write here," Emily says, pointing at a table that we frequently have people working at. Dan, our investor, comes and works sometimes so he can drink beer.

"Too distracting. Got to go, bye!"

I hear Mom and Emily whisper to each other as I leave. It's a lovely day so I walk the mile or so to Gold Roast, excitement flowing to my fingertips.

Whitney will be there.

I can't wait to see her, flirt with her, and get her that much closer to her being in my arms.

When I open the door to Gold Roast, Tara's stare

disarms me immediately. She's handing a cup to a dark-haired woman, whose back is turned to me.

I would know that woman anywhere.

When she turns around, it's in slow motion. I search her face for any sign that she's happy to see me. I see nothing, only a small flick at the corner of her mouth. Her stuff is piled at her table, and there's only one other customer reading the paper by the window.

We stand, staring at each other, like we're at the end of a romantic comedy movie.

"Hi," Whitney says, her voice low and breathy.

"Hi," I say.

"What are you doing here?"

"Well, you said this was a good spot to write. So," I say, holding up my laptop, "I'm here to write. I won't bother you —unless you want me to."

Whitney's eyes narrow. I expect her to be a smartass, but she waves to her table. "Go ahead. But I have a deadline, so I can't talk. I have to finish my words."

"That's fine. Pretend like I'm not even here," I say. Our gaze holds for a few seconds before Whitney steps away, sitting down behind her laptop. She points to it after I sit down.

"Do you want anything, Reid?" Tara asks.

"Sure," I say. "Coffee, black."

She hands me a cup of coffee in a mug, I pay, and then I sit down across from Whitney.

"Do you do writing sprints?" she asks.

"Sprints?" I ask.

"I write as much as I can in a twenty-minute period, I take a five-minute break, then I write again. Repeat until my word count for the day is done."

Huh. I always spent long stretches of time alternating

between staring off into space and typing some words. It's why five hundred words was a good day for me, even if it took four hours.

Whitney is all business, and I can't be distracted by her or distract her. Even though she looks incredibly sexy, even in a hoodie.

"Okay, I'll try it," I say.

She punches a couple keys and says, "Go!"

I open my laptop and go to my documents folder, where *Project Gold Rush* resides. I've had the idea for Flint Turner forever, a bloody tale of a gunslinger in the Wild West who seeks revenge on the outlaw who killed his family. It's *John Wick* meets *Wyatt Earp* and *Tombstone*, all movies I could watch over and over again. I recently got into the TV show *Yellowstone*, and I've been inspired by the character, Rip Wheeler. It's why I grew my beard.

I have no idea where to pick up or how to move forward. The last time I sat down to write, I got so frustrated with the manuscript that I gave up in disgust and haven't looked at it since.

Now, I'm sitting with an accomplished, published author rather than sitting at home with whiskey and pretending I'm Hemingway *without* the writing.

I would much rather be here with this woman.

I start where I left off, but the paragraph before has weird phrasing so I tweak a few sentences in the opening paragraph. The story is so rich in my head, but the words on the page don't match my vision. My character deserves the best story possible, and this is garbage.

I look through my copious notes, trying to pull any kind of research I swore I needed prior to moving forward. I've done so much research for him that it's overwhelming and I don't know what to do with it all so that he becomes the character I imagined in my head.

Flint is a man of honor, a man who takes action when others wrong him and those weaker than he is. He's loyal and strong. He's the man I wish I could be. It's why his story always pulls me back in, why I pull this manuscript out every four months or so to tinker with, even if I don't make any progress or add any words.

I've left off where Flint meets a man who will be his side-kick, a guy who lost his saloon because he owed loan sharks too much money. But I can't figure out the motivations of the sidekick and why he would accompany my main character. It's stumped me for over two years, and it's one of the many reasons I can't move forward.

It's why I've read book after book about the west and the Gold Rush to get inspiration.

I look up. Whitney's focused, headphones covering her ears as she types away. She bites her lip and continues, zoned into her work, unaware that I'm staring at her. That I'm here for her as much as I'm here for the writing.

She's not distracted; she just works. I bet she never gets writer's block. At all.

I stare at the wall. I stare at my screen. What does this character want? I read a book once about goal, motivation, and conflict, but I can't remember the basic details. It might be time to bust it out again.

Whitney's laptop dings, and she looks up with a smile. It's over already?

I look down, and I've added a whole thirty-seven words to my manuscript.

"I got a thousand and five!" Whitney says, her smile beaming.

What?

"That's insanity," I say.

"How much did you get?"

"Not that." I'm in awe of her. "How do you write so fast?"

"It's a sex scene, and I tend to be really good at those. This couple is really hot together." She blushes and rubs her lips together.

"I can't believe you can write sex scenes in public." Saying the word "sex" to her crumples me like a paper ball. I want to have sex with Whitney. I want it bad.

"Believe me, I've had some close calls. When you use words like 'cock' or 'pussy,' sometimes people see that word accidentally and then they have questions. It happened once, and I've had nightmares ever since."

Those dirty words on her lips makes me go uncomfortably hard against my zipper. How can she be so cavalier about sex, writing it out in public, with a stranger reading the paper literal feet from her? I can barely handle my family being in the same room as my printed-out manuscript.

Whitney continues, "I've been procrastinating on writing them since I got here."

"What is happening? In the scene?"

I notice her swallow. "Do you really want to know?"

"Sure," I say. I need to shift in my seat. This might be a terrible idea to ask, but the anticipation is killing me.

Whitney's creamy skin blushes the color of valentine hearts as she looks down. Her voice lowers. "This is their first time together."

I lean in. "Oh?"

"So, they're in the ocean, and he starts kissing her neck. Which is one of my favorite things."

Kissing neck. File that away for future use.

"Then he rips her bikini top off her when she moans."

"Really?" I sound breathy, and this feels wrong to talk about in public, but we're doing it anyway.

"He might use it as a blindfold. I haven't decided yet," Whitney says.

Alright, I haven't done blindfolds per se, but I could be into trying it. Shifting in my seat isn't doing anything to give my growing dick room to exist as Whitney details her sex scene.

Whitney breaks the spell. "That's as far as I got. He's about to lay her on some rocks to eat her out while his enemy, her brother, is mere feet away and can discover them at any moment."

Damn. I take a sip of coffee, but it makes me hotter than I already am. I touch my face. I'm sweating.

Whitney shrugs. "It might change. I let my first drafts be messy. My editor sees an early draft, and then we brainstorm ideas on how to move it forward. I like the scene, but I'm not in love with it."

Now she's back to business, and I breathe out a sigh of relief.

Calm down, Reid. Calm the fuck down.

"You don't go back and edit before moving forward?"

"Absolutely not. I would never finish a book if I did it that way," she says. "Also, sometimes I get ideas as I write, and why make the beginning perfect when I might change it because it doesn't fit the story by the time I make it to the end?"

My mind went from sexy daydreams to a lightbulb moment about writing craft. Is this how Whitney lives?

I look down at the table. Have I been doing it wrong this entire time? This realization shakes me from my arousal in my pants just as Whitney's computer dings and she says, "Go!"

This time, I just let my fingers fly. I don't worry about repetitive word choices or if the prose isn't completely perfect. I just write. Whitney cruises, her typing quick and frantic, while my keys move more slowly. But when she calls time, I laugh out loud.

I got four hundred words. With a wilting hard-on. I can't remember the last time I got that many words in one session, let alone twenty minutes. Not to mention with a hard dick. Am I evolving as a man?

What I wrote is just meaningless conversation between my main character and his sidekick, but it's something. I did learn a little bit more about what the sidekick wanted out of life, so I'm closer than I was when I sat and stared at a wall.

"Not as good as last time, but I did get eight hundred and forty-seven."

"I got four hundred," I say, feeling the embarrassed redness fill my cheeks. It's a nice change from being a sex-crazed pervert.

"That's really good!" Whitney says. "I'm proud of you."

Don't you dare ask about her sex scene. You're close to writing more today than you have this entire year.

"What do you do when you don't know something about a character?" I ask. "I have this guy who is helping my protagonist, and I don't have him figured out. It's tripped me up for a bit."

A bit means two years. Whitney ponders it by tilting her head and then she says, "I usually figure it out in drafting or revising. You could always think about it when you're not writing, like in the car, or on walks. I usually problem-solve then, and it usually works."

That makes so much sense.

I don't have time to ask about her sex scene before the writing sprint starts again.

This round, I let go of my block, and my fingers move even faster. It doesn't match Whitney's speed, but my creativity finally feels alive again. I get through the end of a scene that has haunted me for years, and when Whitney calls time, I can finally move on to my team heading out to exact revenge for my main character's family.

I wrote five hundred and seventeen words this time. I'm nearing a thousand new words. I've never written so much in one day in my life.

"Reid," Whitney says, "I have a manly question."

"Shoot," I say.

"If you emerge from a cold body of water after swimming or whatever, can your dick immediately get hard? Like if you're turned on enough?"

Her question is like Pavlov's bell because my dick gets hard. Again.

"Um..."

"He's now on the rocks by his enemy. He's going to nail the sass out of her."

Does she want me to nail the sass out of her?

"I...uh...I..." I babble, and Whitney covers her mouth. Self-consciousness takes over as Whitney dissolves into giggles.

"What?" I ask.

"You," Whitney says. "You're so cute. One minute you say dirty shit to me, and the next, you're getting all red after I ask you a question about your penis."

"The question was out of left field, is all." Is my collar getting tight?

"I talk about dicks and sex all day long that I forget most people don't," she says. "I'm sorry if that question was inappropriate."

Well, I am now imagining you naked on rocks, and yes, my

dick could be stuck in the iceberg that took down the Titanic and it would be hard immediately if I got to fuck you.

"Yes," I say and cough into my hand.

Her cheeks flush and she looks down. "I'm sorry. I usually ask Brad, but..."

Brad must be the ex-husband. I wonder what kind of guy he is, to let a woman as talented and full-of-life and sexy as Whitney go.

Some men take a woman like that for granted. I would not.

"I meant, yes, after cold water, it can...you know."

"Get hard," she clarifies, and my collar feels like a noose. All I can do is cough and nod.

"Thanks, Finch," she says. "How did you do?"

I sit back, anything to distract myself from imagining myself nailing her on some rocks. With my enemy mere feet away. Trying to stifle her screams because she wants my dick that much. Writing. Let's talk about writing. "I've written more today than I wrote all last year."

"It's the sprints," Whitney says. "They're magic."

"No, what you told me about first drafts is magic. It makes sense. I just want everything to be perfect," I say, motioning to my computer. "I'm so angry the words don't come out like I imagine them in my head."

"I'm writing my twenty-sixth book right now, and my first drafts are always terrible," Whitney says. "You can't expect to be perfect at something you haven't been practicing. Even if you've been practicing, you won't get it right on the first try. Stop putting so much pressure on yourself."

I've heard that all my life. *Relax, Reid. Stop stressing out. Everything will work itself out.*

That's what happens when you're in all honor classes,

and you put pressure on yourself to do everything right. Be perfect.

Sometimes, I'm so focused on getting it done well, that I don't start or I think way too much. Taking action feels fucking amazing.

Like that kiss a few days ago.

Whitney and I have skirted around the elephant in the room, and it's time to act. Now.

"So, you and Thumper..."

Whitney waves it away. "We're nothing. He's into Izzie."

"Great," I say, leaning back. "So what are we doing?"

"What?"

"This?" I move my hand between us. This connection, this flirtation is driving me mad. She's all I think about. I just want to be straightforward and honest, and go after what I want.

All I want is Whitney in my bed.

"We're writing buddies right now," she answers.

"Writing buddies who *kissed*."

Her face does not react. What if she didn't like kissing me? What if it was a mistake?

Take a chance, Reid. Find out now before you're too gone over her. "I really liked it. Kissing you," I blurt.

Her blue eyes look down at her laptop. "You did?"

I nod so hard, my head might snap off.

Her lips form a slight smile. "I liked kissing you too."

My chest immediately lightens. "Telling you to beg might've not be the right move."

"No," she says, with an eyebrow flick. "I really liked it."

"Oh?" I say.

"But it's not you, though. Asking a woman to beg. I think there's a squishy teddy bear in there."

I laugh and place my hand on my chest. "I can be a

squishy teddy bear who wields raw sexual energy."

"Jury is still out," she says. "But I'm cautiously optimistic."

I lean forward and rest my elbows on the table. "So, do you want to go out sometime?"

Whitney leans back, the mirth gone from her body language.

Oh no. This is not good.

"You don't want to pursue me," she says. "It'll just end badly."

"Because we fight?"

Whitney shakes her head. "It will just end badly. We want different things."

What was she talking about? "What different things?"

"I just know it won't work out," she says, crossing her arms. "This can't be anything."

"It definitely felt like *something*."

"I might be up for something casual, but I can't do anything serious right now."

My stomach drops at my strikeout. I do want a relationship and have never been a casual guy. However, sitting here with her, writing on a manuscript I thought was long dead, has been the highlight of my week.

My kiss with her was the highlight of my year. The electric charge we had burnt a memory into my bones, and when I think about it, I'm taken right back to our lips moving together, how she gasped when I grabbed her ass.

This can't be dead in the water.

"I'm not asking you to marry me," I say. "I'm just asking for...exploration."

She smiles, but I know its source isn't happiness. "It's just best we call it at the kiss. Nothing more. Stay just friends."

"Okay," I say. I might try an alpha persona on for size, but that doesn't mean I will turn into an aggressive asshole.

I check my watch, and I've been gone for an hour. My dad wanted to start a brew this afternoon, and there's a missed call from him on my phone.

"I have to get back to work," I say, slipping my laptop in my bag. "Are you going to be here tomorrow?"

Whitney nods. "I'm always here, six days a week."

"Can I still write with you?" I ask.

Her lips press together before she says, "Sure."

"Perfect." I can't help but smile like I'm taking an unironic family photo. "If you won't go on a date with me, I guess this is the only way I can spend time with you."

"I guess so." She rubs her lips together, and my dick tightens again, thinking about our kiss, the frenzy of lips, how my hands roamed up and down her back. How she held me to kiss me like her body already recognized me.

"See you tomorrow," I say.

Gold Roast's door empties into a hallway, since the coffee shop is in an old bank, one of Goldheart's first structures. There is a small window with Gold Roast's logo painted on and when I look back, I see Whitney between "Gold" and "Roast." She's looking at me, holding a pen to her lips. When she notices I caught her staring at me, she flutters her fingers, wishing me farewell.

She thinks it won't end well. I'm not sure what she means, but with the way my mind shifted, the way this woman bewitched me with her lips and her hands, I don't know if I can go back and pretend like nothing happened.

I will come back every day with my laptop until her lips are on mine again.

I'm playing with fire and asking for third-degree burns.

13

WHITNEY

"Where are we going?" I ask, sitting in the front seat of Reid's car.

"It's a surprise," he says, looking over at me. His hand rests on the top of the steering wheel. Reid looks like a model in a high-end car commercial.

Damn it, he is cute.

We've written together almost every day this week, and the flirting has been dialed up a notch with every day that passes. When we sprint, we're focused, pounding words onto the page. I thought Reid across from me would be a distraction, the sexual attraction stalling my fingers and keeping the muse at bay.

It's the complete opposite. My hero now has a beard, because Reid has one.

When we're not sprinting, we're all sexy glances, sexual innuendos, and Reid asking me on a date daily, just for me to say no.

We exchanged phone numbers and trade audio messages back and forth when we're not together. I tell him about random things I see in my day, and he tells me the same.

I know all of this is a terrible idea and this is speeding toward a dead end, but I can't stop.

I was so wrong about Reid.

He loves history, and everything fascinates him. A small detail in his day could become a story. His eyes light up when he talks about his family and his beermaking, even if he didn't imagine his life would go this way. He looks at me like I wasn't terrible to him, and he hasn't let me pay for coffee in two weeks.

I should cut him off completely, be firm that this can't go anywhere.

It's impossible.

Our writing time together is the most fun I've had in forever. No one prepares you for how lonely being an author can be sometimes. Work that felt like a chore is now fun, because I can read sex scenes I've written out loud just to tease Reid.

Saying no to a date has become a game. He asks me every day, and I say no, usually tucking hair behind my ear or giving him "fuck me" eyes as I touch his hand. My nos have no punch, no conviction behind them.

It's Saturday, and he's asked me to go with him to see an old gold mine he mentions in his story to get inspiration. It's become a running joke that this is not a date, and it's been repeated at least fifteen times.

He's talked about the gold mine so much, I wanted to see it for myself. Plus, he couldn't write yesterday when his dad insisted on starting a brew earlier than usual and he couldn't get away.

I missed him. My chest ached, and I moved through the

day with sadness and a heaviness that even Tara at Gold Roast noticed.

"Where's Reid?" she asked.

"He had to help his dad."

"You seem sad."

"Do I?" I asked as Tara sat down my usual order in front of me.

Instead of writing and being in the zone, I talked with Reid over text, sending GIFs back and forth whenever he had a break.

As my day without Reid continued, I looked at his chair. I missed our chats in between sprints, the way his eyes pierce mine, how he flirts with me without saying a word. The words pour out of me when I'm with him. And because I missed him, I'm going to a second location with him, in the woods.

Every true crime lover knows you do not go to a second location, because you're definitely becoming a victim.

Going to a second location with this man means something might happen, and I'm smiling at the possibilities.

I was obsessed with *Twilight* in college. I've written many a love scene in the woods, usually on a checkered, soft blanket, the hero's back muscles flexing as he hovers over his heroine. It's always been a personal bucket list item for me, but I've never had the opportunity. I've scanned this entire car for a blanket and no such luck.

I cannot have sex with Reid Finch. I cannot even *think* about it.

Reid *thinks* he wants me, but he doesn't really want to deal with a woman like me, all broken and destroyed, who writes her childhood trauma in her books.

If my own mother can't love me, there's something wrong with me.

I know Reid's type. He grew up in a functional house-hold, where every holiday was perfect, his parents were happy and in love, and his siblings all got along. Meanwhile, it was me and my dad, eating TV dinners on portable tables, watching the dog show on Thanksgiving, barely talking except to say "Cute dog" every three breeds or so.

My mother left me. Brad left me. A good guy like Reid will leave me.

"I hate this car," Reid whispers to himself as we make a turn.

I was surprised when he picked me up in a champagne-colored sedan, something my dad would drive. He's mentioned here and there that he likes cars and it just seems like a car guy wouldn't drive something so...boring.

"What's your dream car?" I ask.

"I like Fords. I would love a Bronco, especially a vintage one. I've always wanted to fix one up. It's just a low priority right now. This car is fine."

I could read it all over his face. Driving this car is killing his spirit.

I catalog this information for later.

"I would love to see what you like sometime."

He smiles and turns his head toward me. "Really?"

"Sure," I say. He pats my leg and grumbles, and I stare at my thigh, where he touched me. I'm surprised it didn't leave a blaze.

"I'm about to show you my other interest. Since you mentioned the other day you want to learn the history of our town." We pull up a hill to a large structure, crumbling and sunken. We pass a sign, Ernest Wyatt Mine, and we pull over to get out of the car.

Reid opens the door with excitement. "Part of Gold-heart's history. This mine is responsible for the town you now call a temporary home. The men would work here and take a wagon back to Main Street. Where you write is where they used to turn in their gold for the day."

"Wow," I say. The structure is dark and foreboding. I wonder how many dreams circulated this mine, men showing up, day after day, hoping that they would strike gold. It was warm down in Goldheart, but up here, the air is crisp and cool.

Reid looks like he just won a million dollars. "This is living, breathing history. Men came from all over to make a better life for themselves in the West. The energy of this place, it inspires me."

"That's great." My teeth chatter, and my arms wrap around me like a boa constrictor. "Why is it so cold here?"

Reid leans in, his breath hot on my ear. "It's all the ghosts."

"Shut up," I say, smacking him on the chest. His hard, toned chest. "I tell you I think ghosts are real *one time*."

"If there's any place that's haunted, it's this one," Reid says.

I shiver. *Warm me up, Reid. Make me hot.*

No, stop it, you hoe.

"I have something if you're cold," Reid says. He runs back to the trunk of his car and pops it, pulling out a gray sweatshirt with our alma mater, Byron University, on it. He smiles as he hands it to me.

"Here," he says and I take it.

I pull on the sweatshirt, which smells faintly like it's hung out in a trunk for a year, but at least it's warm. There's something sexy about wearing a guy's clothing. It's like he owns me, and I am his.

But I can't be Reid's. It just won't work.

"Why did you bring me here?" I ask, pulling my fists into the sleeves. Anything to keep me from grabbing Reid.

Reid shrugs, walking closer to the structure. "This is my favorite place in town. We used to come on field trips and go inside. I figured you couldn't get the full Goldheart experience without seeing it." He looks up at the mine. "My book is finally coming along."

"That's great," I say, although I know I've written three times the words he has. Still, I'm proud of him.

"I might finally publish it one day," he says, turning to me. "Do you think I should self-publish?"

"It's hard...I mean, difficult," I say. Involuntary giggles leave my mouth. Why did I say hard?

"Seriously, does being a romance author turn you into a twelve-year-old boy?" Reid asks.

"Sometimes," I say. "I once read a colleague's book where she referred to the vagina as a 'snatch,' and I lost my shit in a coffee shop."

Reid laughs, a deep throaty sound from deep within him, and it is making my snatch very, very hot. "What do you call it?"

"What?" I ask, although I know damn well what he's talking about.

Here we go, flirting again.

"Lady parts," Reid says. Why is he stepping toward me? "Va-GINE-a." The way he enunciates the proper medical term makes me laugh harder. Maybe I do have the mentality of a twelve-year-old boy. That's what happens when you decide not to have children. You're allowed to be eternally immature.

"When you say it like that..." I say.

"Seriously, I want to know," Reid says.

"Folds, sex, glory hole."

"You do *not* use glory hole," Reid says, horrified.

I cross my arms, trying to hide my sarcasm. "The actual

line is 'he put his big, hard drill in my glory hole."

"Shut *up*," Reid says, covering his mouth. He wags a finger at me. "You're a better writer than that."

"You didn't think so in college," I say.

"What?" Reid asks.

"You didn't leave any feedback on my last story."

"Oh, that," he says. He looks down. He's going to tell me he hated it. Something close to what he said for the first story of mine he critiqued. I've had hundreds of reviews, Goodreads trolls calling me a horrible writer and telling me to quit writing, but at this moment, his review is the only one that matters.

Now that we're friendly, it's time to revisit the ghost of our creative writing past. Possibly surrounded by pioneer ghosts.

"You hated it," I say.

Reid shakes his head. "No. I was blown away by it."

I could faint right now. "Really?"

"Absolutely," Reid says. "You're a gifted writer. I was jealous and couldn't understand how a romance story like yours could affect me. It moved me."

I can quit writing right now, because praise doesn't get better than this.

"Really?" I ask.

"I would never lie to you," Reid says. "I can't. Except for Jenga."

His eyes soften like butter. Reid's lips part, and I hold my breath.

He shoves his hands in his pockets. "I finished your *Brutal Palace* series, by the way. You are so, so talented."

I hold my breath because this is a fantasy coming true.

He rubs his short hair and turns around. "I really, really

want to kiss you again. But I won't unless you tell me it's okay."

Sparks fly through me, between us. They've been there ever since he pulled me toward him and took my mouth.

"It's a terrible idea," I say. I can't stop walking toward him.

"You're creeping toward me like a raccoon about to steal food."

"Well, you are a snack," I say.

Reid lets out a laugh, deep and contagious. I cover my mouth.

"Don't get too big of a head. There and there." I point to his head and his junk.

"I think we should kiss again," Reid says. "Just to make sure."

"Make sure what?"

"That the first time wasn't a fluke. That it was more than the tequila."

My feet stop. *Be reasonable, Whitney. This man is heartbreak. He might not even like you that much. You're too horny.*

"Maybe," I say, although my common sense is screaming at me.

Reid's feet stay planted like we're at a duel in his book, both holding our lips as our weapons of choice. Who is going to be the first to draw?

"What would a man in one of your romances do?" he asks.

"He wouldn't wait for permission."

"That sounds like permission."

"Just shut up and kiss me."

He charges me, and his hand wraps around the back of my neck, his fingers tangled with my hair. When his lips find mine, his breath is hot, his tongue immediately against mine. It feels exactly like our first kiss outside the bowling alley, utterly consuming. Even more, with all the banked flirting and tension.

His thumb rubs my jaw as he turns his head like he wants to engulf me, take me under with him into a swirl of destruction. His lips move quicker than I can register, but my mouth responds unconsciously. My fingers lace through his hair as his hand goes to my ass and lifts me so that my legs wrap around his waist as he presses me against the crumbling wood of the gold mine. I might be getting splinters all over my body, but I don't care.

All that matters is this kiss. All I want is Reid.

When he pulls away, he does so to kiss my neck as I moan a guttural noise. He presses against me, and I feel an impressive bulge. I try to press him closer, my sex aching for him with the delicious pressure he's applying.

"Oh my God," I say as his hand reaches between my legs and presses the seam of my jeans into me. I better stop this before I'm buck naked and need to be rushed to urgent care for a tetanus shot.

"We can't go further," I say, pushing him off me, my self-restraint shocking and admirable. I want him to fuck me, I want it so bad, but once we have sex, it's absolutely doomed. Someone will compromise, and I'm terrified it will be me.

Also, all the mold and termites hidden in the wood are definitely a health hazard.

In between kisses on my neck and lips, he asks "Do you want me to stop?"

I think way too long about this, the kisses making it almost unbearable, before I nod.

Reid sets me down, and I'm huffing deep breaths, pressing my palms into the wall. He runs his fingers across his hair, and I notice redness splotching his skin, crawling down his neck, disappearing into his shirt.

Don't look at his pants. Do not *look at his pants.*

"Okay, we shouldn't do that again," Reid says.

"Absolutely not."

"I mean, you don't live here."

"I'm well aware."

"Who knows, you might be using me for research."

"Don't get too big of a head. It was fine."

"Fine? *Fine*?" He rubs his beard and it makes me want to sit on it.

I step toward him, and against my better judgment, I reach out to touch him. "Okay, I'm lying. All I want to do is rip your clothes off and get a cool rash as a souvenir."

"Let's do it," Reid says, shucking his jacket off like he's an exotic dancer.

"Hold it there, Magic Mike," I say. "I'm not what you want."

"Don't tell me I can't want you," Reid says. "Because it's too late. I want you in my bed more than I've ever wanted anything."

My first thought is "oh my God." My second thought is "I have to remember that line and put it in a book."

"Well, it can't happen," I say.

"Why?" he questions.

"I don't want kids," I blurt out. Reid does nothing, no shift in posture, no change in facial expression. I brace myself for a million reactions.

"Like now? My sperm is not that strong."

I shake my head. "Like ever."

"Oh," he says. He crumples, body language foreboding.

If Reid tells me he's okay with it, he will be lying to me, even if he said he would never do that. His hunched shoulders, his hands in his pockets—they tell me everything I need to know. There is already overwhelming proof. He was a teacher; he willingly hangs out with children.

"Our kisses were amazing," I say. *Amazing, really?* "You need to know that. And if the situation were different, I would be in your bed. All night. For five days."

"We can still do that. Figure out the big life stuff after we fuck each other's brains out."

God, that's tempting. However, I know I could fall in love with a man like Reid. And he's the type who would fall in love hard. It's not fair to know there's something that can tear us apart and to charge forward anyways.

That kiss, though.

It was a kiss that made me wish I wanted a family. Then, Reid could be perfect for me.

"Are you a casual sex guy?" I ask. "Honestly."

Reid shoves his hands in his pockets. "To be honest, I haven't really tried it."

"That's all I can handle right now. I can't handle love or anything more than that."

This is a test, and I watch him, how his jaw clenches as he thinks. I want to pounce on him, but I also want him to understand this can't be more than sex. This has to be his choice. If he can handle one night, I can handle one too.

"We should get going," Reid says, holding his jacket in his hands, turning away. He stops and doesn't turn, just looking at the dirt.

I want to touch him, comfort him. He just gave me his answer. It's best we don't test it. I'm not sure if I'm relieved or devastated. "It's easier this way. We can still be friends."

"We were never just friends, Whitney," he says, walking away.

My chest heaves and my core clenches at his words. We

14

REID

"Do you want kids?" I ask Cameron as we hang out behind the bar on a slow Wednesday afternoon at the brewery. "With Annie?"

"Absolutely," Cameron says, without a moment's hesitation. "I'm knocking her up the minute she tells me it's okay."

"Why? Like, how do you know?"

Cameron shrugs. "I don't know. I just do."

"What if the woman you were with didn't want them?"

"Well, I don't know any different, and if she was perfect for me, I would just not have them. I want Annie, and Annie wants them, so I want them. With her. I was fine either way, but once I kissed Annie, my decision was made for me."

Same way when I kissed Whitney. Our first kiss felt like the beginning of something, and the kiss at the mine felt like more. Once we stopped hating each other, I realized she was more like me than I realized. She gets the writer thing; past girlfriends just thought it was a silly hobby. Plus, my chemistry with Whitney made me realize all my past relationships were nothing.

Whitney could be everything I'm looking for.

She just doesn't want kids.

I always thought I would have a couple once I met the right woman. We would buy a house, and I would spend weekends doing yard work and going to kids' soccer games. There wasn't another way I imagined my life going. I got a taste of it dating Callie, and I liked it for the most part.

However, I've never been in a hurry. I figured it would happen if it was meant to happen.

There's lots of unknowns about my life but all I know is I want to kiss Whitney again. I wanted to fuck her against the mine, hearing her moan against my ear. But I'm not eighteen anymore. The future is something I have to think about now that I'm firmly in my thirties. I've never been interested in dating casually.

To be honest, I've never tried it.

"What's going on in that big brain of yours?" Cameron asks.

"Oh, nothing. Just thinking."

"Typical you," Cameron says.

"What?" I ask.

"Did you meet a woman who doesn't want kids?" Cameron asks. His eyes light up. "Is it Whitney?"

"No," I say, letting out a guffaw. The lie is thick in my throat.

"You're a terrible liar," Cameron says.

A customer walks up and orders one of our ciders. After Cam pours it and I grab the credit card, Cam picks the conversation back up. "Something's going on with Whitney. I know it."

"Okay, fine. Kinda."

"Kinda?"

"She thinks I want kids and that's why we won't work."

"Oh," Cameron says. "Well, that's a conundrum."

"Conundrum? Where are you getting these words?"

"I'm in love with the smartest woman on this planet," Cameron says.

"Did you picture your life this way?" I ask. "Like with Annie and stuff?"

"Absolutely not," Cameron says. "It's cool, though. I like it when life surprises me. Who knew I would want to get married? Not me."

"Huh," I say. For so long the plan was to find a good woman, marry her and have a couple kids, living a quiet life on a piece of property. That's the blueprint that every one of my classmates took.

The other night I thought about what it would be like not to have kids. I could travel freely like I always wanted to. I could get that car and restore it. I could write books and sleep in.

Still, the dad lifestyle looks fun. I envy the guys on the sidelines at Isaac's games.

I want to see if Whitney and I can be something before I write off my future. Who knows, maybe the sex will be terrible and we'll want to kill each other after a month. Then the decision would be made for us.

"You need to stop thinking about whatever you're doing and just do it. Don't think. Trust your gut for once. You knew Callie was bad news about a year in, but that big heart of yours told you to stay because of the kid. Don't let any guilt fuel you."

"You're right," I say. Cameron wraps his arm around my shoulders and shakes me. Jackson walks out from the back, his dark-rimmed glasses sliding down his nose.

"Reid, tell Jackson what you just told me."

"I told Cameron he was right," I say. Cameron is still jostling me.

"Wow, first time ever," Jackson says. He looks around,

pushing his glasses up his nose. "Where's Shiloh? I thought she was supposed to be on today."

"She texted me and said she found a stray dog, and asked if I could cover for her for a bit while she takes care of it," I tell him.

Jackson scowls.

"I think a loose dog is way more important than our crazy busy taproom," Cameron says, opening his arms to the near-empty space. It won't pick up for another couple hours, when Cameron hosts our monthly trivia night.

"Shiloh said she would be here by five," I say. "It's fine, Jackson. I've seen that dog wandering around before. It could belong to someone."

"Okay," he says. "Let me know when she gets here."

"Sure, will do," I say, saluting him. Jackson nods and walks to the back.

"Does he seem different to you?" Cameron asks.

"Now that you mention it, yeah. I was over at his house a couple nights ago, and he *smiled* when we saw a commercial with a dog."

"Huh," Cameron says. "Maybe we should take him to the doctor."

"No, he's fine," I say. "Maybe he's getting used to Gold-heart again."

"I hope so," Cameron says. "If you need to go, go. I can handle it. I'll let Jackson know when Shiloh gets here."

"What?"

"You're fidgeting like you have to be somewhere. It's fine. I can handle all these people."

I laugh since the only people we have is the group quietly playing Connect Four at one of our tables.

"Thanks, Cam," I say. We hug it out, him slapping my back in encouragement.

"Go get her, little brother."

You need to stop thinking about whatever you're doing and just do it. Don't think. Trust your gut for once. Cam's words ring in my ears as I grab my coat. I'm not sure if Whitney is at Gold Roast or the library, but I won't stop until I find her.

Any kids of mine don't exist at this moment, so I don't know why I'm hesitant about them when a very real woman I can't stay away from is here and available. So I'm going to seize that opportunity. I bust out my phone and open a text screen with Whitney. Our conversations via text have been cutesy, fun. Mildly flirty. Clean for the most part.

Time to make it dirty. I shoot off a text and wait for a response.

15

WHITNEY

"You seem sad," Annie says as we sip our drinks at The Swift. I try to mix up my writing spots so I don't get bored, but every Goldheart spot has been a winner, including The Swift. I'm drafting a new book in a new series about a motorcycle gang. While there isn't one in Goldheart, two Harleys are constantly parked outside the bar, so close enough. But I've seen the men who ride them, and I'm going to have to use my romance author imagination to conjure up better specimens.

After staring into space for more than fifty percent of the time and after multiple Diet Cokes, I texted Annie to see if she wanted to meet me for a drink.

It wasn't The Swift's fault I only got a thousand words today.

It was Reid Finch's fault.

I'm starting to realize he is my good-luck writing charm.

And I am sad. I'm sad about the what-if, devastated Reid isn't The One but he's the one that I want. That kiss outside of Culver Lanes and that makeout session against the mine consume my thoughts.

It doesn't help that I'm writing a book in my dark erotic romance series and I've been imagining Reid in that scene for the past five hours.

"Come on, Whit, tell me why you're looking like that bitch Veronica Hatcher's book is doing better than yours."

I laugh when Annie mentions my author frenemy Veronica, whose real name is Brittany. Veronica and I were cool until she sent her minions after me, spreading a rumor that I was privately telling Bookstagrammers not to read her books.

It was simply not true.

I suspect it was she was jealous that my books were doing so well and I was more successful than her. My fans shut it down, proclaiming that I would do no such thing.

Veronica is still writing and publishing, unfortunately.

"It's not that," I say. "Though that would make me sad."

"Then what is it?"

"Just...things I can't have," I say, staring off into the corner.

"I get that," Annie says, taking her drink. "You'll find what you can have, and it will be great."

"I love you," I say, covering her hand with mine.

"I love you too."

My phone buzzes, and I pull it out.

Sometimes, my mouth does weird things when I smile, so Annie sniffs it out immediately. "Who did you get a text from? You're doing your weird smiling thing."

I press my lips together. "Nothing."

I read it over again.

Reid: If you want to do research tonight, I'm available. I love research.

Heat creeps into my cheeks as I focus, my thumbs flying over the keys.

Me: What about what I told you?

I shift in my seat and take a sip of my rum and Coke to cool down, but it makes it worst. My limbs tingle, my nipples pebble against my bra, my underwear dampens, all because Reid sent me a single sentence via text message.

The three dots flicker for what feels like forever.

The message finally comes through, and I have to cover my mouth as an "Oh fuck" comes out.

"What?" Annie asks.

Reid: I don't care. I can't function until I know what you taste like. Get your fucking ass over to my house right now. I plan to make you come so hard that one night is all we'll need.

Then he provides his address.

There's no way.

Did he just quote my book? I immediately find my copy of *Brutal King* on the Kindle app. I search for the line "**I can't function until I know what you taste like. Get your fucking ass over to my house right now**" and confirm Reid just quoted my book back to me.

This is a terrible idea. This is a horrible idea. I shouldn't do this. I'm going against everything I said at the mine, *multiple* times at Gold Roast.

This is stupid. I can't do this. I...I have to go.

I stand up from my stool and collect my laptop and my notebook, sliding them into my tote. "I have something to do." *Your friend is who I have to do.* "Are you going to be okay?"

"Definitely," Annie says, checking her phone. "Cam is two miles away. He'll be here soon."

"You track him?"

"Like a crazy stalker girlfriend," Annie says. She shakes

her phone in her hand. "He put it on for me so I would know where he was at all times."

As evidenced by my books, stalking can be cute.

"You're okay to drive?"

"Yeah, I only had one." I kiss Annie on the cheek and squeeze her before I leave. "Love you."

"Love you. Whatever the reason for your weird smile, good luck," she yells.

"Thanks!" I say, throwing up my hand in a wave.

This is reckless. I am asking for a broken heart. But I can't help but run to him.

I DRIVE up to Reid's place, which is dark except for one lit window. I wonder if that's his bedroom. I wonder if that's where he'll do the things he promised in his texts.

My body hums with anticipation. It's been almost a year since I've been intimate with a man. It's been even longer since a man went down on me. I wonder what Reid's pussy-eating skills are.

We're about to find out.

He may want to be a daddy someday, but he'll be my daddy tonight.

Only tonight.

I'm so horny, I can't even think.

I knock and shift on my feet. It's so quiet here in the country, sometimes so loud in its quietness. No one comes to the door, and I look in the side window. The front room is dark, the light from upstairs lighting the stairs.

Did I come to the right house? I check the number on the text. Is this a prank? Hearing noise, I breathe out a sigh of relief. I hoist my breasts up in my bra and pull down my shirt. Will he attack me immediately?

My vagina is ready for a beating.

Reid opens the door, wearing a white T-shirt that stretches across his broad chest and grey sweatpants, and all I can see is penis.

A very impressive penis.

"Come on in," he says, opening the door. I brace for his touch as I pause, his hand rubbing my shoulder as I walk in. I shuck my jacket off, and he takes it and my purse from me, disappearing to a room near the entrance. When he comes back out, his hand goes to my lower back to lead me inside.

I love it when guys do that.

"This is my place," he says. "The kitchen is over here, the living room is here, and my bedroom is upstairs."

His cheeks are flushed, and there's a hint of a smirk on his lips.

"Why did you text me what you texted me?" I ask as I rest my arms around his neck. I want him to kiss me, put his hands on me. *Soon, hoe, soon.*

"Well, I was re-reading your book, and I feel just like Sebastian feels about Amelia," Reid says. Nothing gets an indie author going like someone reading their book. He leans his forehead against mine. "I was just thinking... you're right. We need a night to get it out of our system."

I laugh, and he kisses my cheek as I drop my head to his shoulder.

"What's so funny?" he asks, dropping his head so we can look at each other.

"I use that trope all the time in my books. People are crazy attracted to each other and they think one night of sex will vanquish all of the sexual feelings, but it doesn't. It makes them want each other more."

"Oh," he says. "Do you think that will happen to us?"

"I don't know. I've never tested the trope in real life," I

say, looking up at him. His hands on my lower back run up and down my spine, sending shivers and goosebumps with their trail.

"One way to find out." His breath scorches my skin.

"Maybe," I say, wetting my lips.

"Are we going to do this?" he whispers.

I grip the back of his neck, and his mouth crashes into mine.

The kiss sets off a bomb inside me, and I jump up, my legs wrapping around his waist. His forearms create a shelf for my ass, and he carries me up the stairs like I weigh nothing. I fling my sweater off as I kiss him again, like he has the oxygen I need to survive. Moans escape us as we continue to kiss, moving our heads from side to side, hoping one kiss will satisfy, but it's never enough.

Never.

We reach the top of the stairs, and it's dark. He fumbles but manages to stay upright.

"Don't hurt yourself."

"I just might," Reid says. "I don't plan to be gentle."

"Fuck yes," I say, colliding with his lips again.

Somewhere between getting to the top of the stairs and his bedroom, I unhook my bra and toss it aside, knocking something over with a crash of glass.

"I hope you didn't like whatever that was," I say, as he takes one of my nipples in his mouth and I moan, my fingers in his hair.

"If I have to sacrifice my lamp for these tits, then I'll do it."

He bounces me in his arms so I'm higher on him, and he finds the switch with his right hand. Soft light floods the room. I turn and look at the comfortable-looking bed I plan to be fucked on all night long.

It will do.

He drops me on the bed, and I pull his shirt over his head.

Holy shit.

His chest is broad with a sprinkling of chest hair, trailing down to perfectly defined abs, with a V that points right to the cock that will be destroying me tonight. I run my fingers down his chest and growl, and he laughs as he takes my lips again, sweeping his tongue against mine. His mouth breathes hot on my neck, my collarbone, and he takes one of my breasts in his mouth again.

My eyes roll back with the sensations, and I arch my back.

"Do you like that?" he asks, his voice wet as he gently sucks my nipple. All I can do is nod.

He moves to the other, palming the one he just left, and I buck against him, feeling his impressive cock, thick and straining against his pants. My skin is cold and hot all at once, and when his hand drifts down to between my legs, I moan so loud I laugh. I sound like a dying mongoose. I cover my mouth.

He snakes up to kiss my neck, hitting a ticklish spot, and I squirm with giggles as his hand unzips my jeans. He looks down at my lacy underwear, my best pair of baby pink lace.

Thank God it's laundry day.

"I really like these," he says. "So I won't rip them. Tonight."

I bite my fingernail as he pulls them off, my feet kicking to help them. When he puts his hand back where it should be, he rubs my clit in long, strong strokes.

"Whitney, you're soaked," he says.

"I was thinking about what you were going to do to me the whole drive over here."

"Is it living up to your expectations?"

"Absolutely," I say, grabbing his neck, pulling him back to my mouth so I can taste him again. He slides one finger in, then two, so he can feel what he does to me. How turned-on I am.

"Fuck me," I say as his thumb finds my clit, and I pant in a frenzy of desire for this man.

"Well, I promised I would taste you, and I intend to make you come first."

All I can do is nod so hard I think I have whiplash.

He kisses down my stomach and laces his arms under my legs, propping them up on his shoulders. He looks at my pussy first, like he's concocting a game plan.

Without warning, he dives right in.

"Oh my God, Reid," I say, rubbing the short stubble on his head as he feasts on me, licking me and sucking, switching between the two.

He stays focused on the clit like a good boy. His beard is scratchy on my thighs, adding to the sensations.

My breath quickens as the sensations build, his tongue wet but firm between my legs.

Just when a man would get impatient and speed up his pace to make me come, Reid slows down. He moans against my flesh, taking my indulgence to a new stratosphere. Like it's more than duty, it's pleasure.

His tongue goes from my pussy to my clit, flicks against it, and then travels back down again. Every time he hits that sensitive bud, I'm even more frazzled, even more carnal.

"I want to come on your dick."

"But your pussy tastes so good," Reid says. "I could stay down here all night long."

"Reid, I will fucking die if you don't fuck me right now."

He looks up, his mouth glistening from me. He looks manic, like my pussy turned him feral.

I know already this will be more than one night. I don't fucking care.

He doesn't listen and dives back down, inserting a finger into my pussy, and I lose it.

It must look like a demon is leaving my body, because I convulse, the spasms in my walls violent enough to make my back levitate off of the bed in the strongest orgasm of my whole life. He keeps going, licking me, and I have to physically remove his face from between my thighs.

He kisses my breasts before he reaches my lips, hesitant to kiss me, unsure if I'm into it. I grab his face to kiss him, tasting myself on his tongue.

"Did you enjoy that?"

"Goddamn, where did you learn that?"

He massages my breasts and whispers, "Your books."

"Let me see that cock," I say. I pull down his pants, and his cock bobs, more impressive than I guessed. There's a bead of pre-cum on the tip, and I drag it down his shaft, his own groan coming out of his lips.

"Now. I'll die if I don't get to fuck you right now," he says. When I look into his eyes, all I see is emeralds on fire.

"Do you have anything?" I ask. Reid nods and rolls to his nightstand, retrieving a foil packet. I help him roll it on and grip it, giving a playful tug, causing him to groan again.

"You don't play fair," he says.

"That's what drives you wild about me."

"Get on my dick like a good girl," Reid growls.

I don't question where the fuck this came from, I just kiss him as I sink down onto his lap, guiding his cock into me, my pussy ready and willing. He kisses my collarbone as he buries himself in me.

He fills me up perfectly, and we moan together, our gazes locking on each other. His thumb goes to my already overwhelmed clit, making tiny circles that get me closer and closer to ecstasy again. My hands are planted on his firm chest as I begin rocking onto him, while his hands are on my hips, gripping my ass. I place my feet on the bed and piston up and down, bouncing on his cock, letting myself go to a place of bliss.

Reid's groans tell me everything I need to know, lifting me higher and higher to my own sexual pinnacle. He's seen this before when he was between my legs, so he knows I'm close. He grabs my neck, making me look at him.

"Just let go, baby," leaves his lips. I break apart, my mouth stretched as I come again, massaging his cock with my pussy.

"Fuck yes," he says, bouncing me on his dick.

"Holy shit," I say. That orgasm that almost broke me in half.

"Get on all fours," he orders, lifting me off of his cock and turning me over, his hand going to the back of my neck, anchoring me to the bed.

He's behind me and then he's in me again, pumping in and out, reaching around to play with my clit. I don't know how she takes it, but she's ready and willing again.

Seconds ago, I was sure there was no way he could make me come a third time, but I'm dead wrong. It's quicker this time, and his grunts are louder as I come apart, my walls pulsing around his cock as he drives into me at a punishing pace, making me feel every inch of him. This is not gentle; this is primal, full of lust and desire.

When his breathing and thrusts slow, he hugs me, cupping one of my breasts.

I let him slip out of me as I collapse onto the bed, my

limbs jelly. Reid drops down next to me, his forearm across my waist, his fingers playing with my hair.

We do not talk for minutes.

"Well," I say.

"Well," Reid repeats.

"That was wonderful, see ya," I joke, standing up, buck naked.

He grabs my wrist. "You have got to be joking."

"What?" I ask, my face stoic and serious. "That was one time. It was great. It's all over."

"Baby, I am going to need at least twenty more times."

I climb onto his lap, his cock still hard inside a condom, filled with his desire for me.

"Oh, really?" I say, rubbing against him. I can feel him growing hard again, and he lays a kiss on the top of one of my breasts.

"I still haven't kissed every inch of you, and you're definitely sitting on my face at least once."

"Can you handle that? I don't think you can handle that."

"That sounds like a challenge."

"Well, if I get only one night with you, I might as well make you rise to the challenge."

My hand slides between us, touching the rubber of the condom.

I lean into his ear, taking his lobe between my teeth.

"I hope you have a full box."

He picks me up from his lap and turns me over so I'm on my back.

"I got the value pack," he whispers.

"I'm going to be so sore tomorrow," I say.

"I hope so. I never want you to forget how good my cock made you feel."

16

REID

"Happy Thanksgiving," I say, holding up two bottles of liquor.

"Excellent," Cam says, taking the whiskey from my right hand. He turns around and shouts, "Babe, Reid brought the Four Roses."

"Excellent," Annie says, walking out from the kitchen.

I look past my brother to the long table set up in the living room. My mother tends to adopt people without families or folks who can't travel for the holidays. There's at least five extra spots.

Annie casually mentioned that Whitney was traveling to Oregon to see her dad for the holiday and wouldn't be present. She thought my look of relief is because we hate each other, but it's because of something different.

If I saw her again, it might be cataclysmic, because I crave her even more now that I know what she tastes like, feels like. Our night together didn't get her out of my system at all. I play our moments together in a slideshow at the most inopportune times. Me over her, thrusting into her, her begging me for an orgasm, finally releasing her to come undone by my tongue. I've never felt so beguiled by a woman that I lost myself, lost all sense.

I'm the level-headed guy, the logical one. She wiped my mind clean of all worry and thinking, and I just *lived*. With her, I could be domineering, demanding. One "good girl" from me could make her orgasm so hard that she needed minutes to recover.

We've tried our best to avoid each other for the past month. It was one of the conditions of our one night together, that it was best to get some distance before we tried to be writing sprint buddies again. The further we get away from that spectacular night, the more I ache for her, not less.

Annie takes the bottle of wine from my other hand, and she oohs, studying the label as I turn the corner to the kitchen. I kiss Mom and hug Dad, who is busy sprinkling parsley on potatoes like he's a showboating celebrity chef.

"Is Jackson coming?" I ask.

"Um-hum," Mom says, her voice suspicious.

"What's going on?" I ask in a whisper to Cam.

"Supposedly, he said he wasn't sure if he could make it, and Mom went nuclear."

I shiver. Mom rarely gets angry, but if she does, it's Chernobyl and Hiroshima combined. It's why we never pushed her as kids. We saw her anger once, and we've been scarred ever since.

The front door opens, and Olive makes a beeline for Annie, wrapping her arms around her legs.

"Everyone else is chopped liver now," Mom says.

"She's obsessed with Annie," Emily says, walking in. She kisses Mom before she puts down her contribution, her trademarked bacon mac and cheese. If you even look at it, one artery is clogged.

"Hi, Emily," I hear from a voice that haunts my nights. I turn around to see Whitney standing there. Her long dark hair weaves into a braid over one shoulder, next to her fantastic breasts hugged in a low-cut gray sweater I want to peel off of her. She's wearing a lavender cardigan that is unnecessary. Black leggings cover her toned legs, legs that wrapped around me as I fucked her.

"Hi, Whitney! I thought you were going to Oregon," Emily says, taking her in a hug.

"Dad wanted to see his sister in New Jersey. I refuse to see my aunt so I'm here," Whitney says. Her eyes look everywhere but at me. It's been a month since our night together, but I still want to cross the room and kiss her until she can't breathe.

"Who else is coming?" Emily asks, popping an olive from the charcuterie plate in her mouth.

"Shiloh and her grandpa are coming," Mom says, stirring gravy at the stove. "Oh, and Tara and her friend Owen."

Annie smacks Whitney on the forearm, and they make weird faces at each other.

Am I missing something?

"Am I missing something?" Cam asks. Thank you, Cam.

"Tara is 'friends' with the vet."

"So?" Cam asks, still confused.

"They're not *just* friends. They're interested in each other, but both are too chicken to say anything," Emily says. "I can feel it. They just need a good nudge. That's where we come in."

I let out a sigh of relief. If everyone is busy looking at Tara and Owen, they won't study Whitney and me and pick up on the tense "I've seen you naked and I can't stop thinking about it" bond.

Whitney and I catch eyes and Emily gasps.

"What?" I ask.

"You two," she says, pointing between us.

"We hate each other again," I blurt.

"Completely. One-hundred percent," Whitney adds.

"It's Thanksgiving. No fighting on Thanksgiving," Cam says. I hold my hands up like I'm caught with stolen merchandise, and Whitney smirks.

She smirks like she's seen me naked.

I want her to get me naked again.

"We'll be on our best behavior today," she says, nudging my shoulder with her fist as she passes me. The same fist that pumped my cock so expertly.

Gosh, I hope I'm not sweating.

"We won't even talk to each other," I say. It's convincing enough that Annie and Emily circle back to talking about Tara, with Mom chirping in between stirs and checks of the turkey in the oven.

Jackson walks into the kitchen, wearing a long-sleeved shirt and jeans. His hair is *short.*

"Hi man, how are you?" I ask, pulling him in by the hand for a half-hug. "When did you get a haircut?"

He wanders toward the whiskey, examining the cork and looking around for a glass. "This week."

His long hair is gone, his gray temples more prominent now that his hair is shorter. Even his beard is trimmed.

"Doesn't it look good?" Mom says. "I almost didn't recognize him."

"Yeah, it's nice," Emily says. She gets closer to Jackson to study him. "Are you okay?"

"Jackson, let's wait to eat before you open the whiskey," Dad says.

Jackson says nothing as he cuts the plastic surrounding the top and pulls the cork out, finding a short glass to pour a good helping in. Without saying anything, he takes a sip. He may have a new haircut, but that doesn't change the attitude.

"You know what, I'll join you," I say, finding my own glass to pour considerably less in. If I have to spend all night inches from the giver of the best sex I've ever had, I need to be tipsy.

We join glasses and sip, much to my father's chagrin.

I hear a cheerful "Hello!" from the front door.

Shiloh and her grandfather must be here.

Shiloh's grandfather, Earl, was a staple at The Swift for years before his stroke earlier this year. Shiloh's mother has three jobs to make ends meet, so Shiloh volunteered to help him, working at the brewery and taking dog-walking jobs here and there.

Shiloh is the strangest person I've ever met. Relentlessly positive, she can make you feel like the world isn't on fire for a minute when you talk to her. Everything is hopeful. She's bubbly and cute, with blonde hair she wears in braids a lot, and her work pants are always covered in fur because she volunteers at the local animal shelter and fosters dogs constantly.

"Thank you so much for having us, Mrs. Finch," Shiloh says, after giving my mom a good squeeze. "I can't cook worth a darn so Grandpa is really thankful."

"Shiloh can burn water," Earl says. "It's her only fault."

"I have *many* faults," she says. She leans sideways to look around me. "Hi, Jackson. I like your hair."

We all turn to look at Jackson, whose whiskey is mid-lift. Why is she saying hello to Jackson first? Most people ignore him or feel too sorry for him that they feel uncomfortable trying to talk to him.

"Hi," he grumbles. "Thank you for coming."

We all turn back to Shiloh. "Thanks for inviting me. This is wonderful!"

This is going to go down in history as the wildest Thanksgiving we've ever had.

"May I help with anything?" Shiloh asks, pulling off her coat.

"Let's start taking everything out to the table," Mom says, pointing at a few dishes on the island. Shiloh takes the salad while I grab the silverware roll-ups to the table.

Whitney's walking too close to me for it to be an accident. I can smell her perfume and see her cleavage from here.

"Hi," she whispers.

"Hi," I say. "I thought you weren't going to be here."

She leans in, her voice low and smooth, like a sip of whiskey. "Surprise."

I go one direction, she goes another.

Maybe she's remembering our night together as frequently as I am.

Stop it, Reid. Whitney and I cannot be together because we want different things, and we live different places. She may be here for a little while, but it was never meant to be permanent. Even then, she absolutely doesn't want kids, but I'm not sure if I do or not.

Tara and her friend Owen show up with a pie for dessert to join the smorgasbord of baked goods my mother started baking two days ago. I've already eaten two chocolate chip cookies today. I've seen Owen here and there, so I give him a hearty handshake. He points at my glass, and I pour him some whiskey as well.

"Everyone is getting tipsy tonight," Mom says, after Dad joins in, taking some whiskey as well. Soon Annie and Whitney also have some.

"I figured I would join in on the debauchery," Whitney says, sipping from her glass, and her face scrunches with the impact of the whiskey. It was very similar to the face she made when she orgasmed.

I should know. I made her come seven times.

"So, what's up with you, Reid? Seeing anyone special? I saw Callie the other day," Tara says, popping a cracker in her mouth.

I can't help it; I look at Whitney, who tears her gaze away immediately.

"No, just single," I say, sipping my whiskey so I don't cough again.

"Me too," Tara says. She looks at Owen, who is talking to an animated Shiloh. Tara turns her straw in her drink, and oh yes, she definitely wants Owen.

Whitney doesn't know that because she's currently watching Tara like Ted Bundy watched sororities.

"What about Owen?" I ask.

"He's just my friend," Tara says. "I don't think he's interested in me, anyway."

What a lie. I can tell because I've been lying about Whitney all night.

I tried to go thirty seconds without looking at her and fail every time. Her blue eyes, her lips, that ass.

"Hello, Reid?" Tara asks.

"Yes, I'm here. I'm paying attention, I promise."

"I was saying I have a friend coming to visit. Do you want to meet her?"

It looks like Whitney heard that, because her gaze sears me like a ribeye.

I smile at Tara and quietly say, "I was fibbing earlier. I'm actually dating someone. It's new, and we're not talking about it quite yet."

Whitney and I are not dating, but my heart is hers. She just doesn't know it yet. It would be unfair to date any woman other than Whitney right now. All I want is a dark romance author whose kisses send jolts of electricity down my body.

"I'm so sorry. I'm sure I can set her up with someone else. No biggie." Tara takes a step back. "So, who is it? Is it Whitney?"

"No," I lie, adding a laugh to cover my tracks. I'm as fake as my mother's pearls.

Tara looks to Whitney and then to me. "Okay, then." Owen strolls over to her, and she kisses me on the cheek, leaving me alone in my parents' house.

"Dad is carving the turkey so dinner is imminent. Get ready," Mom says, clapping her hands together.

I smile as I scan the room, but my gaze always comes back to Whitney.

Wherever she is, that's where I focus.

All I see in this crowded room is her.

17

WHITNEY

I could rip her fucking hair out.

Tara is pretty, and the way she flirted with Reid makes my blood boil. It was *me* who spent an amazing twenty-four hours with him and milked his cock until he was dry, and there's no way some bitch will sweep in and take what's mine. Yes, it's been a month of us avoiding each other—no more writing sessions, no more sexy trips to the mine. We called it good, and now he's in the same room as me and I'm not sure I can control myself for three hours.

Tara did walk away, thankfully, so I didn't have to make a scene at this very lovely home.

Don't you dare pull him outside runs through my mind, because if I do, I will fuck him.

There's no ifs, ands, or buts about it. I'm so angry that a woman talked to him, hit on him, when he's mine.

Annie practically dragged me to this dinner, but I didn't fight that hard. There's nothing more pathetic than your father canceling on you last minute for a major holiday. It's best I'm not alone tonight, even if I have to fight sexual tension like I'm in an action movie.

We're at Reid's family's Thanksgiving, a time of joyous gratitude. I should be thankful I had that amazing night with him, a night that launched a thousand sex scenes in my future releases. I can think about the acrobatics, the ecstasy, how he kissed my clit as much as he kissed my lips.

Damn, I'm getting horny looking at turkey.

"Come and get it," Kit Finch says, motioning everyone to the table. Reid sits down across from me.

Shiloh sits down next to me and takes me into a crushing hug.

"Whit-NAY!" she says, squeezing her warm cheek to mine. "I didn't know you would be here."

"My dad, um, is in New Jersey."

"Well, at least we got you," Shiloh says, wrapping her arm around the elderly man next to him. "Whitney, this is my Papa Earl."

She leans back so I can shake hands with Earl, a man in his early eighties, if I would have to guess, who has more hair coming out of his ears than his head.

"I just finished your book, *Brutal Lover*. It was so good. Papa is reading it now," Shiloh says.

I don't get embarrassed often, but I turn red at that. He might be my first male reader in his eighties.

"It's really good," Earl says. "Shiloh tabbed off the spicy bits so I could skip them, but I ignored them and I'm so glad I did. Your scenes are *zesty*."

Oh my God.

"I'm glad you're enjoying it," I say, my throat dry so it comes out hoarse. I take a sip of water, but I'm still mortified.

"Which one should I read next?" she asks.

"Um, *Brutal King* is the next one in the series."

Shiloh immediately pulls up an app in her phone,

tapping the screen. She turns the phone toward me to confirm the book, and I nod.

I wish all sales were that easy.

"Done!" Shiloh says, showing me her phone, showing a confirmation page.

"Awesome, thank you so much," I say.

Reid hides a smile, and I want to know what he's thinking. I'm destroyed by the memories of his cock inside of me, how wet I was, how I screamed when I received the seventh and final orgasm that ripped me in half.

There's no way he's not thinking about it. I took extra care to look cute today. I made sure my boobs, his favorite part of me, were on display as a reminder to him.

I don't know why I'm torturing myself like this. It's not like we can be anything.

"Per tradition, we will go around the circle and say what we're thankful for," Kit says, still standing at the head of the table.

Randy, Reid's dad, goes first, then Cam. He says Annie, and Annie says Cam. Jackson is next.

"Pass," he says.

"You have to say something," Shiloh says from beside me.

He glowers grumbles, but ekes out, "I'm grateful for my family, I guess. And whiskey."

From everything I've heard about Jackson, Shiloh's just worked a miracle with him.

I'm next.

If I was going to be honest, I'd say I'm thankful for the sore but happy pussy I had thanks to Reid. How I'm thankful for him. Instead, I go the safe route.

"I'm thankful for Goldheart. This year has been rough, and this town healed me. I'm so thankful for your invitation to join your celebration and for you all making me feel so welcome."

"Oh," Kit says, covering her heart with her hands.

"That was really nice," Reid says from across the table. I want his foot to touch mine, some acknowledgment that we had something. He doesn't do anything, and it kills me.

Shiloh and her grandfather go next, and it then swings around to Tara and Owen.

Owen says, "I'm grateful for Tara for clinching this invite, or I would've been eating leftovers in front of the dog show."

He looks at her with a half-smile. Oh, he wants her.

"I love the dog show," I say. "I used to watch it with my dad every year."

"We can put it on," Kit says. "After dinner."

There's a resounding yes from the table, especially from Shiloh.

"Why aren't you with your dad?" Reid asks me.

"My dad does this a lot. Changes plans at the last minute," I say, rearranging my napkin. I claim I don't want to see his sister, but honestly, I wasn't invited. My aunt makes the Bad Biddies look like Princess Diana. The last time we visited, she tried to pressure me to get pregnant, and told me there was no way a doctor like Brad would stay with me unless I gave him a baby. I blew up at her and stormed out.

Unfortunately, the old bitch was right.

"What about your mom? Are they still together?"

I shake my head. Reid and I never talked about private things when we were writing together. We flirted, we talked about writing, but the icky stuff, the stuff no one knows, stayed hidden. Even Annie doesn't know everything.

"It's complicated," I whisper, clasping my hands together, avoiding his gaze. I still haven't opened the letter my mom sent me before I left Reno. That letter lives with my bras.

Anyone can call or email. Sitting down and writing a letter is a gesture.

"I'm glad you could join us then," Reid says, low and growly, similar to his dirty talk while his cock was inside me. Pounding me, punishing my pussy, making me so sore I walked bowlegged for a day and a half.

"Please pass the potatoes," Shiloh asks, shaking me out of my lurid fantasy.

"Of course," I say, handing her the ceramic bowl full of fluffy mashed goodness. I load my plate as food makes it way around, but my stomach churns.

Every three bites he looks at me, and I smile. The rest of the table is shoveling food in their faces, talking and laughing, oblivious to the covert flirting going on between me and Reid. I want to grab his face and kiss that smirk right off of him.

"Are you dating anyone?" I ask Shiloh, to make small talk.

She smiles and shakes her head. "I just got out of a relationship so I'm taking it easy. Not looking."

Shiloh's gaze drifts to Jackson across the table.

Is something going on between them? No, it can't be. Jackson is at least ten years older than Shiloh, and she's way too bubbly and happy-go-lucky for him. I'm not sure who would be a good fit for Jackson, but I'm sure it's not her. It might just be an innocent crush.

"What about you? Are you seeing anyone?" Shiloh asks.

I shake my head. "No, not really."

"Hmm," Shiloh mumbles, taking a bite of green beans. She studies me intently, and I feel naked, like the dirty thoughts I'm having are tattooed on my forehead. That "not really" meant Olympic-figure-skating-level sex with the guy across the table from me a month ago.

"What?" I laugh.

"Oh, nothing," she says, scooping more green beans past her lips.

My gaze falls on Reid as he adjusts his collar and takes a bite of a roll. His cheek puffed, he looks up at me, just as I catch gravy dripping down my mouth with my tongue. One eyebrow lifts.

Oh, he likes this.

"It's warm in here," I say, pulling off my cardigan, pushing my breasts out as I pull the sleeves off of my arms. Reid flusters as he takes a sip of water.

"I totally get it," Shiloh says. "Lots of bodies in this room."

It's one body that makes me hotter than any others.

Wearing a top like this pumps up my confidence too high, and I want to fuck something.

I want to fuck Reid.

Reid wipes his hands on his napkin and stands up when I lean forward slightly, so he can see the soft lines of my cleavage.

Kit looks concerned. "Where are you going, honey?"

"I need some fresh air," he says, walking to the sliding glass door. When he walks outside and shuts it, he's looking straight at me.

Seconds later, my phone buzzes.

Reid: meet me outside

I throw my phone in my lap like it lit on fire, and Kit stops mid-bite.

"Are you alright, darling? You look like you saw a ghost."

"It's just my dad," I lie easily. "Wishing me a happy Thanksgiving. I can call him back later."

"We don't mind if you need to talk to your dad," Kit says. "This holiday is about family, after all."

Is this the universe's sign that I should go meet Reid? I think so.

Following Reid to the backyard is too obvious. How am I going to get to him? Is he even still in the backyard?

"I'll take it outside," I say, pointing to the front door.

"Of course! Take your time," Kit says.

I pull my cardigan back on and grab my jacket from the extra room. The air is cold when I go outside, and I shiver. When we drove up, I didn't notice a side fence, so I hope I don't have to scale one because I do not have the footwear to do so.

Dammit, there's a fence.

Hands on my hips, I study it. It looks like newer wood, and I can use the trash can by the side. I just hope to God I don't wake up a family of raccoons.

The boots must go. They're strictly for fashion, and I'm less likely to twist my ankle in socks. If I would've known I was climbing a fence, I would've worn a different blouse. Good for seduction, terrible for athletics. One of my tits is bound to fall out. I triple-check my bra straps, making sure I'm stuffed like a Thanksgiving turkey and attempt my ascent.

My socked foot slips as I try to climb the trash can. I'm not tall enough to put a knee on it and press myself up. I wish I had Annie's height right about now.

I'm sweating and cursing when I finally fold myself in half over the fence, my legs kicking, unsure how I'm not going to head face-first to the cement pathway to the Finches' backyard.

Then the gate moves. No, no, no, no.

The gate opens with me still folded over it, and then I'm face-to-face with the man who was the best sex of my life.

"What are you doing, Whitney?"

"Um," I say, still draped over the gate. "This looks easier in the movies."

"Of course," he says, pulling me down by my legs, causing my blouse to push to the top of my head. I'm sure my nipples are as hard as rocks, and I can feel a boob slip out of my shirt, despite my best efforts. Once I shove all my bits back into my bra and put my boots back on, I see Reid's smirking from the glow of a light from the house.

"What's so funny?"

"That's the first time I've had a woman try to climb a fence to get to me," Reid says. "I'm flattered."

"Don't be too flattered. I almost died."

"You could've texted me to open the gate."

"Why are you using logic?" I ask, following him into the backyard, past the trashcans to a tiny shed. He finds the key and opens it, letting me go first. It's dark inside, but I can see tools lined up on the wall, a ride-on lawn mower tucked in the corner. I feel his hands on me, pressing me to his body, feeling his cock along my ass as he kisses my neck.

"We can't do this," I say, as I spin to kiss him, hurried and frenzied, my hands in his hair, his hands on my ass. He lifts me up and puts me on the worktable, burying his face in my tits. I laugh and grab the bulge in his jeans, and he groans.

"I think you do want it. You were pushing those tits out, teasing me at the table," Reid says. My groin tightens, and then he covers his mouth. "I'm so sorry, is that too much? I can tone down the dirty talk."

"Did you like my tits in your face?" I ask. He immediately buries his head in my cleavage. His mouth is hot and firm on my flesh, and I moan.

"I was so fucking hard at the table looking at you," he says, coming up for air before returning his mouth to my breasts. He pulls one out and suckles the nipple, his other hand between my thighs, making the ache more unbearable.

He rips my sweater off, so all that's left is an unlined lacy bra that's always made my boobs look amazing. He pulls the other breast out and knocks them together. I shake them in his face as he works his hand harder on me.

"Fuck," I yell, and he presses a kiss to my neck.

"Quiet, or they'll hear," he says. I drop my mouth to his neck and hum my moan into his skin.

"Good girl," he says. "You like that?"

"Fuck yes," I whisper.

His massages continue, and I could scream the ache feels so good.

"Just one more time," I say, hooking his neck with my arm, pulling him closer, as he drifts down. He tears my boots and leggings off and discovers I have no underwear on.

"Did you go commando because you knew I was here?"

I shake my head. "I just don't wear underwear with leggings. Panty lines."

"Perfect," he says. He lowers his head between my legs, licking me from bottom to top, my leg over his shoulder as he feasts on me. I brace myself on the worktable, leaning back. I'm no longer cold, feeling heat lick up from my clit as I build higher and higher.

By the time I reach the peak, about to spill down into another amazing orgasm, I say, "Reid," and my shouting out his name fuels him, motivates him to continue his torture. When he inserts one finger into me, then two, an orgasm takes me over, causing me jerk like I'm being struck by lightning.

When he snakes up my body, I kiss him, tasting myself on his lips.

"Do you have something?" I ask.

He pats his jeans and looks up. "Fuck, my wallet is in the house."

I unbuckle his pants, dropping them down his thighs. I reach between us and grab him, causing a groan. He's already long and thick, my thumb finding moisture on his tip.

"I'm okay if you're okay. I got tested a couple months ago. Free and clear."

"Me too, after I broke up with Callie. I assume you're on something?" Reid asks, grunting as my hand slides up and down him.

I nod, since we don't have time for me to explain. "Yes."

I spit on my hand, and once his cock is coated with my saliva, I line him up, my pussy dripping wet, waiting for him. When he pushes into me, I gasp, rocking into him as I hug his shoulders.

"I don't think I'll ever get enough of you," Reid says into my ear, and I know it's the same for me. Each thrust satisfies nothing, because I want more, more of him, all of him. I kiss him like he's water and I'm dying of thirst.

God, I hope no one hears us moaning.

"That's a good girl, taking all of my cock," he says, as he thrusts harder, hitting all the right spots and I moan so loud, it startles me. We're arriving at the finish line together, and this might break me.

When we both come at the same time, he places his hand over my mouth so I can't make noise again. I'm so turned on that my orgasm lasts forever, deliciously pulsing as he thrusts into me, my walls milking him with no barriers, nothing separating us.

We're sweaty although it's thirty degrees out, me almost naked except for a shifted bra and Reid with his pants at his ankles. He playfully bites my neck, and I press his face between my hands to look at me.

"I'm sorry if that was too much," Reid says. "Covering your mouth."

I kiss him, full of breath and heat. "It was hot. Perfect."

"Great," Reid says. He kisses my shoulder and then looks at me again. The moonlight illuminates the side of his face and fills in the crinkles around his eyes, his eyebrows bunched together in thought.

"I hated the time we were apart," Reid says. "I want to see you. Like, really see you."

"It's not a good idea," I say, with his dick still inside of me.

"Why not?"

"You know why." I pull the cups of my bra back over my breasts and find my sweater, hanging from a rake. My leggings fell over a wall peg, and there's some kind of residue on them. Reid says nothing as he pulls his pants back up.

"So, what if you don't want kids? We can figure it out. Together," Reid says.

"You don't understand. I can't."

Reid stops moving, and I can't see his face.

As I pull my leggings on, I say, "The reason I let you finish inside of me is because I had a tubal ligation when I was twenty-six. I physically cannot have them."

I'm glad it's dark so I can't see his face. There's no negotiation. I made sure there's no way I can reproduce, even by accident.

"What does that mean, exactly?"

"It means I went to three different doctors when I was twenty-five until I found a doctor willing to do it. It means they cut my fallopian tubes so an egg cannot be released. I cannot get pregnant."

I'm glad it's dark so I can't see his expression.

"I've been questioned my whole life and told that I'll change my mind, that if I meet the right man, I'll want to have kids. I know deep in my gut I do not want them. Even if the perfect guy is standing right in front of me ..."

Now I slap my own hand over my mouth. Is Reid the right man? We've had a few friendly encounters and the sex is incredible, but that's not enough to know for certain. It took two years of Brad begging me to marry him for me to give in. Even then, a small voice niggled at me on my wedding day. I felt sick before I walked down the aisle.

I know what that meant now, looking back.

Now, I'm looking at Reid, who is everything I could want, except one tiny problem.

He wants kids. He was a teacher. He has a large family. He's been a mentor to his ex's child.

He just needs to find the right woman and he'll have a million children.

And I'm not that woman.

It breaks my heart, but I can't change who I am.

"Even if the kids issue wasn't here, you don't want me anyway. I'm messy and complicated and broken..."

"Whitney," he says, stopping me. "You're the most incredible woman I've ever met. This might be my dad's busted old shed, but that was the best sex of my entire life."

He gets closer to me and I might give in. Let this go longer than it needs to.

"Do you want kids?" I ask. "Truly."

Reid pauses for a moment, his big hands on my arms, grazing my breasts with his thumbs. I want to wrap him up in a hug and never let him go. I can't, though. That pause means everything.

Finally he says, "This just seems premature. I haven't even taken you on a real date. We don't need to talk about this now. We should try and revisit this at a later time."

I rub my head with my hand. He doesn't get it. Kids are a big deal, and it should be dealt with early on, before things go too far. Brad lied to me when he told me he didn't want kids either, even drove me to my surgery. He proved my aunt right.

Reid might be the same. He might agree to being child-free, but I'm scared to death he will eventually resent me. As Annie and Cameron have babies and Emily meets a new man and maybe has some more, he'll feel left out and blame me.

Or he'll leave me. Just like Brad.

But my bloodline stops here. My mother didn't want kids, and her mother didn't want kids. I don't want them. This familial cycle of being a mother because society wants you to be ends with me.

"We should get back to the dinner," I say, heading to the door of the shed. He grabs my hand and pulls me back into his arms, kissing me long and hard.

We're breathless when he pulls away, his hands clasped at the small of my back. I don't want to leave. But I have to.

It kills me, but this is the right thing to do.

We cannot look at each other the rest of the dinner, although other guests study us, noticing the shift. The sadness between us. How I've drawn a line, a line strong as iron.

18

WHITNEY

I t's been two weeks since Thanksgiving, and I've barely left Annie's place. Annie is a saint to deal with me, especially with how tiny this apartment is for two people. She's been staying at Cameron's tiny home more to give me space since I've turned into a full-blown hermit.

I've been a writing machine. I finished my second manuscript since I arrived in Goldheart and then edited all one hundred thousand words of it in less than a week, so absorbed in the story that I was sleeping less than four hours a night. I only leave the house to run, and then I'm back, hunched over my computer.

I'm hiding away because if I leave this house, peek out from my manuscript, I'll have to face Reid. Even if I don't run into him, I'll have to face up to the fact that I let go the most amazing man I've ever met, because I don't want to be a parent. And I don't want to take away his ability to be one.

I still haven't looked at or responded to my mother's letter after months, and I thought it was over and she'd leave me alone again, as usual, until I got a voicemail that I haven't listened to yet. At least, I think it's her. It's from a 303 area code, which covers Castle Pines, outside of Denver.

It could be a telemarketer, and I always check to make sure, but I can't bring myself to listen to it.

Watch, it's to extend my car warranty, and I'm worrying for nothing. It's on brand for my mother to make one specified effort and then give up.

I don't hear Annie come in, so when she screams "Hello? Whitney!" inches from my ear, I jump right out of my seat. My hand breaks my fall, but barely. I didn't feel her lift one of my headphones, so my heart pounds in my chest.

"Hi, Annie, I didn't hear you come in," I say. Annie leans in and sniffs me and I freeze. Maybe if I freeze, the stank fumes will freeze as well.

"When's the last time you took a shower?"

"Um," I ask, squinting through one eye. Fog settles in my brain, and my stomach growls. I can't even be certain I've eaten in the last twenty-four hours. I sure as shit haven't showered. And I've been on two runs.

"Take a shower, shave your pits, and let's go out to lunch," Annie says.

"Okay, yeah," I say. "I just have to finish this chap..."

"Now," she says, pointing to the shower. I try to type, and she slaps my laptop closed, almost crushing the moneymakers.

"I may not look like much, but I can drag your petite ass to the shower," she says.

"Yes, ma'am." My clothes crunch as I stand up and realize just how gross I am. She's right. I could fill a car with the oil on my head.

Once the warm water of the shower hits my face, I sob. Full, soul-grinding sobs. My empty stomach cramps with my tears, and my convulsing is so violent, I'm scared I'll pull a muscle. I wish I'd never met Reid. At first, it was because he was the biggest douchebag, but then he turned into the biggest surprise of my life.

A surprise that ripped up my heart. The shreds are all I have left.

I'll pull myself back together; I always do. I just wish I didn't feel like this right now.

Washing my hair and shaving and running a bar of soap over my body helps marginally. When I emerge from the steam like I'm a heroine in an early aughts romantic comedy, Annie claps her hands together.

"Much better," she says. She presents me with jeans, boots, and a sweater. She dresses me like a mother, and I could cry again. Living with Annie fills a hole in my heart I didn't know needed filling. I'm jealous of her future children.

"How are you doing? I'm worried about you," Annie says as she drags me to her car and pushes me into the front seat.

"I'm fine. I'm close to being done with the second draft, so you'll probably get it tomorrow."

"I'll be staying at Cameron's tomorrow, but he usually sleeps right to his alarm so I'll get a chance to read a little bit."

"Okay," I say. "Where are we going?"

"Betty's Cafe," she says. I freeze because that seems like a place Reid would frequent. I'm not sure what I'll do if I see his face again. It will crush my soul.

"You look worried," she says, seeing the pain in my face.

"No, I'm just hungry."

"I get that," she says. "I'm a little hungry myself, I think. I might be nauseous. I'm not sure."

My head whips to her. I know firsthand how much sex Cameron and Annie have—I've walked in on Cameron's bare ass at least twice—and I know damn well she's not on the Pill.

"You're pregnant," I say.

"No, I'm not," she says. "I can't be."

"Did you have sex this month?"

"Yes," Annie says, blushing. I'm not sure why she's blushing. She's a grown-ass woman with a hot boyfriend. Of course she did.

"Do you use protection?"

She says nothing, and I know what happened. Heat of the moment, you can't think, you just want it inside of you.

What a sucker.

"Annie Stewart, you're so knocked up," I say. "You let him put his dick inside you unwrapped, and now you've pulled a *Sixteen and Pregnant*."

"What?" Annie says, throwing her hands up from her steering wheel. "Okay, it was one time. It just sort of happened, but we both want kids, so..."

I nod because I get it. I had her boyfriend's brother's cock bare inside of me, and it felt otherworldly.

Annie and I both know that Finch dick is the best dick.

"I would check before you drink again. To be on the safe side," I say.

Annie smiles, fluttering her eyelashes. While I might throw up if I thought I was pregnant, Annie looks excited. And my heart drops. Annie will make promises that pregnant women have made to their non-mom friends for decades, just to be a slave to the new most important person in their lives.

I will be forgotten. I will be left.

Just like I've been my entire life.

Still, if Annie is pregnant, I will cry with happiness for her. She was born to be a mother, and she's in a healthy and committed relationship. I couldn't think of a better family to add to than the Finches.

It's why I keep my distance. Reid deserves to add his own Finches to the brood.

"Wow, a parking spot right in front!" Annie exclaims. When we walk into the restaurant, we're led to a table by the fireplace, decorated with red and green garlands for the holidays, with fake flames flickering in tall, white candles. Christmas was never a big deal in my dad's house, and I've already told him I'm spending it in Goldheart. Christmas just makes people with broken families feel like shit. I don't need reminding.

"This is pretty," I say, scanning the room for Reid. Instead, I see a group of older women, and the blood drains from my face.

"Oh my God, the Bad Biddies are here," Annie says, shifting down in her seat, raising the menu to cover her face. "If I'm pregnant, they'll figure it out. I swear, they'll be able to smell it."

"Calm down," I say, looking at them. I haven't witnessed their true power, and I just pray they don't know about Reid and me.

One woman waves at me, and I wave back.

"What if they think you left Cameron for me?"

"That's better than them thinking I'm pregnant," Annie says. "I know they would start in on advice immediately. I won't even be able to eat bacon in front of them. They will judge."

I hope to God they don't figure out I'm childfree.

"They're coming over. Oh my God," Annie says.

"Sit up. Women like that can smell fear."

"But hopefully not pregnancy. Crap, it's Miriam," Annie whispers. She shifts in her seat and smiles brightly. "Hello!"

"Hi, dear," Miriam says. "What brings you out today? I love this restaurant. It's the home base for me and my friends."

I flick a glare at Annie, and her shoulders twitch. She decided to test fate, and fate laughed at her.

I keep a smile shellacked on my face. "Annie pulled me out of my writing cave. I've been working a lot."

The judgment wafting off of Miriam makes my arm hair stand on end.

Miriam looks like a mall-walker who asks for a manager everywhere she goes.

"It's so lovely you girls are getting out without your men. So refreshing. I was worried about you, Annie, that you and Cameron were becoming too co-dependent. Oh, is something wrong in paradise?"

Annie stares at me, and I'm not sure why. "Our men?" she asks, her eyebrow arched.

"Thank you for your concern, Miriam, but we're great. Cameron and Annie are stronger than ever," I interject.

"We were worried about him, especially Mrs. Epstein. He's like an honorary son to her, you know, because she doesn't have children. It's so nice to see Reid with a woman like you."

Don't say a word, Whitney. You'll implicate yourself.

And Mrs. Epstein doesn't have kids? I like her so much more now.

I just don't expect Annie to slap the table, making the water glasses jump.

Annie's face is as red as Taylor Swift's lipstick. "Reid, as in..."

Miriam looks at Annie. "Your future brother-in-law, if you ever decide to tell the poor boy yes. I can't believe you turned Cameron down."

"Reid Finch," Annie says.

Miriam looks at me. "You seem like you're slightly out of his league, but..."

And now I'm mad. I turn toward her, trying to think of how to eviscerate her, without scaring this woman to a premature death.

"Reid is amazing, Miriam," I say. "I'm the one who's not good enough for him."

Annie's mouth falls open.

"I'm just complimenting you on your looks, dear. You're just so pretty and seem so smart. I started reading your book, and I bet you're a dynamite in the sack. I'm sure Reid is having the time of his life. We're all very fond of him. He will treat you right..."

"Miriam, will you excuse us?" Annie asks, her teeth grinding down as we speak.

"Of course," Miriam says. "I didn't mean to start anything..."

"BYE, MIRIAM," Annie says emphatically. The woman shuffles away, like she had at least three hundred more words to use.

Where the hell did she see us? We were so careful.

When she's out of earshot, I say, "I can explain."

"How about you tell me why *Miriam Oliver* knows about you and Reid, and I don't?"

"Because..." I say. "Reid and I aren't anything. We're not even friends."

"Have you..." Annie asks.

My chin nods as I grimace, my mouth snarled into guilt. I want to disappear into the floor. She covers her face with her hands and screams.

"Please don't be mad. We didn't tell anyone, because it's not going anywhere. It's over. It's done."

"I can't believe you didn't tell me. Have you done it at my place?"

I shake my head violently. "No, we haven't. We've only been together twice."

"Where?" Annie asks.

"Once at his place, and once in the gardening shed. At Thanksgiving."

"I could punch you in the tit for keeping this from me," Annie says. She waves her cheeks as she lets out a raspy breath. "I can't believe this."

"We decided it was fun, but we're done. It's fine."

"Um, no," Annie says, raising a finger. "You've barely left the house or showered since Thanksgiving. I thought this was part of your writing process, but no. You're sad. About Reid."

"I'm not sad. I don't *get* sad. I'm fine."

That's a lie. I'm sadder about Reid than my divorce, losing my beautiful home in Reno, upending my life. It's why I haven't showered; it's why I haven't eaten more than a handful of Goldfish here and there. It's why I run ten miles just to focus on the burn, rather than the pain in my heart.

"Are you mad at me?" I ask.

"A little," Annie says, looking at the menu. "But once I get over it, I'll be happy about it. And then mad again."

"Why?" I ask, a little too loud, and she shushes me, gesturing toward the group of women who may be listening and/or recording everything we're saying.

"You and Reid make sense," Annie says. "I love Reid dearly, but he's always been with women who've taken advantage of him. You wouldn't. I know that."

"I would never," I say. "Reid is...Reid is exactly the kind of guy any woman should want."

"He is," Annie says. "I spent many years wishing I felt

differently for him, because he would be such a good partner. So giving and loving."

He's giving, all right. Brad rarely licked me down there,
and Reid has done it both times, making me scream. My
pussy remembers, and I have to cross my legs under the
table.

"You need to give him a chance," Annie says. "Unless the
sex sucks."

"It definitely doesn't," I say, taking a sip of my water.

"Okay, use one word to describe it," Annie says, leaning
over the table.

"You use one word to describe your sex life."

"Okay," Annie says, sitting back. I can see the dictionary
flipping in Annie's mind. "Transcendent."

"Oh, that's a good word," I say, thinking myself. "Tragic."

"Why?" Annie asks with a laugh.

"It's so good, and we can't be together," I say.

"Why?"

"The kid thing," I say.

"Oh." Annie stares at the tablecloth for a moment. She
nods once. "He's never talked about wanting to be a dad or
anything. I think he just wants to get married. Why are you
letting that hold you back? You could talk about it."

My throat dries. "I think he might. He's not strong in his
opinion one way or another. But I can't be the person who
takes that option away from him, you know?"

Annie sighs and rests her chin on her hand. "You don't
even know if it would work long-term. Why don't you test
that first before you cut it off at the knees?"

"If it's going to end because of the kids thing, why set
myself up for the heartache?"

I don't bring up my biggest fear, is that I'll be alone
forever because I can't be a mother. That I will never be

enough for someone, that I will not be whole, I will just be left my entire life. It's better to be alone than getting my hopes up, just to be blindsided and devastated.

Like Brad.

"I think my mom called me," I change the subject, holding up my phone.

Annie's eyes bulge. She knows the basics about my mother—how she left when I was three, how the only times I heard from her were once a year, on my birthday, and a disappointing visit when I was nine. That the last time I saw her was my wedding.

"You don't have your mom in your phone?" she asks, seeing the phone number on my screen.

"Do you have your bio dad in your phone?"

"Touché," she says. "What did she say?"

"I don't know. I haven't listened to the message yet. I don't even know if it's her."

"Listen to it. Now," Annie says.

"The nosy women are over there." I point and all the women's heads shift, like they were caught listening.

"Lower the volume on your phone," she says.

"No, I'll do it later."

"You won't do it then. It has to be now."

I roll my eyes while my insides silently freak out. "Okay, fine."

I tap to the voicemail screen and tap on the play button. We both lean over because I have the volume so low.

"Hey Whit, it's me. Your mom." Her voice always unnerves me since it's sweet and unassuming, completely opposite to how I remember her. There's a long pause before she says, "I'm not sure if you got my letter, but your dad gave me your new number. I hope that's okay. I..." She coughs away from the phone before she says, "I really want to talk. Face to face. I know Christmas is a lot of pressure, but Ken and I want to invite you to our home for Christmas. I hope you can make it. It's been too long."

My blood boils. We haven't spoken in years, but she wants to invite me to Christmas, the most pressure-filled family holiday. Frankly the holiday snuck up on me, so I have zero plans for Christmas. I've been focusing solely on my writing, to avoid thinking about Reid.

Now I have my mother to think about too.

After the voicemail cuts out, we both sit back in our chairs, dumbfounded.

"When's the last time you talked to your mom again?" Annie asks.

"Six years ago."

"Wow," Annie says. "I'm jealous. My dad would never."

"Why would she expect me to come to her house for Christmas? That seems a bit much after zero effort for so long. Like it's not weird enough that I've never met her husband, but 'Hey, come to our house for the most emotionally charged holiday of the year'?"

"Where does she live?"

"Outside of Denver," I say.

"You could get some real snow, not just ours that falls and doesn't stick."

"I don't want snow. I don't want to see my mother," I say. My tone has grown agitated and loud. The Bad Biddies are listening but pretending like they aren't. When we look at them, their heads jerk away conspicuously.

"Ask Reid what he thinks," Annie says.

It's so ridiculous, I laugh. "'Hey Reid, I know we've had sex twice, but can you give me advice on my estranged mother and what to do for Christmas?'"

Annie's smile fades, and I brace for the truth bomb I'm about to get. I'm still not ready for it.

"Reid means more to you than sex, and you know it."

I shrug, holding back the urge to cry.

"Just reach out to him. You're miserable without him, and it's your own damn fault. Reid would do anything for a woman. It's you who's being ridiculous."

I take a sip of my water. I can't ask him to give up being a dad *and* get embroiled in my family drama.

"I'm too much," I say. "I'm surprised you've tolerated me for so long."

Stop it," Annie says, holding up a hand. "You are so special to me. I bet you're special to Reid too."

I sniffle, holding the tears in. These last few weeks have been miserable. I wonder what he's doing, how his novel is coming. If he thinks about me.

"Fine," I say. I shoot off a quick text to Reid without thinking.

Looking at it, I want to take it back immediately.

I miss you.

The three dots appear immediately and then an answer. *What are you doing right now?*

Me: lunch with Annie.

Reid: I want to see you.

My hands freeze on my phone. Annie watches me from across the table, examining my behavior.

Fear hovers in my fingertips, making it impossible for me to jump headfirst, arrange a time.

Me: how about tomorrow?

Reid: I'll be at the brewery early. Seven. No one will be there.

Me: Okay. See you then.

"What did he say?" Annie asks.

My stomach responds before my mouth, and Annie looks at me in horror.

"Let's order," I say. "And we're buying a pregnancy test for you on the way home."

"Aren't you supposed to take those in the morning?" Annie asks.

"You're asking *me*?"

We laugh at that. Annie looks past me. "Dang, I think the Bad Biddies heard. We're probably their favorite subjects. Two sluts, out for a meal."

I cover my mouth with the cloth napkin to avoid a very audible cackle. Annie cracks up too and then we're crying-laughing, our heads down on the table as the server comes to get our drink orders.

I order the biggest glass of wine they have, and Annie sticks to water.

The Bad Biddies definitely notice Annie is not drinking. They notice it all.

19

REID

When I get to the brewery and unlock the side entrance, I pull my phone out to read the text again.

I miss you.

It had been two weeks of no contact, no writing together, no possibility of kisses or sex with her, although it's been on my mind constantly.

Believe me, I've tried.

I've stopped reading Whitney's backlist and picked up a thick fantasy tome, but it is not the same. Whitney's books are full of fun and sex, keeping me up all hours of the night. My go-to genre now puts me to sleep. Working out has done nothing to work out the tension or the mind-racing.

I've been consumed by her.

My whole body relaxed like warm candle wax when she texted me. I was home, alone, drinking a beer and watching a basketball game. Watching sports was preferable to thinking about a woman I want and can't have.

Now, she's meeting me here, on my home turf, and I've

never been this jittery. I suggested the brewery to avoid an audience, but the privacy might tempt me in other ways.

Through the glass door, I see she's arrived, her dark hair down around her shoulders, her puffy jacket hiding her curves. She looks around, and once her crystal blue eyes find me, I melt into a puddle.

I unlock the door to let her in. Her clean, citrus scent wafts over me as she slides past me. I want to wrap her in my arms.

Her smile is tentative as she walks up to me, peeling off her jacket. Her long-sleeved shirt and jeans hug her figure, curves I touched two long weeks ago. Her lips look as soft as I remember, and I hold myself back from greeting her with a kiss.

"Hi," she says, her voice like caramel.

"Hi." I grip my travel coffee mug. If I hold that, I won't grab for her hand.

Whitney's eyes cast down and all I want is to keep her gaze on me, feel the heat and connection between us.

"I miss you too," I tell her. "So much."

"What do we do?" Whitney says. "This is impossible."

I shake my head. "It doesn't have to be. I just ask for exploration."

Her eyebrow arches. "Exploration?"

"I don't mean it like that. If you want to, cool. I've read some stuff in your books that I want to try. Not, like, having sex with a dead body in the room, but you know what I'm saying..."

Whitney giggles and covers her mouth.

I should've stopped talking, but I keep going. "Once I make my mind up, that's it. I don't know if I want kids yet or not, but I want to give this a chance. See if you and me could be something. Because for the right person, I will do anything. Absolutely anything."

Her eyes are soft, like she is about to cry. I just keep talking so she can't object.

"If It doesn't work out, all you have to do is say it's not working, and I will leave you alone forever."

"You won't fight me on it?"

I smirk. "I will probably fight you. Just so we can have hot make-up sex."

Whitney's chest heaves, a flush crawling across her collarbones.

"Is that a yes?"

Whitney holds up a finger. "I have stipulations."

"What are they?"

"I can't say yes to a relationship yet," Whitney says.

"Okay..." I'm having flashes of prior women I've been interested in, giving in to them because I was so loyal, so supportive. Those relationships never had the heat that I have with Whitney. So I decide not to be concerned. Yet.

"How do we work up to it?"

"Lots and lots of sex," she says.

Heat fills my cheeks. "Of course."

"I like food so you'll have to take me on dates. And pay for them. I'm old-fashioned."

"Done."

"And you meet my mother with me."

"Wait, what?" I ask. We went from secret sex in a gardening shed to meeting her mother?

"Yeah, exactly," she says, as she looks at my face.

"Is this the mother who..."

"The very one. The woman who gave birth to me and left our family when I was three."

"Oh, wow," I say, rubbing my hand down my face. "I have so many questions."

"I do too," Whitney says, pulling out her phone from her pocket. She places it between us and presses a button, starting a voicemail from her mother. The voice is laced with regret and sadness and desperation.

This woman clearly feels terribly for how she treated Whitney, and I feel sorry for her. But I'm on Whitney's team, forever and always.

"Where does she live?"

"Outside of Denver," I say.

"Okay, let's do this," I say, pulling up the Skyline Airlines app I have on my phone to see flights.

Whitney covers my forearm with her hand. "We're not going there. I'm going to insist she comes here."

"Oh, okay," I say. "Where is she going to stay?"

"I was going to suggest the Goldheart Inn. I checked with the owner, and they have a couple rooms open."

"Oh," I say. My chest floods with warmness. She'll be around for the holidays. I can finally put the bearskin rug to use with the fire going. Drink spiked cocktails and laugh, making love in front of my Christmas tree after playing in the barely sticking snow. We'll get cold so we can heat each other up.

"Have you called her yet?"

She shakes her head, staring at her phone.

"You should just do it. Call her and get it over with."

Her shoulders are to her ears, she's so nervous. I just want to do it for her, but I know it's something she needs to do for herself.

"I don't need to do it right now. I can do it later."

"If you wait, it's only going to get harder."

"You know what I want harder."

"Really?"

"You said no one is here right now, right?"

"Right..." I say.

Immediately, Whitney's hands are everywhere, on my ass, on my cock. She kisses me, long and hard, and I press her against the wall, pulling one leg up, so she can feel that I'm already hard. I've been hard since I got her text.

She grabs my hand and puts it one of her breasts. It feels heavy and full in my hand. I cannot think; all of the brain blood goes straight to my dick.

"What are you doing?" I ask, swallowing the lump deeply in my throat. "You should really call your mom."

"Do you really want me to call my mom? Or do you want me to do this?"

She cups me, and I groan. I don't give a fuck if she calls her mom right now or never.

"Storage room," I say, pulling her by the hand. She scampers behind me, and the minute the door closes, my hands are in her hair as I push her against the shelves. She rips open my shirt and dips her hand into my jeans, and I make a sound so exaggerated that Whitney cackles. An empty keg falls over, and after I double-check it didn't leak, Whitney laughs, kissing me again, her tongue penetrating my mouth.

We're so wrapped up in each other that we don't hear the door open.

20

WHITNEY

"What the fuck, Reid? I thought you two *hated* each other," a male voice says from the door. I peer around Reid to see Cameron and Annie. Cameron's mouth hangs open while Annie smirks.

"Well," Reid says, throwing his hands up.

God, he is sexy.

Annie pushes Cameron out the door, saying "Come on, baby" and stares me down. Reid is quickly trying to button his shirt.

"I'm pregnant, by the way," Annie says, stepping out of the door frame. "Reid, meeting starts in fifteen minutes."

Reid looks to me with a gaping mouth. "Damn it, I forgot we made the meeting earlier today. Fuck. Also, Annie's *pregnant*?" Reid asks, tucking his shirt into his jeans.

"She thought she might be yesterday," I say, grinning. A dream come true is happening for my friend.

"What do I do?" Reid says. "Cam will mention something at the meeting. He can't lie to save his life, and he will out me."

"It's fine," I say, kissing him. "Tell the truth."

"What, that we no longer hate each other?"

"Start with that," I say.

He pulls me to him, and I sink into his chest. It's a shame I won't be banged properly this morning. He kisses my hair and whispers into my ear, "I want to finish what we started."

"We will. What are you doing tonight?"

"Hopefully, you. However, you have to call your mother first."

My stomach churns again. "Not fair."

"What?" he asks. "You're putting it off. Just do it. Call her."

I grumble and huff out a breath. "You're right."

"Say it again," he says. "I didn't hear you."

"You're right!" I yell.

"Love it when you talk dirty to me." He kisses me lightly. "I have to get to this meeting. I'll cook for you tonight if you call your mom."

"I'll do it," I promise.

"Sounds good." Reid walks out and turns back, pointing to my shirt. I look down and readjust my top. I tiptoe out the way I came, the parking lot now full of cars I recognize, including Cam's truck. I'm almost in the clear when I hear Emily behind me.

"Whitney?"

"Hi, Emily, how are you?" I sound guilty. Really guilty.

"What are you doing here?" she asks.

"Nothing," I say, turning back to my car. I don't see Emily's daughter anywhere, so I turn back and blurt out, "Okay, just so you know, I'm fucking your brother."

"Which one?"

"Reid."

"Oh, okay," Emily says, her mouth outstretched.

"Sorry to be frank. Anyway, have a nice day, bye!" I say, rushing to my car like I'm in a dark parking lot.

I see Emily standing there, watching me, as I back up to leave. Saying it out loud, admitting we're involved, drops an anvil from my shoulders.

I can't help but smile.

The smile doesn't last long because I remember I won't have sex tonight unless I call my mom. I've had phone anxiety my whole life, something I got over when I worked in claims. I was stressing out just about calling my bank the other day. Calling my mother, someone I haven't talked to for six years, is way worse than calling any stranger.

My thumb hovers over her number. I can't decide how this is going to go, if I'll be snotty or understanding. Because I will say yes to Christmas, but on my terms. When Brad left, I lost access to his family, a family who wore matching pajamas on Christmas morning and parents so in love with each other, they would hug each other constantly.

Reid's family is like that. Mine is not.

"Just do it," I tell myself. My thumb slips, and I'm calling her.

"Fuck, shit, ass, cunt," I yell to myself as the phone rings. I think I'm almost free and voicemail will blessedly start any moment when I hear a "Hello?"

"Hi," I croak. "It's Whitney. I got your voicemail."

I hear a sigh on the other end. "Hi, Whitney. It's so good to talk to you."

I'm quiet because if I talk, she'll hear the ball of emotion in my voice. She just keeps talking.

"I want to see you. Ken and I wondered if you were available for Christmas. I know that's a lot of pressure…"

"You can come see me if you want," I say, my tone sharp like a hunting blade. "I'm staying in this town called Goldheart, about forty-five minutes east of Sacramento in California. There's a cute little bed-and-breakfast called the Goldheart Inn..."

"Done," she says. "I'll book everything today."

"Why?" I ask. My throat is so tight, I'm having difficulty swallowing. I've never worried about my mother wanting money from me. Even money couldn't get her to talk to me for years. Even after I had three wildly successful releases in a row. Even after one of my standalone novels was optioned for TV and film and I signed a lucrative contract.

She's quiet, and I know she's measuring her words. I've jumped down her throat before.

"It's time," she says. "I figured now that you're not with Brad..."

I want to sob. I want to sit on a curb and let thirty-two years of tears fall. I hold myself back from screaming, from showing this woman anything more than ice-cold indifference. Brad was *not* the reason we didn't talk for six years.

She was.

"Okay" is all I can muster. "I'll send you a link for the hotel. You should book soon."

"Definitely," she says. The line goes quiet, and I pull my phone away to make sure the call is still live. I let the silence hang heavy.

"I'm glad we're doing this," she whispers.

I can't agree. I just remain quiet before I say, "I'll send you the link."

"Okay. Bye, sweetie."

"Bye," I say.

Once the call is over, I pull up the text message screen.

Me: I did it. I called her. She's coming to Goldheart for Christmas.

Three dots appear immediately.

Reid: I'm proud of you.

Reid: Are you okay?

My urge to cry has drifted away now that I'm talking to Reid, although I know I will be a mess when she's in town. I could start crying at any moment.

Me: I'm okay.

The three dots appear again and his text makes me bite my lip.

Reid: Italian or fish?

Me: Italian. I need lots and lots of carbs. And wine.

He sends me the heart-kissing emoji. He's adorable.

Reid will be the buffer, the peacekeeper between me and my mother. It's a lot to put on a guy I've just decided to date, but if he wants to be with me, he needs to know the ugly.

What the ugliest thing about me is.

That my own mother didn't want me. That she broke me. And that facing this trauma will bring out the worst in me.

If he can stand by me, I might just let him love me.

Because I feel like I could with him too.

21

REID

"So, we have something to tell you," Cam says, his arm slung around the back of Annie's chair.

"You proposed again, and she said no again," Jackson guesses. The whole table turns to look at him, unsure if he made a joke or not. Jackson shrugs, and Cam chuckles.

Annie and Cam connected over planning an event for the brewery back in May. At the nineties-themed adult prom, Cam dropped to one knee without consulting Annie, and she said no. They got back together of course, once my brother got his head out from his ass.

Now, they're having a baby together.

"I'm pregnant," Annie announces.

Mom shrieks, piercing my eardrum, and Emily yells along with her. They both stand up and tackle Annie with a hug. Cam smiles like a guy knowing his sperm is strong enough, and Jackson and I just look at each other.

"We no longer matter," Jackson says to me.

"No kidding," I say. Jackson's face is stoic, like usual, and his jaw tightens as we sit at the table.

"I can't believe it. Olive is going to freak," Emily says. "I'm so excited."

"Olive is finally going to have a cousin," Mom says, her eyes immediately filling with tears. Dad sits there, like Jackson and me, not sure how to react or what to do.

"Thank you," Annie says, covering her flat stomach. "We're really excited."

"Does that mean you're going to get married?" Emily asks.

"Uh, we haven't talked about it, but..." Annie's eyes flash to Cam.

"Well, it went so well the last time I asked," Cam says. "I'm waiting for *my* fairytale proposal."

"How would that look, a pregnant woman on the ground, begging her boyfriend to marry her?" Annie asks.

"You better ask soon then," Cam says, licking his lips, a glint in his eye. "For the record, I like diamonds."

Annie smacks my brother on the chest, and my insides squeeze. In this moment, I want the relationship Annie and Cam have, with Whitney. If she would just let me love her, I would.

Without even trying, I've fallen head over feet for her. She's the woman I've been searching for my entire life. It doesn't matter if she doesn't want kids. Wherever she goes, I go. Whatever she wants, I want.

"Reid has news too," Cam says, his eyebrow raising as he rubs his lips together.

"Fuck you," I say under my breath.

Cam cups his ear, like he's trying to hear better. "What's that, brother?"

I swallow. "Whitney and I have been seeing each other."

My sister and mother shriek again, clasping their hands

together, like two girlfriends at a slumber party, bonding over Johnny Depp.

Do people still like Johnny Depp?

"I know. I saw her outside, and she told me," Emily says.

My mother's eyes protrude out of her head.

"She was here visiting me this morning," I explain.

"Yeah, she was," Cam says.

"Shut up, Cam."

"You can't talk to me like that anymore. I'm officially more mature than you."

"I hope so," I say.

"How did that happen? If I remember correctly, you two weren't that fond of each other," Mom says.

I look down. Describing my relationship with Whitney makes me infinitely uncomfortable. I can't exactly tell them it started because I decided to be an alpha like one of her romance heroes.

"We started writing together at Gold Roast. She helped me writing my book, and I'm almost done. It's terrible, but... she is not. I really care about her."

"Wow, Reid, that's great," Dad says, obviously more interested in the book than my relationship with Whitney. It might be all too much for Dad to compute because he rubs his face and then rubs it again.

Annie looks at me, her eyes filling with tears.

"Why are you crying?"

Cam hands her a tissue, and she dabs her eyes. "I love Whitney so much, and I love you so much, and I'm just... so...emotional."

Cam pulls her close so she can continue crying on his chest, and he kisses her head.

"It's new, so we're figuring a lot of things out," I say.

Mom looks at me like I just told her I murdered three people.

"Mom, why are you looking at me like that?"

"Whitney is a lovely person, but Annie told me she's childfree," Mom whispers.

"I know. We talked about it," I say.

"Do you not...want kids?"

I shrug, because I haven't given it much thought. My mother's eyes fill with tears again, but they're not happy.

"Don't look at me that way. *They* are giving you another grandchild."

"I know, but..." Mom says, wiping her tears with a tissue. "I always imagined you as a dad. You would be such a good dad."

"I can also be a really good uncle."

"You can't take my title away from me, man. I'm the best uncle in this family," Cam says, smacking his own chest.

"I'll get Olive an iPad. And your spawn will love me more than you."

"Challenge accepted," Cam says, while Emily rolls her eyes.

"This just makes me sad, is all," Mom says. "Are you sure she doesn't want kids?"

"Yes," I say, pulling my shoulders back. It's none of her business that Whitney had a tubal ligation. It's about honoring her right not to choose motherhood. "She's pretty firm in it."

"I don't like this. I don't like this at all," Mom says.

All the eyes of the table shift to me, staring at me. I've never been the center of my family, I've always flown under the radar, doing what is expected of me. I went to a good college, graduated, worked for the family business with no objection.

Now, the second I start talking of a life different than what they imagined for me, I suddenly matter?

Jackson stands up and sweeps his hands. "Enough, Mom. Reid is a grown man, and he can decide what he wants. He doesn't need you badgering him."

Jackson's words make our mother's face fall even more. I know she cares about me and that's why she's questioning it.

I'm still questioning it as well.

"Thanks, Jackson," I say, patting him on the arm. He sits down again and settles, his hands laced on his stomach.

"I'm sorry. It's a big decision, not having kids," Mom says. "I just want to make sure he's sure."

"He's not getting a vasectomy today," Jackson says. "Relax, Mom. They just started dating."

Funny thing is I think it will go the distance. Whenever I'm with Whitney, I feel like the man I always knew I could be. Writing again, with her, has brought me back to life. Finally pursuing a dream that lay dormant for so long, writing my own books and shooting my shot, it has changed my life.

Now, I'm questioning whether I want to be a parent, a very real decision that I've never thought I would have to make so soon in a new relationship.

Because the woman I love does not want to have them. Therefore, I won't, if we stay together.

My mother still isn't sold on the idea. It's written over her face. Annie and Cam sit and smile, but I know the spotlight being on me is taking away their happy news. While we're sticking up for each other to our parents, I stand up.

"I'm incredibly proud of Cam," I say, slapping him on the shoulder, hard enough to get a squeak out of him. "He's been planning our events like an expert, and we've never had more traffic to the brewery because of him. Now he's making a family with one of the kindest and best women I've ever met." Annie grabs for my hand and squeezes.

"Let's focus on this. We're getting a new Finch. Even if Jackson and I never have kids, that's fine. We have Olive, and now we will have Cam and Annie's baby. They will be perfect. They will be enough."

My mom says nothing, but stands up and hugs and kisses them both.

"Any grandchild is a blessing," Mom says, gulping back sobs. I hold out my fist to Jackson, and he bumps it.

After tears and hugs finish, we start the family meeting, discussing new hires, new brews, and upcoming events. Emily confirms she has the Christmas gifts for our employees ready to go for the party when Jackson says, "I have Shiloh's taken care of."

"*We* have Shiloh's taken care of," I say. Jackson suggested something for Shiloh as a gesture, and I had to help. Jackson wanted to be the one to tell her.

"Okay," Mom says, studying Jackson. Our meeting morphs into a brainstorming situation for names for Cam and Annie's baby.

My phone buzzes with a text. Whitney called her mom. I breathe out, a smile on my face.

"Looks like Reid is texting her right now," Emily says, her arms crossed.

I neither confirm nor deny as I type out plans for tonight.

She answers immediately.

"Oh my God, I think Reid is in love," Emily says, covering her mouth. Damn, this family is relentless, and they have the memory span of a goldfish.

"Stop it, Emily. Mind your business, like Jackson said," I say.

Annie starts sobbing again. She waves her hand in front of her face. "I'm sorry, but any time I think of my best friend with my other best friend, the waterworks go crazy."

"This is just the beginning of the hormones," Emily says. "I hope you're ready, Cam."

"Of course," Cam says, pulling Annie to him. "This is my best friend. And the love of my life."

"Marry her then," Mom says.

And we're right back to the loop of arguments and side conversations that go nowhere and why what should be a ten-minute meeting takes an hour.

As they continue to bicker, my mind drifts to Whitney and spending time with her tonight. I don't know when the best time to tell her I'm in love with her, but I need to. Soon. So she knows what she means to me and that I'm serious.

I will give up an unknown future, if I know she will be mine.

22

WHITNEY

I get the text, but my hands are shaking so violently that the words are a blur.

"You read it. I can't."

I hand the phone to Reid. He reads, "'Ken and I are here in Goldheart. Can't wait for dinner tonight.'"

I swallow back the bile in my throat as I take my phone back.

"Baby, it will be okay," Reid says, his hands massaging my tense shoulders and his lips in my hair. The breath I release is loud and heavy as my hand drifts down my face.

"You don't understand because your family is so great," I say. "I don't think you understand how truly messed up this situation is."

"It will all be okay," Reid says. "What if you and your mom can have a relationship now? It's not too late."

I laugh at his optimism as Reid's hands skate across my arms. It's been a lifetime of being ignored by my mom. Staying with a dad who'd assumed my mother's feelings would change when I was born, to find he was wrong and he was left holding a toddler.

Then she divorced him and married Ken, a bachelor fifteen years older than her with grown children, living in a state I've never been to. And now she's here.

"Baby, just breathe," Reid says, pushing my hair to the side so he can kiss my neck as we sit at his dining room table. My coffee quivers in my mug as I raise it to my lips.

"I'm just so nervous," I say.

"Eat," Reid says, pushing some toast in my direction. My stomach churns, and I take a bite, the bread dry and scratchy in my throat. I eat until the piece is gone. Last night, I was too stressed to eat, and this morning, the toast feels like a lead brick in my stomach.

"Are you sure you want me to come with you tonight?" Reid asks.

"Yes. Please. I need moral support," I say.

"I will be that for you." He kisses the side of my head and refills my coffee mug. My anxiety has been at an all-time high leading up to Christmas, and caffeine is making it worse. However, Reid knows the tossing and turning I did last night. Because he was there.

Ever since the night of pasta and sex after our storage room incident, I've been staying at Reid's. I have a drawer there, and my toothbrush lives in his stand. He keeps my favorite non-dairy creamer in the fridge, and he bought a new pillow for me after I woke up with a stiff neck one morning.

I've never been taken care of like that by a man, ever.

It's been wonderful so far, snuggling at night after the lights go out, making coffee and sitting on the porch. We actually get up at the same time, which is a miracle. I've always been an early riser and Brad loved to sleep in, but it's been nice to seize the day together with a partner.

It's a lot of pressure to be in a new relationship leading

to the holidays. Pile on some parent abandonment, and I can't believe Reid is still here.

He's seen all of my ugly and hasn't run away. He's run toward me.

It's the day before Christmas Eve, and I have something planned, but it may fall through. Nothing feels enough for what he's given me. What he's shown me. Facing my estranged mother with me is such a huge gift, there's no way I can repay him.

I'm going to try, though.

I don't make it a habit of talking to children, but I caught Isaac in the brewery during one of his homework sessions and he gave me the perfect gift idea. It's just about finding it.

When you have a couple million in the bank and TikTok has been promoting your entire backlist for months, you can afford to be outrageously generous.

Reid takes me in a hug and I settle in his arms.

"Thank you for doing this," I say.

"It's not a problem."

"What if she tells me she's sick and that's why she's finally reaching out?" I ask. "I don't know what I'll do if she's sick..."

"Don't let your big, beautiful brain go there. I will be there to support you, and *everything will be fine.* The holidays make people realize things about family. That it's the most important thing."

His words cause my breathing to slow down, and a strange calm comes over me. This will be fine. This will be great. This is a step in the right direction. Now that I'm divorced and don't have any children, I need all the family I can get.

But the anxiety is still there. "We can just stay home

instead, and I can lick whipped cream off of your body, and you know I found that special porn for research..."

Reid groans and walks away, circling back. For a second, I think he might indulge me. He shakes his head.

"You're not getting out of this," Reid says. He points to his package, one of my favorite parts of him. "This can be your reward."

"Well, when you put it like that..." I say.

Reid looks at me, and his face is odd. Like he wants to say something, but he's deliberating.

"What's going on in that big, beautiful brain of yours?" I ask, scratching the short stubble on his head. He takes my hand from his head and laces his fingers in with mine. Our hands rest on the table and he looks at it, and then at me.

He really looks at me.

"I love you," he says. His thumb rubs the back of my hand.

My heart flutters, and I blink rapidly. "What did you say?"

"I love you," Reid repeats.

My hand grips his like we're watching a horror movie. "Why?"

"What do you mean 'Why'?" Reid asks. His face cracks into a smile. "You're literally the most dynamic woman I have ever met. You're so talented and beautiful and witty and funny and everything I'm looking for."

He presses his forehead to mine, drinking in my gaze. "What's going on in that big, beautiful brain?"

I swallow. I was not expecting this today, between seeing my mother for Christmas or Reid's "I love you." My skin crawls with discomfort, with the dread I've spent my whole life fighting.

That my whole life has validated.

Nothing good ever lasts for me. Everything good ends.

"What about kids?" I ask.

"If it means having you, I will do whatever it takes. All I want for Christmas is you."

"Did you just quote Mariah Carey?"

"Maybe," he says. That sly smile has been my downfall since I met him, has made me forget the major themes of my life.

"You are the best man I've ever known," I say. It's all I can do right now. If I say those words back to him, we will be at the point of no return. There's no exit. Still, tears fall from my eyes. This incredible man loves me. Will give up being a dad for me.

It's too much to ask of him, but I know what I feel. So I say it.

"I love you too."

His lips are immediately on me, kissing my mouth and my tears.

I love him for how he has fit into my life without trying, without effort, without friction. Yes, we hated each other for a while, but two artists are bound to have strife and heat between them. Being here with me, helping me face my demons, has been more than any man has given me.

Reid is the man I have been waiting for.

Still, asking him to give up being a father, because I'm terrified of repeating my mother's mistake, one she is apparently trying to fix, plagues me.

I believe Reid feels this way now, but what's going to happen when his family gets married, has their own babies, and we're without?

He would choose not to be a father, just to make me happy. To be with me.

That might be too big of a present to accept.

23

REID

"You look beautiful," I say to Whitney, as I take her in my arms. We're about to leave for dinner with her mom and her mom's husband, but I want to be late, if Whitney will let me.

Telling her I love her couldn't have gone better. She said it back, and a smile has been tattooed on my face since then.

Looking back, I don't think I loved anyone before Whitney.

She is my new reason, making me want to be better, stronger. Being with her gives me direction. I finished my novel this morning, and I've already ordered a proof and paid an obscene amount of money for the company to do a rush on it.

It will join a bunch of other items for her for Christmas. I'm ready to spoil her.

There's no diamond ring yet because I learned from my brother, but that's not far off from me. I get it now.

I'm excited to meet her mother. Meanwhile, Whitney looks like she's going to vomit.

"I have one goal for tonight, and that's to keep my emotions about me," Whitney says.

"I'll be with you. No need to worry. Just hold my hand," I say. She brushes her lips against mine, and we leave, getting in my car to go over to the restaurant.

I grab her hand and hold it over the console as we drive. "It will be great," I say.

"I hope so," she says. Her hand shakes in mine.

We picked a small restaurant that's new on Main Street called Bistro 530. The owner, Burke, just moved from the Bay area to open his own restaurant, after never setting foot in Goldheart. The Bad Biddies have already tried to set him up with all the single women in town, but he keeps to himself.

When we enter the restaurant, a man lifts his hand in greeting, and we approach the table. The man is all smiles as he shakes my hand and introduces himself as Ken. He looks at Whitney like she's a celebrity.

I can't help but stare at Angie, Whitney's mother. The resemblance is uncanny. They have the same bright blue eyes against pale skin and dark hair, though Angie's is streaked with gray. And the same petrified expression on their faces staring back at each other.

"Wow, you look just like your mother. It's so wonderful to finally meet you," Ken says, staring at my love. She looks him in the eye, bold and confident.

"You too," Whitney says, sitting down opposite Angie, her mom.

Angie fidgets and doesn't say anything. No hugs, no hellos.

"Hi, I'm Reid," I say, extending my hand. I shake Ken's first. Angie's hand is small in mine, and her eyes stay on her daughter.

"Hi, Whitney," Angie finally says.

"Hi," she says, staring at the menu, her eyes flicking to her mother for a second.

"The menu looked amazing online. Has this been here for long?" Ken asks.

"It's a new restaurant to us," I say. "My family owns a brewery, and our beer is actually on the menu." I point out Gold Dust, and Ken nods.

"I can't wait to try it."Ken seems like a nice man. He wraps his arm around Angie, and I can see the love he has for her. He's much older, with a bald head and gray in his mustache, and looks like your nerdy uncle who reads lots of fantasy.

"The bed-and-breakfast is nice. Thank you for the recommendation," Angie says, trying to not to stare at her daughter.

The server appears. "Hey folks, can I get you something to drink?"

The silence hangs over our table. I speak up. "Should we get a bottle of wine for the table? Or two?"

Angie's shoulders relax. "Please."

I pick a red I'm familiar with from a neighboring winery, and the server brings it for the table. It's dry on my tongue and a great wine to relax and forget deep-seated issues for a couple hours. Ken also gets a pint of Gold Dust.

"Wonderful choice, Reid," Angie says.

"Truly, this beer is fantastic," Ken says, the foam in his mustache.

"Thank you, Mrs. Singleton, Mr. Singleton."

"Please call me Ken."

"And please call me Angie."

"Okay," I say, although calling her Angie didn't feel right. Whitney calls her Angie.

Whitney grips my thigh under the table, and our hands join, my thumb rubbing her skin, telling her everything will be okay. That I'm here. That I'm in love with her.

"So, you're friends?" Angie asks, looking between us.

I wrap my arm around Whitney's shoulders, and she relaxes and melts into me. "More than that."

"Reid is..." Whitney says, her voice cracking. She leans in and kisses me, and when she pulls away, her eyes droop and tell me everything I need to know.

"You two seem so happy," Angie says, holding her wine glass with both hands.

"I know I am. It's new so..." I say, kissing Whitney's temple. Whitney says nothing, and so I say, "Right?"

"Right," Whitney says, kissing me quickly. She must be nervous, because her lips are tense when they touch mine. *Just let it go. She's nervous.*

"It's so nice you found someone. After Brad. I still don't know what happened," Angie says.

I take a swig of wine. That's the only way I can listen to Whitney talk about her ex, the bastard who let her go because he changed his mind.

My mind is made up.

When Whitney agrees to marry me, we're growing old together, we're going to have matching oxygen tanks as we sit and remember all the travel we did, all the chances we took, how full our life was without having children.

"Brad wanted kids, but I didn't," Whitney says, drinking some wine. She looks at her mother and says, "I'm not having children."

Her mother nods. "I fully support that. If you don't want kids, you shouldn't have them."

"Unlike what you did?" Whitney asks. Her head tilts, and I can see Angie's heart sink at her daughter's words.

Here we go.

Ken and I look at each other, and he nods once. "So, your mother tells me you're an author. What do you write about?"

"I write romance," she answers. "Mostly dark. My last series was a mafia romance."

"Wow, those are popular?" Ken asks.

Whitney nods vigorously.

"Who publishes them? Like, what publishing house?" Ken asks.

"I publish them," she says, sitting up straight in her chair, her wine completely gone. She pours more.

"Like self-publishing?" Ken asks. His tone isn't accusatory, but Whitney, who runs on high emotion, may take it the wrong way.

I've seen Whitney become visibly flustered when people suggest self-publishing isn't real publishing, or romance is just smut. It's why we hated each other for eons.

I've learned now, and I would love to have half the success Whitney has. To be read, to be loved, to connect with readers. I see how much joy Whitney has doing what she loves and I cannot wait to experience it for myself.

"Yes," Whitney says, ripping her hand away from mine. She needs two hands to discuss it. "I'm more successful than I would ever be if I tried to traditionally publish. I have an agent for foreign rights and audio rights..."

Ken smiles nervously and holds his hands up. "I'm so sorry. I don't know much about it, you see. I read but..."

"We are very proud of you," Angie says, reaching across the table to Whitney. Whitney's hand stiffens under her mother's, but she doesn't pull it away, which is a good thing.

Maybe we're getting somewhere.

"Reid, can I talk to you for a second?" Whitney asks.

I follow her outside, even though the temperature has dipped below thirty degrees and we can see our breath. I pull her toward me so we can create heat to keep us warm.

"I need you to go," Whitney says against my chest. I hope she can't hear how my heart pounds.

"Are you sure?" I ask.

"I think I need to discuss things with my mother. Alone. I'm going to ask Ken to leave too."

"Okay," I say, although my stomach churns. "I can stay. Hold your hand during whatever you have to say."

Whitney's glacial eyes capture mine. She found the courage to face her mother because I was by her side, but she needs to continue alone. I understand, and I respect that.

"Do you need me to come get you?"

She shakes her head against my chest. "No, I'll see you at home."

Her calling my house "home" makes me smile as I pull her in again, kissing the top of her head. "You call or text me if you need anything."

"I will," she says. She leans in, and her lips are soft and warm even though it's below freezing out. It kills me I can't be there for her to protect her from the emotion she's feeling. I wish I could feel her pain so she didn't have to.

When she goes back into the restaurant, she turns back to me and blows a kiss. I catch it just as a dusting of snow begins to fall.

MY PARENTS' house glows like a fireplace when I pull up onto the gravel shoulder. The Christmas tree peaks through the window frame, and my mother's many bows and foliage decorations are sprinkled throughout the front porch and door.

The snow has stopped, and snowflakes dust their lawn. I pull my jacket tight around me as I walk up to the front door and knock. My parents aren't expecting me so I assume Mom is reading while Dad is tinkering in the garage. It takes a few moments for someone to reach the door, and Mom is clearly surprised to find me here.

"What's wrong, Reid?"

I say nothing, and I hug her. I squeeze her in the warmth of my childhood home, surrounded by holly and plush Santas decorating the foyer.

"Did something happen, Reidsy?" she asks, using my nickname from childhood.

"Nope, I just wanted to tell you I love you," I say, taking my mom in a tight hug.

Her hand swipes against my short hair, and I can hear the beginnings of a sob. "I love you too."

"I have something else to tell you," I say, pulling away. My mom studies my face. I look down. "I'm in love with Whitney."

Her eyes soften like a baking chocolate chip cookie. "I know, dear." Her hand cups my cheek like she used to do when I was a boy.

"Me not having kids isn't because you were a bad mom, you know," I say. "It's because you were a great one."

My mom pulls me in and cries softly against my shoulder, and I let her. No matter how much meddling she does, she has always been there for us. Our family is not perfect, but it is full of love.

When we break apart, she wipes the tears from her cheeks. "I'm sorry I got emotional. I just don't hear that from you kids out of nowhere."

"I'm sorry about that. I'll try to get better about it."

"Come in," Mom says, pointing to the kitchen. "I was going to brew a cup of tea if you want some."

"That would be great," I say, following her. I notice the Christmas cards on the fridge, a picture of Annie in Cameron's lap, another of Olive and Emily standing together in front of the large oak tree on her property. I hope next year a photo of Whitney and me will be on the fridge. Maybe we'll do a cheeky one on vacation because we will be childfree and therefore able to travel whenever we feel like it.

I sit at the kitchen island as the teapot hisses on the stove. Mom moves it to an inactive spot and opens the cabinet where at least twenty types of tea live. I point to the green, and she pulls out two bags.

Once the water is poured, my mom looks down at her mug.

When she looks up, I see glassiness, and her eyebrows crinkle like she's confused.

"Does Whitney love you?" Mom asks, dunking her tea bag into her water.

I nod.

"That's good," Mom says. "I've always worried about you, you know."

"Why?" I ask.

Mom shrugs one shoulder. "You've always dated people who didn't care as much as you did. You have so much to give, Reidsy. I'm glad Whitney recognizes that and loves you for you."

"She does, Mom."

"Good." Mom walks to my side and slings her arm around me. She kisses my head, like she used to do when we were little. "My sweet boy."

We both sip our tea. Mom asks, "Where's Whitney right now?"

"She's having dinner with her mom. I met them, but she asked me to leave. She needs to talk to her mom alone."

"That must be hard," Mom says. She blows on her tea, and it steams around her. "Annie told me a little bit about her situation."

"It is. Her mom left when she was three, and they haven't spoken since her first wedding."

"That's too bad," Mom says. "I don't understand how any mother wouldn't want to be involved in their child's life, especially when that child is Whitney."

"I don't get it either," I say, sipping my tea. "Because she is everything."

My mom smiles with her lips to the coffee mug. "That makes me giddy to hear."

"It's the truth," I say. "I think I'm going to marry her."

My mom begins sobbing again.

I have the best mother in the world. If Angie can't be a mother to Whitney, my mom will adopt her and she can be a part of our family.

She can be a Finch if she wants to.

I'll try to make her one as soon as she's ready.

24

WHITNEY

A ngie and I sit across from each other. Our wine glasses are empty, tinted with the wine long consumed. A half bottle sits between us, but we have not refilled.

Ken left shortly after Reid, understanding that we needed to talk one-on-one.

As the silence grew, I didn't know how to break it. I could talk about benign things, innocuous and unimportant. Or I could go for the kill.

"I read your book. *Brutal Lover*," she says. "Brad sent me a copy with no note."

I freeze. The heroine's relationship with her mother is so rough, she kills her toward the end. It was deeply cathartic to write, but I never thought my mother, the inspiration, would read it.

A tear drops down her cheek. "It was really eye-opening. How you view me."

"It was hard. Growing up without you."

She nods once, pouring more wine. She offers me some, and I take it.

I blurt out, "Why did you have me if you knew you didn't want children?"

My gaze flicks to her and her mind turns, as I watch. I will finally get answers.

"Once it happened, I thought it was a sign. That this was meant to happen to me." Angie says. I hear her deep intake of breath. "I always figured that if it happened, it was the universe telling me I should be a mother.

"When you were born though, I couldn't stop crying. When you were screaming in the middle of the night, I screamed with you. I tried so hard to make it work. Every woman I know made being a mother look so effortless, and here I was, so sad I couldn't get out of bed to feed you. I couldn't comfort you."

She inhales, exhales and continues. "It was your third birthday. You were obsessed with horses. I got you a horse cake and decorations and made it perfect for you. All the moms complimented me, saying you were so beautiful and the party was great. They didn't know I cried every day. That I thought multiple times a day that I had made a mistake. That your dad and I fought all the time, but we waited until you were asleep."

Angie wipes her nose. "I knew if I stayed, it could be bad. Very bad. I couldn't screw you up."

My voice is quiet when it finally makes noise. "I was screwed up with you leaving, though."

"You were better off without me," Angie whispers. My mouth gapes. How dare she think that.

"You're my mother," I say. "I needed you. There's so many things Dad didn't get, and I had no one to talk to. About boys or mean girls or what to do about my life."

"You seem to be doing okay, though," Angie says. "You have your career, and you have Reid."

The mention of his name slices through the pain I'm feeling. I want to know what Angie sees, if it's all in my head or if I'll be crying in a few months when he leaves me like everyone else does.

"He loves you," Angie says. "Really. He looks at you like any mother would dream of a man to look at her daughter."

My heart threatens to leap out of my chest. I love Reid more than any man I've ever known.

And that fucking terrifies me.

"I'm so mad at you," I say, my eyes filling with tears.

"That's fair," Angie says, reaching out for my hand. It's the second time today I've let her touch me. "I'm here now. I've been doing a lot of work in therapy and I want to be here now. I want a relationship."

I breathe in deeply to calm myself as tears slip from my eyes.

"Why did you let six years go by? You didn't get in touch on my birthday or when Dad let you know I was getting a divorce."

"After that fight we had, I..." Angie's voice cracks, and she rubs her forehead with her palm. It was the day after I got married and Brad's parents hosted a day after brunch. My mother refused to come because she claimed she wasn't welcome. I remember being so happy she showed up to my wedding, but the wedding reception was tense with her there. Brad even commented on it.

She acted awkwardly, refusing to speak with anyone. Acting more like a stranger than my mother. No matter what happened between us, she should've been better. She should've tried harder.

She promised she would show up to brunch, but she didn't. It led to a huge blowout over the phone where I said

some hurtful things and hung up on her. Told her to stay
gone from my life forever.

I wanted her to try harder, to show that she gave a shit
about me, but she never did. She let six years go by before
sending a random letter. A whole life happened in the time
she missed, just because she assumed one fight had crum-
bled the shaky relationship we had.

In the first year, I reached out twice to apologize. I gave
up when she didn't return my call and my email went
unanswered.

I spent many years wishing she'd never come to my
wedding. It got my hopes too high.

"I wanted you to fucking try," I say. "You spent my entire
childhood taking the easy way out. You are the villain in my
life."

"I deserve that," Angie says. "I'm here now. Trying. I
want to get to know you. And Reid. I want to visit this beautiful town again."

I fold my arms across me. "How do I know you won't
disappear again?"

She says nothing. For a split second, I devolve to that girl
in pigtails who wanted to make her mother proud, make her
love her. Who got more than just the child support checks
and the annual birthday phone call.

Angie shifts in her seat, and I can see the hurt in her
eyes and how her mouth turns down. How she slumps here,
taking the beating I'm giving her.

"Just because I wasn't cut out for motherhood doesn't
mean that you aren't."

I fold my arms across myself. "I come from a long line of
women who shouldn't have had them. I'm breaking the
cycle."

She's weighing something, whether to confess or to keep it to herself.

"Did you love him?" I ask. My dad, quiet and stoic, did the best he could. Reid reminds me of him.

Her breath is a lifetime of relief. "With my whole heart."

"What happened?" I ask.

"You were an accident. We were so careful, but you still happened. Your dad was excited, so I tried to be excited. I had a shitty childhood with your grandmother. You're right about the long line of women who shouldn't have been mothers."

"What happened with Grandma?" I ask, the word foreign in my mouth. Ginger was cold at best and a mean bitch at worst. I always knew there was a deeper story there, but it was too painful to be around her to stay and find out.

"She shouldn't have been a mother." My mother smooths out her napkin, and I see a small tremor in her hands. "I was terrified I would turn into her if I stayed. If I hurt you like she hurt me..." She quiets. "I couldn't live with myself. Because I love you. I love you so much, Whitney."

Don't cry again. Don't cry again, I tell myself, but emotion constricts my throat and I cough into my hand.

"Your grandmother was an unhappy woman. My father was not nice, not like your dad. I kept questioning if your dad was right for me. He wanted kids so badly and I didn't, but I loved him. I let him sacrifice for me, until I sacrificed for him.

"When I told him I wasn't sure I wanted to have kids, he said it was okay, but I knew he wanted to be a dad. When I got pregnant, his eyes lit up, and it crushed me. I knew I would have you then. I hoped I could change how I could feel because I loved him so much. And I loved you. But as you got older, it became clear to me that you were better off without me than with me. So I left."

She looks down, and when she looks back up, her eyes are filled with tears. "Just make sure you're careful with Reid if you really don't want to have kids. Don't repeat my mistakes."

"I can't get pregnant," I say. Angie's shoulders droop, and I add, "I got a tubal ligation at twenty-six."

"And what about Reid? Do you know if he wants to be childfree too?"

He wants to be with me, and he will do everything in his power to make sure we're together. Will he change his mind? Will he realize one day I'm not enough? I'm not worth the resentment and the big life choice.

I don't know if I could weather another divorce. Or partake in motherhood to keep the most amazing man I've ever met.

Everything in me is saying to go for it, date this man, marry this man. The part of me that knows in my soul that parenthood is not for me says this will never work.

Angie grabs her wine glass and brings it to her lips.

"Don't make my mistake. Because saying goodbye now is a lot harder later when more is at stake."

She means me. I was what was at stake.

"If he might want kids, even a little bit, end it now before it's too late."

We sit with our wine, silent, as the entrées come.

Her words are full of regret, of a decision made that changed the trajectory of her life.

She basically said she wished I wasn't born.

If I wasn't born, maybe her and my father would've made it, and she would've never met Ken. My parents would still live in Oregon, going on vacations and working on their careers and hobbies.

If I wasn't born, Reid would date someone else. Find

someone else.

Some uncomplicated woman who wants to have children, who had a good childhood, who has parents who are dying to be grandparents. Not like my Grandma Ginger, who snarled when she saw me. Not my dad who didn't know what to do with me when he had to be a mother and a father.

I'm just a woman who shook him loose from what he thought his life could be like.

Reid thinks he wants me, but he doesn't. Not really.

"This looks so good," Angie says when the food arrives, stabbing her chicken with her fork.

Eating a meal with my mother feels weird, but also illuminating.

I can't end up like her.

I need to leave Goldheart. And Reid.

25

REID

I see the light from the kitchen before I hear her.

The paperback I was reading is splayed over my chest. I search for my bookmark on my nightstand, and then get up to see what she's doing.

After talking to my mom, I know I need to tell Whitney how serious I am about her. Anyone can say they're in love.

When I say I'm in love, that means I want to love them forever.

That I see her here in Goldheart. That I could see myself dropping to one knee someday, when we're both ready. Spending the rest of our lives together, sharing a home and a bed, being each other's family.

The light assaults my eyes when I open the door. Whitney is sitting at the counter, drinking a beer from a Woody Finch Brewery pint glass. This is the first time since we've started seeing each other that she doesn't smile when she sees me.

"Hi," I say, walking over to her, kissing her head. She flinches with my touch and I pull away.

This is not good. Maybe we need to talk about whatever

is bugging her first before I blurt out *Please move in with me permanently and tell me you'll say yes if I ask you to marry me.*

Now is not the right time, though.

"How was the rest of the dinner with Angie?" I ask, standing in my kitchen, leaning on my hands. She can't look at me.

"It was fine," she says. "I'm not sure if I feel better or worse."

"I can see that," I say. "Is she staying? For Christmas?"

"I think so," Whitney says. "Ken's kids are visiting his ex-wife this Christmas, and they don't have anything else to do."

"Are you going to see them again?"

Whitney nods. No matter how long I stare at her, she won't look at me.

"What's wrong?" I ask.

With that, she looks at me and there's tears in her eyes. Definitely, not good.

"Do you want kids?" she asks.

I pause. "I always thought I wanted them. Goldheart is a small town, and that's what you do. You get married to the first person you date and you have a couple kids and you stay put. Since I met you, though, I'm seeing my future differently. I want you. If that means not having kids, that means not having kids. I'm at peace with that."

"I don't want you to ever resent me, though," Whitney says. She wrings her hands, and I can hear her breath. I cover her hands with mine.

"Look at me," I order, and she does. "I won't. I promise."

Whitney stands up and rips her hands away. She paces the length of my living room, her arms folded in front of her like she's cold. I stay still, although I want to envelop her in my arms until she believes I want her. That being with her is enough for me.

"Everyone thinks I'm selfish for the choice I've made. Everyone. I don't think it is. I also know I can't be selfish and ask you to give up your vision of your life."

"I'm never going to find anyone like you. What we have is so rare. I want to have a beautiful life with you, if you will let me. I'm so in love with you."

"I can't risk it," Whitney says. "I can't risk you hating me for making you sacrifice. Or ending it in a few years because you change your mind and decide you want kids."

"When are you going to believe me? I will give it up to be with you."

We stand still, and Whitney's eyes cannot look at mine. Her voice is small when she speaks.

"I think we need to end this."

Time stops. My thoughts scramble to say something, anything, to get her to take those words back. I've never stopped a woman from ending it with me. I don't force people to be with me. There's nothing I can say if she wants to leave.

"Reid," she says. Her voice is shaky. "I just want to let you know I've enjoyed getting to know you..."

I tune her out. It's like every other relationship I've had. I've given a hundred percent while they've given less. Whitney says she loves me, but she doesn't believe me when I say I love her. That'll I'll give up kids. For her.

The kids issue is just an excuse. If she loved me, she would believe me when I said I would sacrifice a hazy future, a future I didn't even see clearly, until I met her. She's breaking up with me because she doesn't feel enough for me to believe me.

I turn my head, and I see her stuff collected in a corner,

like her mind was already made up. Like I had no say in the end of the most powerful relationship I've ever had, even though it was so short.

"So that's it, then," I say. "We're done."

"Yes," she says, the word ending with a hiccup. I rub my hand down my face. I didn't think I could be in so much pain from one word. It feels like my chest will break open and my heart will explode.

"Why don't you believe me?" I ask, looking at her. Her arms are wrapped tightly around her like a straitjacket.

"I do," she says. "But I'm not sure if you really understand."

I stand and look at her. "You're just scared. Look, you're shaking."

"I've been down this road before," she says. "I have one failed marriage under my belt because he changed his mind about kids. I don't want another one."

"It's different with us," I say. "Please tell me it's different with us."

Tell me to erase the last ten minutes from our history. I will, if you ask. If you tell me to forget it, I will.

She doesn't. Instead, she disappears into the darkness of the bedroom and emerges with her suitcase, stuffed haphazardly with her clothes. Clothes that were folded neatly in one of my drawers an hour before. "I'm going to stay somewhere else tonight," Whitney says. "I just can't be here."

She heads to the door, but I have to say what's on my mind. A lifetime of holding in my thoughts, letting people walk all over me. Assuming I'm fine.

I'm not fine.

"It was different for me," I say. She stops and turns. My hand goes to my chest. "You are the only person I will ever love."

A sob builds in my throat, but I can't cry in front of her. I'll wait until she's gone before I break down with a bottle of whiskey. She moves like she's going to leave, but instead she runs into my arms.

I hear a whimper, and I realize it's me.

"I'm sorry," she says into my shirt. I pull her into me and touch her hair because it's the last time. She feels so right in my arms. How can this be happening?

I'm losing her.

Like I've lost every other woman I've been with.

But this is the one I know I'll never recover from.

26

WHITNEY

"She's awake," I hear as my eyes open, my neck and back stiff from the restless night. My vision is blurry as I look to the side.

Annie and Cameron stand with cups of coffee in their hands, watching me sleep.

"Merry Christmas," they both say.

Annie broke her lease at her bungalow to move in with Cameron at the tiny house, and now I'm freeloading again. My mother offered to get me a room at the inn, but I declined, more comfortable in cramped spaces with my best friend and her boyfriend than with her.

"We didn't think you would wake up," Cameron says.

"What time is it?"

"Nine-thirty," Annie says, sipping amongst the steam. "It's very unlike you."

"Yeah, well..." I say, sitting up. Try seeing your estranged mother and breaking it off with the best man you ever known, and then contemplate how you will ever get out of bed again.

"Are you going to see your mother today?" Cameron asks. "You are always welcome at the Finch house. Even if..."

He knows. I fell apart in Annie's arms last night after breaking it off with Reid, my chest cracking open from the pain.

"No, thank you. I can't," I say. I grab my phone, that sits on the arm of the couch. I flip through my notifications to see a text from my mother.

Angie: Are we seeing you today? For Christmas?

I answer yes, and we arrange a time.

My heart must be decimated if I'm going to willingly see my mother to avoid feeling like this.

Annie gets a look on her face and escapes to the bathroom. Her morning sickness started a couple days ago with a vengeance, so Cameron and I are in each other's presence, unsure how to address that I broke up with his brother.

His amazing, incredibly sexy brother who I love.

"So, you're going back to Reno?" Cameron asks.

I nod. "I think so."

"Okay," he says. "It might be better for Reid if you're not around."

"It'll be good for me too." I pause before I say, "I've really loved Goldheart. It healed me."

Cameron looks down at his coffee. "You're always welcome, no matter how much time has passed. I hope you know that. And my brother... I know he would love to have you back."

Cameron disappears into the loft they use for storage and reappears with a large box full of gifts.

"Reid dropped these off this morning while you were sleeping."

My heart drops knowing Reid was outside this house,

giving me gifts when I had nothing to give him. After I broke his heart.

"That's...so much," I say. The presents overflow from the top of the bag. I didn't even get that many presents from my mother my whole childhood.

"My brother never does anything half-assed. Once he commits to something, he pours his whole heart in."

I'm not sure if Cameron is talking about presents or me.

It makes me feel terrible I wasn't able to find his present in time. I haven't stopped my search, though.

Cam hands me the bag, and I take it. Damn, it's heavy. I try to count, but I lose track of the items in the bottom. They're all wrapped in paper featuring raccoons wearing mittens and Santa hats, holding candy canes.

"I gave him the wrapping paper," Cameron says, pointing with pride.

"It's cute," I say. I stand up and offer my arms to Cameron. He takes me in and squeezes me.

"If you want to get me anything for Christmas, I could really use Thane's story."

"The bodyguard?" I ask, pulling back. Thane is a background character in my *Bad Royals* series, and Thane appears in many scenes, but he really doesn't have a backstory. He's just a steady presence for the main family.

"Yes," Cameron says. "I totally have a thing for bodyguard romances. Even since *Brutal Knight.*"

I laugh for the first time I since leaving Reid's house. A tear slides down my cheek, and I wipe it away. "Thank you."

"You're welcome," he says. He points to the bathroom where we hear faint retching sounds. "Annie wants it too. We talk about Thane all the time."

I laugh again and slap Cameron's back. I'm going to miss them so much.

"Hi," Angie says, opening the door to her hotel room. I try to smile, but my lips do not work.

"Hi," I say, as she opens the door wider to let me in. I walk past her and shrug off my coat. The Goldheart Inn has a couple rooms with kitchenettes, and I made sure Angie and Ken booked one of them. Dinner is on the stove and a bottle of red wine sits on the counter, open and ready for me to drink it all down.

"Ken ran out to get some rolls. We forgot them at the store. Goldheart's little market is so cute."

I remember Reid dropping an egg on my foot there.

Do not cry. Do not cry.

I say nothing as Angie walks over to the wine. "I assume you need this."

"Definitely." I told her about Reid and she's not asking about it, which I appreciate. She pours a generous amount and hands it to me, then pours her own. We clink glasses and drink. The fruit and alcohol dance on my tongue, and I drink slowly but deeply.

"Slow down, Whitney, or you won't be able to drive."

I want to cry. That's the first motherly thing she's said to me this whole trip. It seems like something that would annoy an adult child, but I've been starved of maternal care for so long, it feels nice.

"Do you want to talk about it?" Angie asks. I shake my head.

"Okay, then," she says, walking over to the glass table under a vintage light fixture. I look around the room, capturing this piece of my history. I will remember Goldheart fondly, for so many reasons.

Thinking about leaving makes me drink faster.

I hold my glass of wine close to my chest, and I walk around, examining the pictures on the wall. Above the little sitting area, there's a photograph of a man from the past, standing in front of the mine Reid took me to.

I wonder if that man had a family, if they worried about him until he came home from his shift. My thoughts drift to the time we spent at the mine. How it was the first time I knew I was in trouble with Reid. How he kissed me with his whole being.

"Are you okay?" Angie asks, standing next to me. I bring my hands to my cheeks, smearing makeup off my face with my tears. Her arm wraps around my shoulders tentatively, and a sob leaves me. She sits down with me in her arms, and I cry.

I cry because something about leaving the town and Reid does not feel right. But I cannot take parenthood away from him. He would make such a good dad, a better parent than either of my parents were.

"Is this about Reid?" she asks.

I nod, sniffling against my hand. "I don't know if he'll change his mind. What if he resents me later? I can't be abandoned again."

We stay quiet together, her arm still around me. It feels awkward and comforting, in a jumble of emotions swirling within me. I'm sitting with my first abandonment, and she doesn't say anything, try to explain it away. The past happened and silently, it's forgiven.

I've always been so sure about my life and its trajectory. Now I have no idea what to do, where to go. What's in store for me.

"From what little you told me, you and Reid are not the same to me and your father," Angie says.

"We want different things."

"I get that." She smooths down my hair away from my face.

"What if I'm making a mistake?" I ask.

"Then you'll realize it, one way or another. Just give it some time."

My tears slow, and I look at her. Really look at her. Her blue eyes crinkle at the sides. Freckles dot her nose, and her skin folds around her mouth from years of smiling. I notice the gray at her scalp and her jingle bell earrings. Her perfume is not the same from the visits we had when I was a kid, but it smells familiar. I know my memory of this night will be haunted by the smell of lavender.

"You know, I always regretted I wasn't there for your first heartbreak. To tell you that it will all be okay."

"You weren't missing much," I say. "Justin Trouser. What a punk."

"Tell me about him." She pulls her bent leg onto the bed. I turn toward her.

"He said he was so into me for two months. Then I caught him making out with my best friend Courtney. Afterwards, I heard that Courtney was talking crap about me and spreading rumors. Claimed I knew she had a crush on Justin and I went for him anyway. For the record, I had no idea."

"Sounds like a winner," she says with a laugh. I laugh too and take a sip of wine.

"I locked myself in my room and listened to heartbreak country for days. Dad left food outside my door."

"I'm so sad I wasn't there," Angie says, taking my hand in hers.

"You are here. That heartbreak wasn't important, but this one is." I hear a sniffle from her. "I don't know if I will ever get over Reid. I just feel so...broken. Even if the kids weren't the issue, I'm not a whole person."

"Oh, Whitney," she says. "I will spend the rest of my life undoing all the harm I caused."

I shake her hand in mine. "You're already helping."

Ken came back to the room shortly after with another bottle of wine and a loaf of French bread. We sat and laughed, and the awkwardness drifted away.

Today, I'm cautiously optimistic that as I let one relationship go, I'm getting one back in its place.

And when my mother suggests video conference family therapy between her and me, I say yes in a heartbeat.

Then, right before I fall asleep on a roll-out the hotel manager delivers around ten, I make my own appointment with the therapist I stopped seeing three years ago.

It's time to not suffer alone anymore.

THE NEXT DAY, my mother and her husband pack up and head home, and then I pack up to head back to Reno.

Annie and Cameron stand in front of his tiny home, their hands in their pockets, watching me pack up my car with my two suitcases. Cameron makes sure Reid's presents are in the trunk, a bag I'm not sure I can look at any time soon, maybe ever. Once my last possession, my computer bag with my notebook, is in the front seat, I turn toward them.

Cam hugs me first, whispering in my ear, "Take care of yourself."

"Thank you," I say.

Annie is sobbing before we even hug. She holds me for minutes, rubbing my back, squeezing me like she's never going to let me go. When she pulls back, her face beams bright red, making her freckles disappear.

"I love you so much. Your heart must be aching."

"It is, but I'll survive," I say. "I love you. Take care of my niece or nephew for me."

"I will," she says, holding her stomach. After Annie told me she was pregnant, I mentioned being an only child and how I will never be a fun aunt. Without skipping a beat, Annie says, "You can be my kid's aunt. Aunt Whitney."

"Thank you for inviting me. This town has brought me back to life," I say. "Take care of Reid for me."

I hiccup a sob as we say our final goodbyes and hold out my hands in a last-minute reach. I get in my car and wave one last time as I drive away.

Main Street is the opposite direction of the freeway, but I visit it anyway. I see Gold Roast one last time and The Swift. I pull up the directions to the mine, and when I arrive, no one is there.

It's the perfect spot to break down and sob.

27

REID

"Why the long face, Reid?" Shiloh asks as she dries glasses fresh from the dishwasher.

It's the second week of January and I'm still not sleeping well. Every day has a gray haze over it, as I go through the motions. I can't read; I haven't been able to write.

I've never been this sad and folks are starting to notice.

The Bad Biddies even invited me to a lunch at Betty's that I almost accepted so I wouldn't be alone with my thoughts.

"I'm going through a breakup," I say.

"With Whitney?" Shiloh asks.

My head snaps toward her. "How did you know?"

I didn't announce that I was seeing her, and while it's no longer a secret, it wasn't public knowledge either.

"I figured. I saw you the way you two acted at Thanksgiving, I knew there was something going on," Shiloh says with a smile. Her hand rests on my shoulder. "I know we don't know each other super well, but I'm a great listener. I might be able to help."

"Thank you. But I'm more of a 'suffer in silence' type."

"Got it." Shiloh still smiles. "I'm sure you can work it out. All you need is love."

I let out a chuckle. Sometimes love is not enough. Sometimes there are things people can't overcome. Sometimes there could be so much love, but it doesn't mean it will last forever.

"It's complicated," I say.

"I'm always here if you need to talk," Shiloh offers again.

Here is this person I barely know, wanting to hear about what happened. Since Whitney moved out and left town, everyone has traveled large circles around me, giving me space. Ignoring my heartbreak like nothing has happened.

It's actually nice to be pressed to talk about it. About her.

"People have problems a lot worse than mine," I say. "Mine are insignificant."

"Just because you haven't been through the worst of the worst heartbreak or trauma doesn't make it less valid. You're allowed to feel heartbroken."

Shiloh goes back to drying the glasses like she didn't say something so profound to shake me out of myself.

This may be the greatest heartbreak of my life, and I'm downgrading it, making it smaller.

"Give me a hug. I promise it will make you feel better," Shiloh says, holding out her arms. She is short, so I fold myself down to hug her. She smells like shortbread cookies.

She pats my back in a sisterly way and pushes me away by the arms.

It's no wonder everyone at the brewery likes her.

"See? A hug makes you feel better, right?"

"It did," I say.

"Good," Shiloh says.

"How did you get so wise? Aren't you, like, twenty-one?"

"Twenty-six," she says. "Let's just say I had opposite upbringing to your family. But I like to look for the light in the dark. It makes me feel like everything is going to be okay, no matter how bleak it gets."

I don't know what is good about this situation. I had a taste of forever love, just for it to end like the others. My heart is smashed again, but I'm not sure if I can put myself back together.

"Thanks for the pep talk. And the hug."

"No problem," Shiloh says, playfully punching me in the arm. "If it's right, she will come back to you. Promise."

For the second time today, Shiloh goes back to drying like she didn't say something that wiped away my smudged future.

I had a few short months with Whitney, but I still want it all.

I just don't know how to get it all.

I barely notice Mrs. Epstein in the corner of the brewery until she waves me over. I've never seen her outside of the library, so it takes me a minute.

Shiloh nudges me with her elbow. "Oh, she wants to talk to you. You should go. I can watch the bar."

Nodding, I walk out from behind the bar to Mrs. Epstein's table. Her legs are crossed, and her purse sits on the small table next to a vase full of flowers, a touch Emily takes care of every three days. I lay a small kiss on her cheek.

"How are you holding up?" she asks.

"Fine," I say, shrugging. She must've heard about Whitney leaving.

"Sit." She motions to the chair across from her. I sit down tentatively. "Why did you let that girl go, son?"

I crumble with those words, letting the weight of Whitney's absence take me over.

"I don't know if you know this, but Whitney is childfree," I say. "I said I would give up kids for her, but Whitney doesn't believe me. She left."

I wait for Mrs. Epstein to say something about changing minds or some solution that would result in Whitney giving up her prerogative. Instead, Mrs. Epstein pats my hand.

"You know, Arthur and I never had children."

"Really?" I ask. I always assumed their kids lived in other parts of the country and didn't visit. She never mentioned any so I assumed it was a sore subject and never asked.

Mrs. Epstein nods. "When I met him, I was head over heels within a week. I knew he was the one. I knew it in my bones.

"He told me on our fifth date that he was sterile, that he couldn't have kids. He asked me to think about it and take some time. We broke up after that. I saw some other men here and there, but nobody made me feel the way Arthur made me feel."

I think back to my times with Whitney. Singing karaoke at The Swift, visiting the mine, all the laughs and times writing at the coffee shop. Whitney is my Arthur. I just don't know how to make her believe me.

"What happened? What did you do?"

"I really thought about being a mother. I realized I didn't *yearn* to be one like my friends did. If the situation was different, if I had fallen in love with another man, I would've had them and tried my best. However, the life I wanted included Arthur, so I made that decision, independent of him.

"I showed up on his doorstep like a crazy woman and told him I didn't care if we had zero or a hundred kids. I just wanted to be with him. We got married four months later. I wouldn't trade that man for anyone. You know Arthur died last year, and he was it for me. I knew I would regret not going after Arthur. So I did."

I grab her hand and hold it, feeling a deeper connection to her than I've ever felt before.

"Do you love her?" Mrs. Epstein asks.

I nod. "Very much."

"You want to spend the rest of your life with her?"

"Yes."

"How do you feel about kids?"

"I said I didn't want them because of her, but now, I don't think I want them period," I say. I think about all the things I want to do. Vacations I want to take. Books I want to write. I can still be a friend to Isaac, I'm about to have another niece or nephew. As Olive's uncles, we've all taken turns being a father figure.

That is enough for me.

I look at Mrs. Epstein and say, "I think I'm childfree."

Mrs. Epstein leans forward, taking my other hands in hers. "Congratulations."

"Thanks."

A wash of calm comes over me. All my life I've been doing what others expected of me, being who I thought they wanted me to be.

At the end of the day, the people who matter just wanted me to be happy.

This is the right decision for me.

"I need to go get her," I say.

"I agree," Mrs. Epstein says, patting my hands. "And when you do find her, tell her we're featuring her book for February. And *every member* finished it. It might be a book club miracle."

. . .

AFTER MY PEP talk with Mrs. Epstein, I head to Cameron's tiny home on our sister Emily's property. When I get out, I check for Emily's unofficial pets, two raccoons named Thelma and Louise.

With a sigh of relief that no raccoons will bum-rush me at three in the afternoon, I walk up to Cameron's dark blue tiny home and bang my fist on the screen door. Cameron appears at the door.

"What's going on, Reid? You okay?"

"I'm fine." I shake my head. "No, actually, I'm not."

"You want a beer?"

I nod, and my brother disappears, returning with two dark brown bottles. We really enjoy an IPA that comes out of Washington, but we keep it a secret from Dad. If Dad knew we were drinking anything but Woody Finch, he would...do absolutely nothing but give us big puppy dog eyes like we disappointed him.

We sit on Cameron's deck in two white wire chairs, looking out at the tall trees. It's cold, but the beer warms me. Plus my newfound determination to get Whitney back is creating a fire within me.

"What's going on?" Cameron asks.

"I think I'm childfree," I say. "I mean, I know I am. I don't want kids."

Cameron takes a sip of beer. "Who would've thought. Me the dad and you get to be the fun uncle. That's wild."

"I know, right?" I say, smiling for the first time in weeks.

"Does Whitney know?"

I shake my head. "I told her I would give up having them for her, not that I'm actually childfree. She thinks I'll regret not having kids."

"Damn," Cameron says, taking a sip of beer.

"What's going on?" Emily asks, walking out from her house.

I peer around her. "Where's Olive?"

"Baking cookies at Mom's so I can fill some orders. I may or may not have taken a nap."

Emily has a successful Etsy shop where she personalizes necklaces. The bulk of her clientele are moms who want necklaces with their kids' names on them. Emily wears a silver one with Olive's name on it.

She also loves good gossip, and seeing us drinking beer together is probably way more exciting than slapping labels on packages.

"You want a Space Dust?" Cameron asks, offering the contraband beer.

"Yes, please," Emily asks. "Dad would be disappointed if he knew you were drinking that."

"No kidding. That's why we're implicating you." Cameron walks inside and comes back with an open bottle. Emily sips it, grimacing slightly at the bitter hops, but still smiles.

"I heard Whitney left," Emily says, slapping me on the knee. "What happened?"

"Reid didn't fight for her," Cameron says. "That's what happened."

Emily's forehead creases and she looks between the two of us.

"She thinks I'll regret not having kids. She doesn't want them," I say. "I just talked to Mrs. Epstein, and I need to find her."

"Wow," Emily says. She looks down at Cameron's small deck and props her hand on her hip. That's Emily's thinking stance.

We wait for a few minutes, watching her, and then she turns to me.

"Do you love her?" Emily asks.

I nod vigorously.

"And you don't care about having kids?"

"I think I'm childfree. Like I don't want them."

Emily stops in her pacing, and her face crinkles into a sob.

"Oh no." Cameron lifts off of his seat with anxiety. "You will not start crying."

"It's just..." Emily lets out a sob. She covers her mouth. "I can't get over how much you two have grown up."

"Emily, we're older than you." We can't admit she *is* more mature than us, even though she's the baby of the family. But Emily has a child, owns her own home, and runs a successful small business.

"I know." She waves her face to fan away the tears. "It makes me happy to see you two figuring things out. You were both drifting for so long..."

Behind her, I see Jackson approaching Cameron's tiny home, and Cameron and I look toward each other.

What the hell.

Emily turns to see what we're looking at, and the sob gets louder. "Why is Jackson here?"

"Hey," Jackson says, shoving his hands in his pockets. The dark circles that always accompany his eyes are gone, and he looks...good. Like he's getting sleep. Like he might actually be happy.

"Hey, big brother," Cameron greets.

"Aren't you supposed to be helping Shiloh today?" I ask.

"Shiloh predicted you might be having a hard time," Jackson says. "She basically told me to find you."

Emily's tears dry as she looks at Jackson in shock. He hasn't listened to anyone in eighteen years.

"Whitney broke up with Reid. Left town," Emily says.

"I figured something was going on. Well, you have to go get her then," Jackson says. "Be Flint."

At Christmas, they let me talk about my book. I'm surprised Jackson was listening.

"Yeah, what would Flint do?" Cam says, although I know he's going along with it and doesn't really know what's going on.

"Who's Flint?" Emily asks.

"The main character in Reid's book. He told us about it at Christmas."

"Oh, that's right," Emily says. "Reid, you'll have to tell me about it again. I think Olive was having a meltdown or something."

This is blowing my mind right now, since this has never happened. I've never been the one in the spotlight, and now they're cheering me on. Treating me like I'm more than a cog in the machine of our family's small business.

"So, what do I do?" I ask. "What's romantic? What says, 'I want to go on vacations with you and not impregnate you'?"

We stay quiet as everyone thinks, and then Jackson claps his hands together.

"I got it."

"Well, what is it?" Emily asks.

The corner of Jackson's mouth tips up in a smirk. "It's simple. Go see her."

"It's perfect," Cameron says. "Straight to the point."

Emily looks between all of us. "Should we all go?"

"Um, you have a child," I say. Emily immediately picks up her phone and starts frantically texting. I point to the rest of them. "And Dad would shit if we all go up there. That night of karaoke was a fluke."

"The Finch siblings deserve a day off at least once a quarter," Jackson says. "For bonding."

My head snaps to Jackson. "Who *are* you?"

"Hell yeah," Emily says, putting her phone down and slapping the chair. "Mom said she would take Olive tomorrow."

"We *do* deserve a day off," I say. "And tomorrow is Wednesday. Our slowest days. I have some stuff to do tomorrow, but..."

"Make the call," Cameron says, seriousness in his voice.

I can't remember the last time I took a random day off in the middle of the week. "I can get it done tonight. Cam, can Annie check that Whitney is in Reno?"

"On it. She's currently with Dan, but I'm sure she'll pick up," Cam says, holding up his phone to his ear. "Hey, honey. I'm good. Listen, is Whitney in Reno right now?"

Cameron listens and smirks. He puts his phone down.

"Why are you smirking?"

"Oh nothing," Cameron says. "She just said something dirty."

"So, we're going tomorrow?" I ask. I bounce in my chair; I'm so excited.

"Yes, we'll go tomorrow," Cam says. He's still smirking.

28

WHITNEY

J odie jostles me awake, and the light assaults my eyes when I open them. I can barely lift my head, my neck is so stiff.

Jodie and Lucy let me crash on their couch as I look for an apartment. There were some beautiful options, but I can't pull the trigger and pick one. Reno was home for a little while during Brad's residency, but it was never my first choice.

It's just familiar.

I considered moving to a completely new city, a city that holds no memories, but my brain and heart can't handle a new place when my heart is in Goldheart. Reno, while holding lots of sad memories, also holds a lot of good ones.

Being in Reno feels like being in your rattiest but comfiest sweats.

I take walks at the Reno Riverwalk and feel the memories wash over me as I walk amongst the snow and the barren trees. My bestselling series was born on these walks. My creativity is alive no matter how sad I am, at least; I've been writing in hipster coffee shops in midtown. I snuggle under lots of blankets and read my friends' romances until dawn cracks through the blinds of the living room and cry with every happily ever after.

Because I can't have mine.

It's when I'm quiet and alone that I think about him. I haven't cried much since I left him, but if I let myself, I stare off into space and replay our days and nights together. I remember our time at the mine, how we used to laugh during writing sprint breaks. Thanksgiving.

My time for Reid was the kind of love I write about but thought was impossible for a normal, healthy relationship to feel like.

But it did.

And then I left.

I still question if it was the best decision.

"I can't handle you being like this," Jodie says. "It's one o'clock."

I squint as I sit up, my body stiff with the supine position I've been in for over twelve hours. My e-reader is buried in the cushion, and it's been digging into my back the entire night. Wincing, I sit up and toss my e-reader on the ground.

My friend's Dachshund Twinkie sniffs it like he's not sure if he should bark or not.

"I'm sorry," I say. I rub my face with my hand. "I'm seeing two apartments today. I promise I'll pick one soon and get out of your hair."

"No, no, it's fine if you stay with us," Jodie says. "It's the moping around and acting like you didn't do this to yourself that's annoying me."

"He might change his mind one day!" I shout, smoothing my hair away from my face. "I can't take that away from him. I can't ask him to give that up."

"What if he wants to give it up?"

"I don't believe him." I fold my arms, my body tingling with anxiety.

"Why?" Jodie asks.

My mother, Brad. It's hard for me to trust, period.

"When are you going to believe that people love you?"

When they stop leaving me."

"You drive me nuts," Jodie says. She points to my bag, full of presents from Reid. "You haven't opened that giant bag of presents yet. I'm going to make you. It's January, Whitney."

"I'm...waiting."

"Here," she says, shoving a glass full of whiskey. "Drink that. We're opening your presents."

"Nooooo," I yell like it's at a dumb heroine in a horror movie.

"Yes," Jodie says, waddling since she's carrying a bag of presents between her legs.

She dumps it in front of me, and I notice the presents were wrapped with precision. Jodie picks up a slim package and hands it to me.

"If you don't open it, you can sleep at GSR tonight." GSR is short for Grand Sierra Resort, a large hotel off of 580, about fifteen minutes from her house.

I have nothing against GSR, but I like Jodie's house better.

My heart beats against my ribcage, and I stick my finger under the flap and tear it, my heartbeat speeding up. When I pull out the papers, I don't know what it is right away. Then, my eyes fill with tears.

And they don't stop coming.

It's my story from the creative writing class. With Reid's feedback.

He kept it all these years.

My vision is blurry as I read the comments.

Wow.

This sentence is beautiful.

This imagery is fantastic.

On the second page, in the margins, is written: *You're the best writer in this class, Whitney.*

The ink is old and worn, faded on the paper. He wrote that back in college.

There's also new writing too.

The word "love" is circled everywhere it's mentioned. I stop breathing as I reach the final page, the blank space that you would typically find feedback from other students.

Reid's message to me filled that space and continued to the back page. I look up and sniffle, but snot and tears drip onto my blankets.

Whitney, I'm sorry I didn't give you this sooner. I was blown away by this story, and I was so envious of how you weave stories together and your use of language. You're the most talented person I've ever met, and that is evidenced by your loyal readers who love you.

I love you. I love you for your drive, your passion, your essence and your soul.

You are what I've been looking for my entire life.

You are what is missing.

You're the love of my life.

I understand that this is scary. You've been left for reasons that feel like they're about you, but they're not. Your mother, Brad. It wasn't about you. The reason I'm staying is because of you.

I want to be your hero. I want to show you the love you write about and that it can happen in regular, everyday life.

A romance author deserves a happily ever after.

If you're in, I'm in.

I sob harder and hunch over, grabbing my stomach.

"What does it say?" Jodie asks. I hand it to her and she reads it, then looks up with tears in her own eyes. "Goddammit, Whitney. If you don't go find him, I'm taking you out of the will."

I can't speak. My throat is tight, and all the tears I've been holding in are rushing out like a burst water pipe.

"Time to cry some more," Jodie says, handing me another package.

I rip it open to find a book.

Not just any book.

His book.

He got a simple cover made, and the proof banner runs through the top of it. I'm not sure if he plans to publish it right away or if this is just a gesture, until I open the front cover.

Whitney, you inspire me every day. This is the first book I've ever completed a draft for. It's because of you. I wanted you to be the first person to read it. The character Lila is inspired by you.

The tears stop, and I find a tissue, wiping my cheeks and blowing my nose. I hand it to Jodie, and she examines it.

"Well, shit."

"'Well, shit' is right."

I pull out another square box, and when I rip away the paper, I notice the insignia. He didn't forget. My sandals, the ones he ruined at the Goldheart market. He said he would replace them, and he did.

My hand runs over the smooth leather. I look up. "I think I fucked up."

"I think you did."

I open another couple items, including a necklace with my name on it from Emily's jewelry line, and a beer in a simple can, marked with the name *Romance Author*.

"Holy shit, did he brew you your own beer?"

"I think he did," I say. These are the most gifts I've received ever from a man. Each one is thoughtful and special.

My head pounds, but I don't know what to do. How to fix this. I wonder if it's even fixable. If Reid could ever forgive me for leaving.

"Do you want Reid back?"

I nod and cover my eyes with my hand. "How do I say I'm sorry?"

"First off, get him a present. I've never been with anyone who has gotten me as much stuff as you have."

I haven't checked the website lately I've been monitoring for my idea for Reid's gift. Something tells me to check.

There it is. Exactly what Isaac told me to get. An hour passes as I message with the owner, who lives in Ukiah, California. I could swing by there before going to Goldheart.

I scroll through my phone and hold it up to my ear.

"Are you calling Reid?" Jodie asks.

I shake my head. "Thumper."

"Who the fuck is Thumper?"

29

REID

I t's nine o'clock and I'm still in the brew room, finishing up my Wednesday work so we can go to Reno to see Whitney. I've tried to be focused, but all I can think about is her. How excited I am to see her. How I hope she believes me when I say I'm now childfree.

I'm writing my script in my head when I hear footsteps.

"I'm almost done," I say.

"Good," a female voice says, and I turn.

There she is.

Whitney is wearing a hoodie, her dark hair piled on top of her head. Her hands clasp in front of her as she looks at me, her lips parted.

I remind myself to breathe, deep inhales and exhales. Whitney looks down, her plump lips slightly parted, examining her cuticles, something she does when she is nervous.

"Reid, I..." Whitney begins and coughs, clearing her throat. "I got your feedback. I finally read it."

I step down from my ladder. "I'm sorry it's twelve years late."

"Or just in time," she says, then pauses. "I've spent a lot

of my life on my own. I had to figure out a lot of things on my own. Even married, my ex worked so much that it felt like I lived alone most of our marriage. I don't know how to depend on anyone, how to trust anyone. I haven't been able to trust anyone. And you bore the brunt of that. And I'm sorry."

She looks up and our eyes catch, and I'm done. I might as well crumple to the floor.

"You can depend on me. You can *trust* me."

She holds up her hand to stop me.

"I want to," she says. She laughs in a way that she can't believe she's saying what she's saying. "I may get scared. I might lash out. I need you to be there. Through anything I throw at you."

"I will," I say.

She looks at the ground. "I just know I'm hard to love."

"No, you're not," I interrupt. I reach out to cup her cheek. "You're so easy to love. It happened before I could stop it."

A tear trickles down her cheek. "I love you, Reid. I'm so unbelievably in love with you. I—"

I kiss her, before she finishes. Tension in my body whooshes away as I sink into her, my arms around her frame. I pull away, tilting her chin to look at me.

"You're enough. Exactly as you are. I love that you don't want to have kids because I don't want them either. It took you to make me realize that about myself. If I had them, I think I would've tried my best, but a life with you, full of adventure and fun sounds way better to me."

I squeeze her oh so tight.

"I love you," leaves my lips one more time as I kiss her, long and deep, squeezing her tighter and tighter.

There's wetness on her cheeks, and I wipe the tears away

as I kiss her for what seems forever. The door creaks open behind us, and there's a gasp.

"That was easy," Cameron says, crossing his arms. Emily appears at his side, covering her mouth with her hands. Jackson steps to the other side of Cam, matching him in stance.

"Are you back together now?" Emily points a finger from Whitney to me.

"I think so," I say. Turning toward Whitney, I say, "Right?"

"Yes," she says, kissing me.

"This is bullshit. Annie needed way more convincing," I hear Cam say.

"You all knew," I say.

Emily nods. "Sure did."

That's why Cameron smirked on the phone.

"I have one more thing," Whitney says. "Thumper is hauling it right now."

My jaw drops. "What?"

"I was a total asshole for not getting you a gift," Whitney says. "So I'm making it up to you."

She hands me her phone to show me a beat-up 1969 Ford Bronco. My dream car.

"Where did you find this?" I ask.

"Some guy in Ukiah had it sitting on his property. I swung by there before coming back to Goldheart and it's legit. It's in terrible shape, but I figured this could be a project for us. Thumper is dropping it off at your house, as we speak."

I can't believe it. I just kiss her.

"I'll pay for the restoration," she says. "That's included in my present."

That's thousands and thousands of dollars. I shake my

head. "That's too much."

"No, I want to. I want you to have it, exactly the way you want it."

"Sounds like Reid got a sugar momma," Jackson says from the doorway.

"Get out of here," I say, shooing away my siblings. They all linger, but finally leave. It's then that I can kiss her, pull her into my arms.

"I guess I need a place to stay," Whitney says. "My car is completely packed."

"Move in with me," I suggest, pushing her hair back from her face so I can kiss her neck.

"I thought you would never ask," she says, kissing me back. "I was going to move back to Goldheart, no matter what you said."

"Goldheart is pretty awesome. But I have a long list of places I want to see."

"Best part about not having kids is we can go anywhere we please, when we please. We have the rest of our lives," Whitney says.

"Are you proposing to me?"

"No," she says. "However, you will marry me one day. I may not want kids, but I definitely want to marry you."

"Same, honey," I say. "I love you."

"I love you too," Whitney says.

I hold her for moments, maybe hours. It feels like a dream that a woman like Whitney loves me and I love her right back. It makes sense why it didn't work out with others.

She's not only the woman I've been waiting for, I needed to meet her.

She brought my words back. She showed me there's another way to live.

I can write the rest of my life the way I want to, with Whitney by my side.

EPILOGUE

WHITNEY

"Happy Mother's Day!" I shout at the table, full of people I love.

The Finches, my adopted family, cover one side, while the other side includes my mother, Ken, and Jodie and her wife Lucy. They recently adopted a three-year-old from foster care, and he sits on Jodie's lap. Annie is round with child, a flower on her plate from the restaurant, although she has two months to go.

I sit down next to my love.

Reid and I have settled into domestic bliss since I moved to Goldheart officially in January. I've released two books, including the one I sprinted with Reid. He's been revising his book, getting it ready for beta readers. He's talking about trying to get an agent, to traditionally publish.

I read it, and while it has some ways to go, I love it. I can feel Reid's love for me in the pages with how Flint loves Lila, and how he's willing to fight for her.

We're in the middle of the restoration to Reid's dream car. We built a new engine and we're getting close to getting it painted. It's been a fun project we can do together, although I just watch Reid bend over most of the time.

I can't wait until it's done so we can take it out for long evening drives.

"It's so wonderful we can get everyone together," Kit, Reid's mom, says, holding up her mimosa. Everyone lifts their glasses.

"What I wouldn't give for a mimosa right now," Annie says, rubbing her stomach.

"Soon, baby, soon," Cameron, her husband, says, kissing her on the head.

They came to family dinner last week and announced they went to the courthouse and got married. After Cameron's botched proposal, both of them were at a standstill on who would propose to who, so they just went to the courthouse and did it. Kit sobbed when she found out because she wanted to be there to witness it.

"We'll do a big party once I have the baby," Annie told everyone. I'm not sure if that will happen.

Everyone is eyeing us now about when we will get engaged, but it already feels like we're married.

We're not, though, and that's a point of contention right now.

My mom is on my left, and Reid is on my right. I take my mom's hand, holding it like I wished for so many Mother's Days before. We did start therapy together, and Reid and I went and visited her and Ken in Colorado last month.

I wish I could tell thirteen-year-old Whitney that she would find a man who loved her even though she didn't want children, and that her mother would come back into her life. That she would be working on dismantling the trauma she experienced. That she would live in a house on a lake with a man she loves, and she gets to tell stories for a living.

It's really everything she could want.

"I want to make a toast," Reid says, standing up, holding his own mimosa. The table quiets, watching Reid, my soft-spoken man who growled in my ear this morning. He looks around, and I can read his tense body language.

I'm learning his body as well as I know my own.

"I know some amazing mothers in my life," Reid says, looking around the table. "My mother, Kit Finch, and my sister, Emily. My new sister-in-law and best friend, Annie. You are all so special to me, and I celebrate you today, for all you have given this family and will continue to give this family. I love you all."

"Cheers," the table says, clinking mimosas and orange juice and coffee. The Finch family have gotten better about taking time off.

I like to think it's because of Reid.

"That was a lovely speech," I say, fluttering my lips against his ear.

"I tried," he says. His hand lands on my thigh, and I feel liquid warmth flow through my limbs.

I love that this family supports my and Reid's decision, that we won't be getting those "when are you having kids" conversations when we get married. That we will be free to being the best aunt and uncle to his siblings' children.

"Happy Mother's Day," I say to my own mother, pulling her toward me in a side hug.

"Thank you for having me. It's so nice to be here." Her eyes fill with tears, and she wipes it away with a napkin, taking a sip of her mimosa. "I couldn't have dreamed that I would get to do this. After everything."

My mother kisses me on my head. She points to my love,

who is smiling and talking to his niece. "I'm so glad you found Reid. His family seems really nice."

"They are," I say, looking around the table. My best friend is cherished by Cameron, who's rubbing her belly as much as she does. I see Olive talking with her hands, telling Reid about a book she just read. Emily sits and smiles, though there's always a thin layer of sadness with her that no one wants to acknowledge. Jackson, who was incredibly closed off and quiet when I first met him, is now laughing with Randy, their dad, as they slap each other on the shoulder.

I'm incredibly grateful for all of this.

Not only do I have my own mother back, but I'm part of a bigger family now.

I'm so grateful to the man who fought for me.

A man who left his browser history open, clear as day, on the exquisite diamond ring he's planning on purchasing for me. Even though I would marry him with paper rings.

I pull Reid to me and kiss him slowly. He pulls away and looks to me. "What was that for?"

"For being you." I snuggle up against him as the table grows loud with laughter.

A table full of my family.

I excuse myself to go to the restroom, and as I lather soap in my hands, Miriam Oliver appears behind me.

"Hi Miriam. Happy Mother's Day," I say brightly. She rubs my back and kisses me on the cheek.

"Hello dear," she says.

When the Bad Biddies discussed my book a few months ago at book club, they came clean about trying to set me up with Reid. Ever since then, It's been a quiet few months from them. We still see them at Betty's Café once in awhile, but there honestly hasn't been that great of gossip lately.

Miriam pulls out a tub of lipstick. "How is Jackson faring these days?"

Well, I lied. There's been gossip about Jackson.

"He's hanging in there," I say.

Miriam nods. "I mean this in the nicest way possible. He's finally happy again and he messed it up. Big time."

I can't argue with her because I agree, but my allegiance is now with the Finches. While I don't understand Jackson's actions, I have to respect his decision.

"Good to see you Miriam," I say, cutting off the discussion. She's gotten better about respecting boundaries so she just smiles.

"Good to see you too," she says.

~

"A MOTHER'S Day karaoke is a little strange, isn't it?" I ask my mom, who just shrugs.

"Don't question it," Emily says, standing next to me.

"Mom, can I do Britney?" Olive asks, bouncing on the balls of her feet.

"No," she says.

Olive turns her lip down and runs off, tugging on Cameron's shirt.

"Just watch. Cam will say it's okay."

Kit walks toward us with a portable microphone. No one is on the stage right now, and I look around.

"Aren't mothers supposed to sing today?" I ask.

"It's my karaoke day, and I want you to sing. Consider it your initiation into the family," Kit says, handing it to me.

Oh fuck. I haven't done karaoke since our disastrous duet at The Swift. I may be named Whitney, but I sound like a drowning cat. What is with this family and karaoke?

"I had to do it too. It's tradition," Annie says.

"What's the tradition?"

"Just get your cute ass up there," Emily says, pushing me to the stage. I look back to my mom to save me, but she laughs as I'm dragged up by Kit, a woman I hope to have as a mother-in-law one day.

"What do I sing?" I ask Kit.

"I don't know. Maybe pick something for Reid."

I find him in the audience, laughing and trying to cover it. He gives me a thumbs-up, and I want to die.

I swallow a lump the size of a golf ball as I scroll through the offerings. I almost pick "A Whole New World," but there's one song that I heard again recently and it fits us perfectly. I remember being young, hearing it for the first time, and wanting to love someone like that.

Alanis Morrissette's "Head Over Feet."

I hold the microphone to my mouth.

"This is for the sexiest Finch," I say, pointing to Reid. "I love you, baby."

I begin to sing, and it's terrible. But the way Reid looks at me, the way I feel about him... It's why musicians write love songs. it's why I write romance novels.

I'm accepted. I am loved. I am complete.

THE END

WANT MORE?

To keep up to date with Jenny and get more Whitney and Reid and the rest of the Finch family, please go to jennybuntingbooks.com to subscribe to her newsletter!

Loved *Gold Rush*? Please consider reviewing on your favorite retailer! It helps others find and enjoy this book.

Curious about Cameron and Annie? Their book, *Fool's Gold*, is available in ebook and paperback!

Come find Jenny on socials! She has a readers' group on Facebook called Jenny Bunting's Adultish Readers, a Facebook page called Author Jenny Bunting, and she's on Instagram at @jennybuntingbooks. She always loves connecting with readers.

ACKNOWLEDGMENTS

This book was difficult to write and I'm so glad I had people along the way to help me and guide me to the final product you just finished. A huge thank you to Sarah from Lopt & Cropt Editing who continues to push me, although we're eight titles in. Thank you for your suggestions. No matter how mad I get, I'm forever blessed to have you in my corner.

Another huge thank you to Horus Copyedit and Proofreading and Kari March Designs. You both are such pleasures to work with.

My beta readers—Candice, Erica, Allie, and Goddess Divine. Thank you for beating the whine out of Reid and making the book what it is today. I appreciate your time and your comments to help my story become fully realized.

Thank you to my author friend Natasha Bishop who named Whitney's novel, *Loves, Lies, and Contracts* and thank you to my reader, Rachel, who named Betty's Café in my readers' group. Love you guys.

Thank you to my husband's Uncle Jim, one of the coolest childfree people I know. He knows enough about "brewing to be dangerous." He also validated that Night

Music was a great name for a stout and stroked my ego, so there's that.

To my husband. Loving you has taught me so much about myself. I thank the Universe every day that you weren't set on having children. I love our life together.

For all the mothers—the ones who worry, who love, who cherish their children. I'm in awe of your tenacity and drive to be the best you can be for your family. It's an impossible job and you all make it look so easy. I respect you and I admire you.

For my people, the childfree. We are rebels and rebels have never had it easy. Deciding not to parent is an act of selflessness, no matter what the haters say. I'm glad that you realized parenting did not set your soul on fire and resisted the societal pressure. This book is for you.

ABOUT THE AUTHOR

Jenny Bunting is the author of six full-length romance novels and three romantic comedy novella titles, all self-published. Jenny has had over thirty jobs, including working at a newspaper, teaching, and adjusting claims in the insurance industry. She hopes to be a full-time author one day and is a fan of hazy IPAs, brewery games, and *Yellowstone*. Jenny lives the childfree life with her husband and their German shepherd in the suburbs of Sacramento, California.

Made in the USA
Middletown, DE
11 January 2023

21389652R10170